Double Play
&
Perfect Victim

Kelley Armstrong

This is a work of fiction. Names, characters, businesses, places, events and incidents are either the products of the author's imagination or used in a fictitious manner. Any resemblance to actual persons, living or dead, events, or locales is purely coincidental.

All rights reserved. No part of this book may be reproduced in any form or by any electronic or mechanical means, including information storage and retrieval systems, without the written permission of the Author, except by a reviewer who may quote brief passages in a review.

Copyright © 2017 KLA Fricke Inc.

All rights reserved.

ISBN: 1974060276

ISBN-13: 978-1974060276

Author's Note

This is a compilation of two Nadia Stafford novellas. Both are set after the events of the book trilogy: *Exit Strategy, Made to be Broken* and *Wild Justice*.

The second novella, *Perfect Victim*, includes a character from my Rockton series—yes, it's my first crossover story! For those who haven't read the Rockton series, Tyrone Cypher is introduced in book *2, A Darkness Absolute*. At the back of this book, you'll find seven chapters from the first Rockton novel, *City of the Lost*.

Also by Kelley Armstrong

Nadia Stafford trilogy
Exit Strategy
Made to be Broken
Wild Justice

Rockton series
City of the Lost
A Darkness Absolute
This Fallen Prey

Missing
The Masked Truth

Cainsville series

Otherworld series

Age of Legends trilogy

Darkness Rising trilogy

Darkest Powers trilogy

The Blackwell Pages trilogy
(co-written with Melissa Marr)

Contents

Double Play............................1

Perfect Victim...................173

City of the Lost excerpt......347

Double Play

Chapter One
Nadia

"So we're watching this show, about a woman hiring a hitman for her husband, and I tell Hank that's what I'll do the next time he leaves his dirty socks on the floor."

Stella's pickup rolled alongside me as I jogged down the empty dirt road, her window down so she could talk.

"And he says, go ahead, just make sure you ask Nadia Stafford to do it."

A moment of silence, filled only by the rumble of the old engine and the pant of the two German shepherds at my side.

"Why?" I asked finally, trying for a laugh.

"Because Hank says that's what damned fools like me always do. Go looking for a hitman. Hire a cop by mistake."

I did laugh at that. It was true. Finding an actual hitman is nearly impossible for the average citizen, and people almost always end up talking to an undercover cop instead. It's not as if you're going to find a hired killer living down your street. Or jogging alongside your truck.

"Well, I'm not a cop anymore," I said. "Just keep letting Hank eat at the diner. It'll kill him soon enough."

That got a guffaw loud enough to startle Rex. Scout looked at me, rolling her eyes at his puppy nerves.

"How about that new man of yours?" Stella said. "Is he good with a gun?"

"Um, yes . . . but . . ."

She grinned. "Don't worry. I won't try to hire him either. Hank was just wondering if he wants to go hunting sometime. He do that sort of thing?"

"He . . . has."

"Well, ask if he wants to go hunt wild turkeys with the boys next month. Hank said since it seems you're keeping him around, he ought to be more neighborly. Invite him to turkey shoots and poker games."

I made a noncommittal sound and said, "How about we have you and Hank to dinner? John's in the States right now, but he'll be back by next weekend."

"I won't turn down Emma's cooking."

"Good. I'll call you later this week."

Back at the lodge, I could hear guests slowly waking,

roused by the smell of coffee and Emma's cinnamon rolls. I popped in to grab a roll and dog treats. This never impresses Scout and Rex, who seem to think if dog treats are so great, I should eat them, too. The handbook says not to give dogs human food, though, and I'm very good at following the rules. Well, in some things.

A quick word to Emma—my lodge housekeeper—and then I zoomed off before any guests could wander down and declare they'd like an early morning canoeing lesson. They'll have my guide services for the rest of the day. This is my time, with Jack's daily check-in call.

Granted, that conversation wasn't exactly deep. Any phone call with Jack is almost entirely one-sided—that side being mine. I got used to that in the years we'd worked together. Did I expect it to change when we moved beyond friendship? Yep. Which proves that I'd misunderstood the purpose of the conversations altogether. Jack wasn't calling to talk. He was calling to listen. Calling to hear me chatter about the lodge, about my day . . . The very average life of Nadia Stafford, ad nauseam. Can't say I see the appeal, but compared to dating a guy who doesn't give a shit, I'm happy to oblige.

I headed to the site where we're building our private chalet. It's right on the edge of our cell service periphery, intentionally so, because as nice as it'd be to live out of contact sometimes, we really can't.

I retrieved the cell phone from its hiding spot. Rex

nosed around, as if hoping for more interesting buried treasure. Scout sighed. Scout is my white German shepherd, a year old now. Jack bought her for me. I retaliated—I mean, reciprocated—by getting him Rex, a black-and-tan shepherd, for Christmas. Yes, he named his dog Rex. Not surprising for a guy who, when given the full array of cool hitman noms de guerre, went with Jack. He didn't even need to think it up—it's what his family used to call him as a diminutive for John.

Phone in hand, I climbed to the half-finished balcony and took a seat on the edge, my legs dangling. The view was perfect. It should be, given how damned long Jack spent picking our building site. He'd actually hauled out a ladder to find the best balcony viewpoint. Hitman perfectionism for you. And it was absolutely right—the morning sun over the lake, leaves whispering in the breeze, not a single structure to mar the illusion that you were in the middle of endless forest. I uncapped my thermos, poured my coffee and took a bite of my cinnamon bun while the dogs snuffled through the forest under my dangling feet. A minute later, Scout let out her "someone's coming" growl and Rex echoed it. I followed their gazes to see a figure coming through the trees. I checked my watch. Three minutes until Jack's call at nine.

Shit.

I rose in a crouch, ready to scuttle back inside the chalet. Not very dignified. Or very polite. But I only got these few minutes each day to touch base with Jack and remind myself that no matter how messy my life might be, it was, at this moment, everything I wanted it to be.

I was halfway through the doorway when a man's voice called, "Nadia?"

I left the doorway. "Hey, didn't see you. Let me come—"

I stopped. Even in the forest shadows, I could tell the guy wasn't a guest. Not when he was dressed in a three-piece suit.

"Let me come down," I said.

As I did, I took my time and turned up the volume on my phone. It was nine o'clock on the dot. If I stalled for a few moments, my visitor would hear the ring and I could excuse myself to answer.

I picked my way through the piles of wood and supplies inside the building.

9:01.

I frowned. Yes, that's not exactly late, but Jack is precise. Like let's-sync-our-watches precise.

"Big dogs," the man called up.

"Don't mind them. They're fine."

To have Scout and Rex on the property with guests, they need to be perfectly behaved. They're trained to warn of intruders with growls only, and then keep their distance. They're friendly enough, but they'll only approach strangers when I give the signal.

I checked the time again—9:02—cursed under my breath and stepped out. I still couldn't see the man's face, but despite the suit, I could tell he wasn't some salesman who'd wandered over from the lodge. He was fit and trim and his right hand rested awkwardly—a man accustomed to having a sidearm within reach.

Law enforcement.

I took a deep breath, plastered on a cheerful lodge-hostess smile and ducked under a tree branch. Then I saw his face.

Diaz.

I don't know his given name. He very likely *was* law enforcement, but he moonlighted for the Contrapasso Fellowship, a secret organization of law enforcement officers, lawyers and judges who looked at failures of justice and said, "I could fix that." So they did. Vigilantes of the highest order. They'd been trying to recruit me for a while and had successfully recruited my ex, Quinn, a US Marshal.

"Nadia," Diaz said. "I'm sorry to approach you here. I know—"

"You sure as hell know," I said, bearing down on him. "This is my *home*. Contrapasso may know more about me than I like, but you are supposed to at least pretend otherwise. You do not show up—"

"It's Quinn."

I stopped. "What?"

Double Play

"It's Quinn. He's disappeared."

Chapter Two

Jack

It'd been thirty years since Jack had left Ireland and now, crouched on a rooftop overlooking Dublin, he was counting the hours until he could get the fuck out again. Which wasn't what he'd expected. Yeah, thirty years ago he couldn't wait to wash the dust of the city from his boots. But he'd been a kid then. Twenty years old, hating everything about his country, hating what it'd done to his family.

No, hating what *he'd* done to his family. He could blame the politics, and what it'd done to four young men who'd wanted better than the dirt-poor lives of their parents. Boys who'd wanted what they thought the world owed them. But the world didn't owe them fuck all. You make your choices. You make your mistakes. And sometimes, those mistakes lead to a boat bound for America with no plans to ever return because the sight of those green hills reminds you of what you did. Of the fact that your family lies cold in their graves and it's no one's fault but your own.

Yet the boy at twenty isn't the same as the man at fifty, and Jack had started looking back on Ireland with something he wouldn't quite call nostalgia, but definitely a yearning for lush emerald hills and sooty old cities. Back when he and Nadia had become friends and she'd talked of travel dreams, he'd often thought of saying, "How about Ireland?" But he hadn't, of course. Fuck no. Even when he'd invited her to Egypt, he'd cancelled, buying a hot tub for her lodge instead. Because that's what people did, didn't they? Bail on a trip and replace it with a hot tub? Yeah, it'd been a fucking long time since he'd done the friendship thing.

He still couldn't believe she'd let him move *past* friendship. Kept waiting to return from a job and find his bag at the door, some higher power correcting a miscalculation that had awarded him a prize meant for a guy who hadn't spent his life as a hired killer. Instead, the only thing waiting for him was Nadia herself, jogging out to meet him, grinning like he'd returned from a three-year tour of duty.

His phone buzzed, a reminder that in minutes, he could make his daily check in. He smiled, something he did much more readily these days, but still really only for one person.

He paced along the roof, as close to the edge as he could get without casting a shadow below. Tomorrow, he had to meet an old friend at the cafe across the street, to discuss a hit while sipping cappuccinos or some shit.

Fuck, he was getting old. Starting to sound like a crotchety old man, muttering about the good old days, when if you wanted someone killed, you met in a seedy pub and talked business in a dark back room.

The truth was he didn't mind cappuccinos. Better than some of the swill they passed off as beer. He was just cranky today. He'd been supposed to meet Cillian this afternoon, only to have him call and reschedule for tomorrow, which put the entire fucking job a day behind and left him with busywork like this.

He checked his phone. Three more minutes. He surveyed the street, squinting against the early afternoon June sun as he searched for something interesting to tell Nadia. *Know what I saw today? What I heard today? Learned today?*

His gaze traveled along the narrow road. *Nope. I got nothing.*

He exhaled and resisted the urge to pull out a cigarette. He'd been cutting back for years, with no real intention of quitting. It was his outlet for stress and his one vice. Well, his second vice if you counted murder as his first, and he was well aware most people did, but that was work. He was down to a couple of cigarettes a week and at the lodge, he didn't even need those, though he still smoked them because they were shared with Nadia, and that meant something to him. Those shared cigarettes had been their first step from colleagues to friends, when he offered her his cigarette, seeing that ex-smoker hunger in her eyes. A simple, small act of intimacy that had felt as huge as inviting her into his bed.

Maybe he'd mention that when he called. Something about grabbing a couple of cartons. His brand was still Irish, and it was a bugger to get in Canada. Yeah, he'd tell her that. Not exactly scintillating conversation, but she liked it when he added something, even if he'd be happy spending an hour listening to her talk.

His phone blipped the second alert, but he was already dialing. It was an untraceable number, one that'd reroute a few times before ending up at an equally untraceable phone. Jack didn't understand the technology, but he trusted Felix, the guy who set it up for them.

The line connected. One ring. Then a soft click, and he closed his eyes and waited for her voice, for the reminder of what he had waiting for him. Nadia. The lodge. The chalet. That chalet was important. So fucking important. It meant he wasn't just shacking up in Nadia's bedroom at the lodge. They were building a home together, literally, and he still wasn't sure it meant the same to her—was as permanent for her—but it was a start in that direction.

Nadia. A home. A life.

The phone rang again.

What the fuck? He'd heard the line connect, hadn't he?

No, he'd heard a click and jumped on it, like a fifteen-year-old calling his crush, praying she'd answer.

A third ring.

He frowned. Nadia never let it ring more than twice.

Yeah, actually, she did . . . if she wasn't there to

answer. It had only happened a couple of times before, but it *had* happened. Once, she'd been putting out a fire—an actual fire. Some moronic guest decided it was a little chilly by the lake and started a blaze he couldn't control. The other time, it'd been a failure of technology.

A fourth ring.

Fuck.

Five.

Jack hung up. Then he paused, his finger over the redial. That was against the rules. His rules, for Nadia's safety. One call per day at the arranged time. If he couldn't place that call or she couldn't answer, then they waited until the next morning.

Still, his finger hovered over the button. The click suggested it just might not have gone through. Another tech-fail. And if he didn't call, she'd worry.

All valid excuses. Which were exactly that: excuses. He put these rules in place to protect her, and the moment he started making exceptions, he'd never stop. Setting limits and sticking to them was the price he paid for his past, and it was a small price, all things considered.

He pocketed the phone, made one last loop around the roof, checking out the scene for tomorrow's meeting. Then he headed down to find something he could tell Nadia tomorrow. Something interesting.

Chapter Three

Nadia

No call from Jack, and as much as I knew it almost certainly meant nothing, I couldn't help fearing the worst. I always did. But now I had Diaz standing there, telling me Quinn was missing and that *was* a big deal.

As a federal agent, Quinn cannot just "take off." When he does a job for Contrapasso out of driving distance, he has to take vacation time and use Felix's gadgets to reroute his calls. Hellishly complicated, which is one reason why, like me, he doesn't pull more than a couple of hits a year.

"Where's he supposed to be?" I asked Diaz.

"On Thursday he was teaching in DC. After that, he'd booked a long weekend."

"He was on a job, then. For you guys?"

Diaz shook his head. "I know he was working something—he has to run all moonlighting past us. He was supposed to call in and talk to us yesterday on a separate matter. He didn't, and we couldn't get in touch. That's when we checked out his tracker. We aren't getting a signal."

Contrapasso implanted trackers in their operatives . . . usually without them knowing it. Luckily, Quinn discovered that before signing on, so he'd refused the implant. Instead, he'd agreed to an external one, attached with waterproof tape. At the time, I'd wholeheartedly agreed with that. Now, though? Now I was realizing the advantage to the implant. If Quinn had it, Diaz and I wouldn't need this conversation.

"Let me go warn my housekeeper I'm busy," I said. "I'll meet you at the gazebo. Head for the lake. Big body of water—you can't miss it."

When I reached the gazebo, I turned the heater on low and served coffee and cinnamon buns.

"So what are you doing on my doorstep?" I asked. "If Quinn's missing, I want in on the search, obviously. But telephones work, even up here."

"Your name was on his calendar for Friday morning, along with a flight confirmation number. We thought maybe that's why he'd taken a long weekend, and that he'd just forgotten our call Saturday."

"And the tracker?"

"Either it coincidentally died or he removed it temporarily, not wanting anyone to know where he'd gone, which considering . . ." He cleared his throat. "I know you two had a romantic attachment and that Quinn is convinced your relationship with Jack is . . . temporary."

"So you thought he snuck up here because we're screwing around behind Jack's back?"

"I had to consider that. Or simply that he was attempting to change your mind."

Quinn and I were still friends. Would he come out here unannounced? He *can* be impulsive, and if he got it into his head that he could fix this "Jack nonsense" by talking to me face to face, he might very well hop on a plane. I highly doubted it, though. Not while Jack was here.

Except Jack wasn't here.

To say Jack and Quinn don't get along is an understatement. The problem is ninety percent Quinn's. Jack's uncomfortable with Quinn's hard-core vigilantism, but his real issue is Quinn's complete disinterest in hiding the fact that he thinks vigilantism grants him the moral high ground. To Quinn, I get to share that ground with him because I mix vigilante jobs with "victimless" mobsters-killing-mobsters gigs. To Quinn, Jack's the worst kind of criminal—one who kills for money he doesn't even need.

When it comes to the job, ideologically, I prefer the vigilante work. But I'm still killing people for money. There is no justification that clears that particular moral slate.

I've come to a better understanding of my motives—the deep-seated need for the justice my cousin, Amy, was denied when she was raped and murdered twenty years ago. She wasn't the only one raped that night, and I'm sure there's some of my own rage there. I survived. Amy did not. And now with both her killer and my rapist dead, little has changed. I haven't taken a job since, but I will at some point. I don't kid myself on that. It has become part of me.

That's no excuse. In this, I'm closer to Jack. As a teen he'd been recruited by an organization that made the IRA look like Boy Scouts. He joined because his brothers had, and once the group saw his crack marksmanship skills, they made him a killer. When he tried to get out, they murdered his family. No surprise, then, that the kid who felt he was only really good at one thing—killing people—turned his rage into a career doing exactly that. Yet he never uses that as an excuse. He made a choice, like I did. There is no justification.

Given Quinn's opinion of Jack, it's not surprising he's convinced our relationship is just temporary bad judgment on my part. Really bad judgment. Quinn believes Jack took advantage of a low point in my life, smarting from our breakup and dealing with the truth behind my rape and my cousin's murder. That means Quinn just has to wait for me to come to my senses. And this, not surprisingly, was why we were struggling to keep our friendship from imploding.

"Jack isn't here, as you may have noticed," I said. "But I hadn't told Quinn that and Jack left after Quinn would have arrived. Quinn didn't disable his tracker or 'forget' his appointment. He wouldn't. Ever. If he's vanished . . ." I inhaled sharply. "We need to find him."

"Do you know what he was working on recently? As a Marshal?"

I nodded. "He doesn't give me details but he shares enough that I know what sort of cases he has. Nothing on his current roster is the type where someone would want to . . . to stop him." *Kill him* is what I meant, but I couldn't bring myself to say the words.

I continued. "First thing we need to know is whether he got on that flight. Can you check—?"

"We have. He didn't check in or cancel it."

"Yet you followed his trail up here anyway?"

"I had to be sure he hadn't bought a new ticket under an alias on a different flight in to keep under Jack's radar. And if that wasn't the case, then showing up here is the best way to get your help. You know him better than we do. You know how his mind works."

And it'd be much harder for me to refuse in person.

Which only proved Diaz didn't know how *my* mind worked either. A phone call would have put me on this trail. Whatever problems Quinn and I had, I wouldn't have considered sitting on my ass and letting Contrapasso investigate on their own.

"When will the Marshals' office realize he's missing?" I asked.

"He's supposed to be back at work Tuesday. We can extend his absence with a falsified call, but I'd rather not."

"So we have about sixty hours before they realize something's wrong. The problem is that it's Sunday and I have commitments here. I can conduct research today, but I can't get away until tonight."

"Understood. I'll get started and meet you in Virginia tomorrow morning."

Chapter Four
Jack

First thing Monday morning, Jack was back on the roof. Smoking this time. Not just a cigarette to settle his nerves. He couldn't remember the last time he'd needed that. Work didn't cause him stress. Life did. Work was simple. Life was not.

But today? Today the two melded, and he was already on his third cigarette. Which was a fucking bad sign. He wasn't overly concerned about his aborted call to Nadia. If anything really bothered him about that, it was the fact he'd spent far too much time yesterday coming up with ways to guarantee daily contact, like a second phone or a backup time to call. That was pure selfishness. He had to stick to the plan because a plan is safe. It wasn't a concept he'd ever struggled with before.

He tapped his cigarette on the ventilation shaft and looked down at the cafe. Ten minutes to go. Two hours until he could call Nadia again. It wasn't just about talking to her, however much he liked that. It was about stilling his anxiety better than nicotine could.

It'd been nearly thirty years since he'd spoken to Cillian. Cillian had been a mentor in those days. He'd helped Jack get out of Ireland and set him up with his first jobs. Which meant Jack owed him. Half a lifetime later, Cillian was coming to collect.

As for what he'd ask Jack to do? That was the real reason for the chain smoking.

Cillian knew Jack from the time when he'd pull a hit for any reason—when he didn't even *need* a reason. As long as it wasn't a family or a kid or an innocent bystander, he didn't give a shit why someone wanted his mark dead. He'd worked fueled by the rage of a twenty-year-old kid who'd gotten his family killed and blamed everyone else, hated the world, but deep down only blamed himself, only hated himself. All the bullets in the world couldn't fix that shit, not unless the barrel was aimed at his own head.

That blind rage had passed. He'd grown up. Calmed down. Within a few years, he'd started needing a reason. But that was a matter of self-protection. He wasn't going to off witnesses for a cartel—that shit comes back on you. Kill a guy's business partner to give him control of the company? No problem. Then he met Nadia, and began scrubbing his client list until, while it might not be up to her standards, he wasn't worried about her scrubbing *him* from *her* contact list.

And now . . .

Fuck.

He stubbed out the cigarette and pocketed the butt. This was stupid—worrying about possibilities before he even talked to Cillian. Part of being a pro meant mapping out every contingency and planning a response. Great for the job; bullshit for real life.

While he didn't tell Nadia about his job—she was always safer not knowing—she'd be okay with it. He refused to pull any hit he wouldn't want her finding out about. That vow stood. Even for Cillian.

Fuck, Cillian. Know I owe you. And I do. But I'm getting out. Retiring. Can't do that kinda shit. Too dangerous. Still owe you. But not that.

Then he'd walk away. Because he could—that was the reward for being at the top of the food chain. He'd owe Cillian an explanation for his refusal, which was more than any other client would get. But if Jack said no, Jack meant no. End of discussion. That was the rep he'd earned.

At five minutes to eleven, Cillian strolled around the corner, and all Jack could think was, "Fuck, he's gotten old." Which was, sadly, what he thought about most of his former colleagues these days. Cillian couldn't be more than seventy but fuck if he didn't look eighty-seven. A long and hard life.

He was about to do one last perimeter check when he saw Cillian nod, as if to someone passing on the street. Except there was no one on that particular stretch of road.

Fuck.

Jack strode to the roof edge and adjusted his position so neither he nor his shadow would be spotted. Then he peered into the dark alley below and . . .

Fuck.

A guy stood in the shadows. Youngish—early thirties, Nadia's age. Young compared to him, a fact of which he was not unaware.

The guy leaned casually against the brick wall. Just a guy enjoying a smoke. Nothing to see here. His sight line, however, lined up perfectly with Cillian's table.

Fuck.

Don't pull this shit, Cillian. Tell me you just got nervous. Asked one of your boys to keep an eye on this meeting because, hell, it's been thirty years. You don't know me anymore, so I'll allow the backup, even if I'm kinda insulted.

The problem? The really big problem? If that guy in the shadows wasn't just there to protect his boss.

Fuck.

Jack crossed to the other side. He hopped from the roof to the fire escape balcony. Okay, yeah, "hop" was pushing it. He was in fucking good shape for fifty-one, but still not at the age where one "hops" off roofs. Still, he managed the descent easily enough and took no small amount of satisfaction in that.

Off the roof. Down the fire escape. Hop onto a Dumpster. And that *was* a hop, being only a two-foot drop. A little more than a hop in the descent to ground level. Then through the back alley, heading toward the one hiding Cillian's thug. When he reached the corner, he peeked around. The guy was still there, still looking toward the road.

Jack sized up the distance between them. Thirty feet. There was another trash bin, maybe ten feet this side of the guy. He flexed his ankle, the one he'd broken last spring. Just a little sore from jumping to reach the fire escape. A necessary reminder he wasn't twenty anymore and couldn't pull stupid twenty-year-old shit.

He took three careful steps across the alley, then three quick ones to get into the shadow of that trash bin. He climbed onto it with surprising ease—*Don't get cocky, Jack*—and held his breath for two seconds, making sure his target hadn't caught the movement.

The guy checked his watch.

Yeah, I'm late. Give me a minute . . .

Jack eased along the trash bin, each step taken with extreme care so the metal didn't creak underfoot. Now the tricky part. Step up to the edge, crouch and . . .

He leapt and hit the guy in the shoulder, knocking him down. Then he grabbed the guy's leg and hauled him behind the bin, which might have been the toughest part—the guy was not small. He wasn't too fucking smart, either. Instead of going for his weapon, he just flailed, as if he could throw Jack off.

Jack tossed him behind the bin and the guy finally remembered he had a gun. He didn't even get it out before a barrel pressed against the back of his neck.

"You got anything to say?" Jack asked.

"What?"

He spoke slower. "Got anything to say?"

"You fucking—"

Jack slammed his foot between the guy's shoulder blades. "That's a no." He patted the guy down, taking a gun, two knives and brass knuckles. People still used brass knuckles?

He shook his head and pocketed the weapons along with two cell phones. The guy squawked, saying, "Private property, you—"

Another slam sent him face-first into the dirt.

"Last chance. Anything to say?"

"Just that you're a—"

Jack didn't wait to find out what he was. He already knew. Just like he knew this guy wasn't giving him answers and he didn't have time to beat them out of him. He hit the guy again. No anger behind it. Just shutting him up so he could speak, because he really hated to repeat himself.

"You've been put down," he said. "By a guy old enough to be your father. That's humiliating. But you know what's worse? Telling your boss about it. You can cross that road with me and do it. Or . . ."

Jack stepped back. The guy pushed to his feet and looked Jack up and down in hopes of saving his ego by seeing that Jack was younger than he'd heard, bigger than he'd thought. The result of that onceover said Jack didn't look *that* old and he wasn't small. But nor was he twenty-five and six-foot-four. The guy grunted and crossed his arms.

"Take off down the back alley," Jack said.

The guy said nothing, but when Jack stood his ground, he stalked in that direction. Jack watched him go, then turned toward the street.

As Jack walked away, he kept his ears attuned for any sign the thug decided to circle back behind him. His attention, though, was on the guy's burner phone. On the text message the guy had received from Cillian.

Make sure you're ready.

Jack exhaled. He'd still been giving Cillian the benefit of the doubt. Presuming he'd only told his boy to protect his back. But Jack was not an optimist. His gut had said the Cillian he remembered would never admit he was concerned about a meeting with an old friend.

Jack knew his own reputation, too. It came partly from prowess. He was damned good at his job. But more than that, he was fair and he was trustworthy. Cillian would know that much. Which meant he knew Jack would never double-cross him.

And *that* meant Jack was the one being double-crossed.

Fuck.

The thug's phone buzzed with another text.

Where are you?

Jack sent the reply. *Pissing.*

Get the fuck back to your post.

Jack picked up his pace to a jog. He headed back the way he'd come. Down two alleys. Circled another building. Exited far enough from the thug's post that it wouldn't look suspicious. When he reached the sidewalk, he slowed to a purposeful stride.

As Jack approached the cafe, Cillian looked up, his head tilting as he squinted. Then he went back to his newspaper. He hadn't recognized Jack. Not surprising after thirty years, but even less surprising given that Jack wore a disguise as he always did for a client meeting.

Jack pulled out the chair across from Cillian.

"That's—" Cillian began. Then another squint over his reading glasses. "Jack?"

Jack sat without a word. He endured the obligatory appraisal, that oncever from an old friend that wasn't so much seeing how he'd changed as seeing how much he'd aged, while hoping the answer was "more than I have." A tightening of Cillian's lips said he couldn't have that satisfaction.

Jack wondered if all people did this. Go to a high-school reunion and size up your classmates, hoping they showed their age more than you. Or was it just guys like them? Guys who needed to reassure themselves they were still men to be reckoned with.

"You look good," Cillian said with obvious reluctance.

"Not here for a date."

Cillian snorted a laugh and reached for his cigarette, burning on the side of a small plate.

"You know they don't allow smoking here?" Cillian said. "Even on the patio? Fucking world, huh?"

Jack set one generic, unmarked allergy capsule in front of Cillian.

"What the fuck's that?" Cillian said.

"A choice."

"What?"

"Cyanide pill. Gun. You pick."

"Gun?" Cillian's gaze followed Jack's arm and registered the gun was under the table, pointed between his legs. He shoved back his chair.

"You move," Jack said, "I fire. Pull that chair in."

Cillian did, sweat breaking out on his upper lip as he said, with a hint of a whine, "What the fuck, Jack? This better be some kinda dementia—you getting paranoid in your old age. Because threatening me—"

Jack tossed the thug's burner phone on the table. "He's not taking a piss."

Cillian went still. That beading sweat formed droplets, sliding down the side of his ruddy face. He reached for his coffee, and then stopped as he noticed his hand trembling.

Fuck. You haven't just gotten old, Cillian. You've gotten soft. Lost your nerve. No excuse for that. There just isn't.

"Third option," Jack said. "You talk. Tell me what's going on. Might still shoot you. Might make you take the pill. Not going to let you walk away. But . . ." He shrugged. "Options. I'm flexible. Convince me not to shoot."

"It isn't what it seems, Jack. I'd never—"

"Skip the bullshit."

"But you gotta understand. It isn't—"

"Don't care. You wanna make me happy? Talk. Fast."

"I got into some trouble, Jack. Things have changed. It's not just about knowing the other guys in town. Everyone's global these days, and I'm just an old boss trying to run—"

"Give me facts. Not excuses. You owe money. Favor. Yes?"

Cillian swallowed and nodded.

"They found out you know me," Jack said. "Can call in a favor. You've bragged. Fucking disrespectful. But you did it. No changing that now."

"I needed credibility, Jack. It's all about who you know, and you're somebody. Being able to say I helped you get your start? That's gold."

"Someone told you to get me here. Why?" He peered up at the surrounding buildings. "There a rifle pointed at my head?"

"No, nothing like that. You're no use to anyone if you're dead."

Which Jack knew. People wanted him for his skills.

If you want revenge for a hit, you go after the son of a bitch who called it. Jack was just the faceless guy behind the gun. Still, there was always a chance. He'd known that when he walked over. Also known that the sun's position would make it a tough shot. Not impossible—Nadia could do it—and maybe knowing that, he should have walked away. But if someone wants you dead, you'll be dead. He knew that better than anyone. You want to stay alive? Tackle the problem that's going to get you killed.

"Talk," Jack said.

"They want to hire you." Cillian rambled after that, appealing to Jack's ego, as if that might nudge aside the bullet currently aimed at a place he didn't really want to get shot. He said Jack was the best. The absolute best goddamned hitman alive. Which was bullshit. Jack figured he rated about third. That's what Evelyn told him, which was supposed to incite him to do better. First, third, tenth, what did it matter? Who the hell figured out the rankings anyway? Market research survey? On a scale of one to ten, how do you rate your satisfaction with the services of the following hitmen . . .

Cillian kept nattering on. Jack was *such* a big name, and if someone wanted his services, well, it wasn't easy to do, was it? Cillian himself had to jump through hoops, and he was an old friend. But he understood. Yes, he did. A man like Jack had to protect himself. But Jack also had to understand how that could lead people to take desperate measures to get his attention.

"Stop talking."

Cillian's mouth shut with a click of his teeth. He was sweating enough now that Jack could smell it. Letting him ramble hadn't been a kindness. Jack had been allowing the older man to dig himself deeper, getting increasingly anxious as he struggled to explain and Jack's expression didn't change. Now Cillian sat there, breathing out of his mouth, panting slightly as he waited for Jack's next command.

What the fuck happened to you, Cillian? I was scared of you back in the day. Scared shitless. Wanted to be like you. The tough bastard nobody screws with.

"They want to hire me," Jack said.

"Don't ask me details about the job. These people aren't like you and me. If they want something, they get it."

"So do I."

Cillian shifted. "Sure you do, Jack. I didn't mean it like that. Yes, they want to hire you. They'll pay your going rate." A nervous laugh. "I don't even want to guess what that would be. Off my pay scale. A few years ago, I thought of asking if I could sell that favor you promised me. Would have made my retirement, I'm sure. A guy like you—"

"—is not someone you fuck with."

Sweat dripped into Cillian's coffee.

Jack continued, "Don't care about the job. I'll tell them to fuck off. Better yet? You'll tell them. That's how we'll handle this. You tell them fuck no. They don't like the message?" Jack shrugged. "Say it nicely. Maybe that'll help."

"You—you don't understand, Jack."

"Yeah, I do. I understand my old friend fucked me over. I understand he might not survive that message. And I don't give a shit. Can't." Jack rose. "Also, tell them—"

"They've gone after your girl."

"What?" he said, slowly and, he hoped, calmly.

"Your girl. The hitwoman. The one you trained."

"Dee?"

A short laugh. "You're fucking more than one? Lucky guy."

Jack's cold stare made Cillian shift. "Sorry. Yes, Dee."

"She's my protégé."

Ever since word got out that he was Nadia's mentor, everyone presumed sex was part of the arrangement. Otherwise, why the hell would you bother with a girl? They couldn't entertain the possibility Jack might have trained her because she was good. Easier to say he was sleeping with her. Now that he *was*, it got tougher to work up righteous indignation, but he still managed enough that Cillian ducked his gaze and muttered, "That's what they think. Whether it's true or not—"

"Not."

"That doesn't matter, Jack. They're going through her to get to you. Well, through Quinn first."

"Who?"

"Quinn. The Boy Scout. That's what they call him, right? Fucking vigilante—"

"What about him?"

"I only know what these guys told me. I don't keep my ear to the ground the way I used to—"

"Quinn. Dee. Connect them."

"Okay, so these guys know—uh, presume—you're sleeping with Dee. Only, apparently, getting to her is almost as tough as getting to you. But she's rumored to be pals with this Quinn, and he's much easier to contact. So that's their plan. Set Quinn up. Take him hostage. Bring Dee running. Use her to make you do whatever they want. Complicated, I know, but this shows how badly they want you, Jack. The lengths they're willing to go."

Don't panic. Don't fucking panic.

I can fix this. Will fix it. Dodged a bullet. A fucking well-aimed bullet, but consider it dodged. Nadia is fine. She will continue to be fine. I just need to make that call . . .

That call . . .

The unanswered call. The click on the line.

Jack's head jerked up. "When is this supposed to happen?"

"Now, Jack. It's happening now."

Jack yanked out his phone. Then he stopped and switched to the thug's prepaid.

"That won't help," Cillian said. "They know the number you were dialing. Her phone won't accept incoming calls unless they place them."

He hit the numbers anyway. The phone rang. A soft click. Then it continued to ring. He hung up and started dialing the lodge only to stop himself again. They could get access to the phone record and trace any call he made.

He'd have to get to a payphone. Or buy another cell.

Was *that* safe?

He'd make sure it was. He'd stop this before Nadia was in danger.

This is exactly what you always worried about. Exactly what you convinced yourself wouldn't happen. How long did it take, Jack-o? Six fucking months.

"It's too late, Jack," Cillian said.

Jack turned to him. That's all he thought he did—swung his gaze to the guy. But whatever Cillian saw in that gaze made him jerk back and the legs of his chair skittered on the ground.

Cillian swallowed. "I'm going to help you, Jack. Anything I can do, I will. I regret this. I really do."

"You have not fucking begun to regret this."

Cillian flinched. "I-I know but—"

"Talk. Make it useful."

"R-right. S-sorry. I know you're trying to figure out how to contact her, but it's too late. They took this Quinn fellow Saturday. Last night, that phone you use to contact her started moving."

"Bullshit. GPS is disconnected."

"Right. Or they could have used it to find her. That's smart, Jack. Got some high-grade tech there. Can't even imagine what that costs."

"Stop. Start again. Facts."

"They know she made a few calls on the phone last night. Which suggested she knew about this Quinn guy and was doing some research. Whatever you've got installed won't tell them where her calls are coming from. But they can tell the phone's on the move."

Because Nadia was going after Quinn.

Didn't matter. She'd have her real cell phone. She needed it to contact the lodge and—

And Felix had programmed that high-tech phone to

let her make and accept calls to her legitimate cell number . . . while still rerouting that signal so she couldn't be traced.

If these guys knew the number Jack used to call Nadia and her real number went through the same device, could they block that? Fuck if he knew. He'd have to contact Felix—

Yeah, Felix, who was a known confederate of his. Same as Evelyn. Same as anyone who could help him get in touch with Nadia. If he called them, that call could be monitored.

Fuck!

There had to be a way. It was a fucking *phone call*. Or he could send a text. An e-mail. Something. Anything.

"Whatever you're thinking," Cillian said. "You can't take the chance. You know that."

Jack turned that look on him, the one that made Cillian quail.

"You want to be fucking useful?" Jack said. "Tell me something fucking useful."

"Just do the job. Your girl will be fine. She's busy chasing this Quinn fellow, and as far as these guys know, you and I are talking about a hit you'll do for me. You're supposed to spend a day or two on research, me having you check out this fake mark. As soon as they get your girl, they'll come and tell you what's what."

"Yeah?"

"Yeah, Jack. It's real easy. You take a couple of days off. Hell, anything you want, it's on me. Whiskey, girls, horses . . . not a bad way to spend a couple of days."

"So I do that. Drink. Fuck. Gamble. Wait until they take her. No big deal."

"Exactly. Live it up at my expense and—"

Jack leaned across the table. "I lied. She's more than my protégé."

Cillian only gave a sweaty smile. "Okay, so you really will be worried. But all the more reason to indulge, right? Get your mind off it. I know a couple girls—twins— who'll get your mind off pretty much any—"

"Take the pill."

Cillian blinked.

"Count of three," Jack said. "Take the fucking pill. Or I pull this fucking trigger. It won't kill you. Just make you wish I had."

"But—"

"Pill. *Now*."

"Jack, please. I—"

"Anyone watching?"

"W-what?"

"Are there fucking eyes on us?"

"N-no. Just my boy."

"Take the pill. It's slow-release cyanide. You'll have an hour. Swallow the pill. Walk with me. Tell me what I want. Everything I want. I might give you the antidote."

Cillian stared at the capsule.

"Take it. Now."

Cillian picked it up, put it in his mouth and took a swig of coffee.

"On your feet. Walk."

Cillian obeyed. Once they were in the alley, Jack spun and slugged him in the stomach. Cillian went down, gasping and hacking.

"What the fuck, Jack?"

"Making sure you swallowed it. Now get up. Walk."

Chapter Five
Nadia

I spent the rest of Sunday looking into the case Quinn was working. Well, that and conducting my lodge-hostess duties. I couldn't escape those, no matter what else was going on. The lodge is my real job. I never forget that.

So I skated between responsibilities all day. Show guests the budding wildflowers. Grill Diaz on what he knew. Give shooting lessons at the range. Call Evelyn for background on Diaz. Take a group white-water rafting. Research the background on Quinn's case.

Yes, maybe calling Evelyn wasn't absolutely necessary. Maybe I'd mostly been checking in to see if she'd heard from Jack. She's a retired hitman and his former mentor. If I claimed Jack is the closest thing she had to a son, she'd treat me to a diatribe about the uselessness of children while getting in a few digs at Jack on the way. But theirs is the longest and closest relationship either of them has ever had. That didn't mean he would call to chat, not unless he needed her help. He hadn't.

Diaz knew the basics of the case Quinn had been working on the side. As I researched, I could see why Quinn had jumped at it. Those with a vigilante bent often lean toward specific crimes. For me, it's ones involving women and children, not surprising given my history. Quinn's focus is similar, without the personal experience to explain it. If I whipped out my psychology credits and analyzed, I'd say it's the frustrated family man in him. He had been married once, to his teenage sweetheart. They'd split before having kids, which I'm not sure is as much a symptom of the problem as a cause. Quinn comes from a tight-knit family and grew up expecting that for himself: wife, kids, house in the suburbs. It hasn't happened, and while I think part of what he channels into his vigilantism is what made him become a cop, as it is for me, another part is that frustrated instinct to protect.

It had been that sort of case that started Quinn's vigilantism. A family friend's daughter had been murdered by her abusive ex. When the ex was acquitted, the man asked Quinn to "help him find justice." Quinn refused. The father killed the ex-husband and went to jail. His wife committed suicide. Quinn blamed himself.

For the case Quinn was now investigating, take that old one and multiply it several times over. An abusive husband had murdered his wife, and everyone in his town knew it. Yet the police couldn't dig up enough evidence to charge him. His wife's brother had tried to take matters into his own hands. The perp shot and killed the brother, and the DA decided it was self-defense. The perp remarried and started knocking around wife number two. She disappeared. Again, no one could pin it on him. Then his daughter from his first marriage accused him of sexually abusing her. He accused her of fabricating a story because she blamed him for her mother's death. The police didn't press charges. The daughter killed herself.

It's easy to blame the cops in a case like that. But if the police can't find the evidence, they can't lay charges, as much as they might like to.

For Quinn, this was a local case, about a hundred miles from his home. He'd have known about it and almost certainly would have thought, "I'd like to take that bastard out." When someone came and asked him to do exactly that? He'd have accepted the job. No question.

My research ensured Diaz was being straight with me—the case existed and it was one Quinn would take. Jack doesn't trust Contrapasso—we butted heads with them on our last investigation—so I was extra cautious. Yet from everything I dug up, this was on the level.

I also made sure Quinn really was out of contact. I phoned his personal cell. Phoned his work cell. E-mailed. Texted. I was careful in all of that, the calls going from the phone Felix gave me, which would scramble and reroute. Even then, I left no messages on voice mail, and my text and e-mail were vague, "Hey, you around? Call me."

I left the lodge right after dinner, but hit a post-weekend backup at the border and missed my flight. Diaz rebooked me on the first morning one, and I found a hotel for the night.

I woke in the middle of the night to a text from Jack.

Fucking tech. All fine. Home as planned.

After a few years of knowing Jack I've become fluent at text shorthand, because that's the way he talks most of the time. From this message, I interpreted that he was having trouble placing outgoing calls on his phone. He didn't like texting—it left a permanent record of a conversation—so he'd only make this one exception. I wouldn't hear from him again until he got home "as planned." But I hadn't thought he'd set a date for his return. The last time we spoke he hadn't gotten his job details.

I puzzled on that until I decided I was overthinking it. He'd said he expected to be a week at most. Evidently, that was still all he knew. He'd make contact when he landed.

Knowing not to expect a call didn't mean I wasn't hoping for that nine a.m. check-in. My flight was due to land at 8:30. A delay in takeoff meant we were still descending at 8:56. I turned on my phone early and, yes, felt guilty about it, despite knowing it wouldn't send the plane into a tailspin. I got service at 8:57. By 9:08 we were unloading. No call from Jack. I sighed, pocketed the phone and prepared to disembark.

Chapter Six
Jack

Jack took Cillian three blocks before finding a suitable building to shove him into. The section of Dublin they'd met in was an old one, mostly empty, with sporadic attempts at "revitalization." He took three blocks to choose a spot because he was trying to figure out what the fuck he was going to do next. A rare bout of indecision, rising from the pounding knowledge that he'd fucked up. Fucked up so bad.

He'd spent a year telling himself he couldn't make a move on Nadia, that on the very offside chance she actually reciprocated, he couldn't endanger her by advancing their relationship. Then he'd told himself as long as he took precautions—scrubbing his list of anyone who might be even a remote concern—she'd be fine. But that didn't help against those who were trying to get *on* his list, did it?

As he walked, he kept telling himself the same thing

he'd told Cillian. *Stop whining. Give me something useful.* Yet all he could think about was how to contact her. Anything he did would be risky. But he had to warn her. Had to.

Do you?

Of course he did. Fuck, what kind of stupid question . . .

Except it wasn't a stupid question. Because Nadia wasn't stupid. Yes, she'd go after Quinn. But that didn't mean blindly chasing leads into a trap. She cared about Quinn. But, fuck, Nadia cared about *people*, in a way he admired, even if he couldn't fathom it. He'd seen her do something dangerous because she'd been focused on saving a victim, and he'd given her proper shit for it, in a rare fit of temper. But even then how much danger had she actually been in? Minimal. He just didn't like her taking risks.

Nadia knew what she was doing. And Quinn was not some helpless victim. Like Nadia, he could take care of himself.

Moral of the story, Jack? Chill the fuck out.

Jack prodded Cillian to a building. They walked in and Jack squinted against the near darkness.

"Back there," he said.

"Here's good. There's some light and—"

"Back there."

Cillian's shoulders slumped and he made his way to

the back room Jack had noted. He paused in the doorway, looking around, and Jack had to give him a shove inside. The second room was darker, filthy and full of crates and debris. The condition of the room wasn't the issue. It was what that room said—that it made a really good place to dump a body.

"How's it going down?" Jack asked.

"What?"

"Letting Dee know Quinn's gone. How's that happening? Can't just wait around. Hope she figures he's missing. Not fucking happening. Not on this timetable."

"Uh..."

Funny what a difference time and perspective makes. Thirty years ago, Cillian had been almost twice Jack's age and to Jack, he'd seemed the ultimate ball-busting, take-no-prisoners tough guy. The reality? Cillian was a third-rate thug, a big fish whose small pond dried up years ago. A complete fucking moron who'd gotten where he'd been through brute strength and brass balls, and when one failed, the other took over.

Cillian had no idea how these guys planned to lure Nadia in. Apparently, he really *had* just figured she'd magically realize Quinn was missing. This was, of course, the same guy who believed an antihistamine pill was slow-release cyanide.

What was that old saying about never meeting your heroes? It also applied to not *re*-meeting them thirty years later.

Of course Jack didn't drop it at that. He kept asking. He shattered Cillian's kneecap. And fuck if he didn't feel bad about that. But he had to be sure he was getting honest answers, and he'd always found that rather than threaten to do a thing, you should just do it.

"Fine," Jack said. "Forget their fucking plan. Which you should have asked about. Due diligence."

"You—you broke my goddamned knee," Cillian heaved between gasps of pain.

"Yeah, but at your age? Probably need it replaced. Easier now."

"You've lost your soul, you know that? All those years of killing, and it's gone. Just gone. What would your brothers think? Or your parents?"

There'd been a time when invoking his family's memory would have hurt. Hurt like hell. But Jack hadn't lost his soul. Yeah, he'd misplaced it for a while. Lacking a soul meant you knew the difference between good and bad, you just didn't give a shit. But Jack knew and, in this case, he felt bad. However . . .

"You fucked me over," Jack said. "Did nothing to deserve it. All about you. What you wanted. So now it's about me. What I want. To protect Dee. Who's only in this mess because of us. Your backstab. My carelessness."

"But she'll be fine. That's what you aren't understanding here, Jack, that if you just do what they ask—"

Jack walloped his pistol against the old man's busted knee and then shoved his jacket over Cillian's mouth to stifle his screams.

"That's a no," Jack said. "Suggest it again? You'll need both knees fixed. *If* I give you the antidote." He checked his watch. "Thirty minutes left. You feeling it yet?"

Cillian swallowed and nodded.

"Useful information," Jack said. "That's the key. What's the timetable?"

"Uh, I keep you busy for a couple days doing recon work. They contact me as soon as they have her, and that's when I give them an address and they move in to talk to you."

"You have contact info?"

Cillian nodded. "But you can't just call—"

"Give me everything. I'll decide what to do with it. When are you due? To contact them?"

"They'll call when it's clear on their end."

Which meant no one expected to hear from Cillian.

"How're they making contact? Your phone?"

Cillian nodded. Jack patted him down and took the phone.

"They Irish?" Jack asked.

"Fuck, no. They're from—"

"We'll get to that."

What mattered right now was that, not being Irish,

they'd only expect to hear an older man with an Irish accent when they called.

"Contingency plans?" Jack said, and when Cillian's face screwed up, he couldn't tell if it was because he didn't know the word or because he didn't understand the concept. Both seemed equally likely.

"Backup plan? If they don't get her? If I refuse your job? If I refuse theirs?"

Cillian blinked, and Jack fought the urge to sigh.

"Start with the first," he said. "If they don't get her?"

"I . . . I don't know. I suppose, then the plan fails and they'll just kill that Quinn fellow."

Jack considered that, maybe longer than he should. But, no, Quinn's death would not be a positive outcome. It would upset Nadia.

"If I refuse your job?" he said. "Walk away? Or quit? Or never showed up here?"

"Uh . . ." Cillian paused before seeming to realize all the questions led to the same general conclusion. "I'm supposed to make sure you stay."

"But if I don't?"

"I'm supposed to make sure," he said. "By any means necessary. That's what Petey was for."

"But now Petey has walked away. What if I do the same?"

More blinking, as Cillian propelled his mental wheels faster. Then his eyes glinted, a hint of that crafty thug coming back as he said, "Then I call them, and they know where you're staying, and they'll come get you, and it'll go bad then, Jack. Really bad."

"Bullshit. If they knew my hotel? They'd know how to get to me. Avoid all this crap."

Cillian kept insisting they *could* get to Jack. Covering his ass because the truth was that they hadn't said what they'd do if Cillian failed. The answer was obvious. Cillian failed, Cillian died, so he was trying very hard to convince Jack there was no escape here.

As for the last question—what if Jack refused their job—he supposed there was no need to ask that. They'd take it out on Nadia. Compel him to accept by threatening her. By torturing her.

Which meant there was only one answer here. Only one variable he could control.

Get the fuck out of Ireland and find Nadia.

Chapter Seven
Nadia

There are places you hear about so often that you can picture them. I remembered when Jack and I talked about going to Egypt, seeing everything we'd read and heard about. I have images of all those historic sites. The reality would probably be a disappointment because I can't help but picture them in a historic setting, with endless sands and smog-free skies.

Yet I have mental images of other places, too. More personal places. Quinn's condo is one of them. He's never talked about it specifically. My images come from scattered bits of conversation.

You're painting the lodge? Yeah, I need to do that, too. My walls are builder beige . . . and I'm the second owner.

Hold on, I'm moving into the living room. Someone's having a BBQ out back and they sound like they're on their third case of beer. Let me close the patio door first. That might help.

Nearly broke my neck on the stairs today. Who the hell carpets stairs?

Trust me, you don't even want to see my basement. There's one corner for my weights and the rest is floor-to-ceiling crap. When my family needs to store a few boxes, they bring them to my place.

I moved through Quinn's condo, and it was like being in a dream version of a place I've visited a hundred times. Not quite right, but familiar enough.

Diaz and I came here to hunt for more information, but I'd taken a few minutes alone to orient myself. It was uncomfortable, being here. I'd never visited before, and even if that had been my choice and not his, this felt like an intrusion. This place was unmistakably Quinn's, in a way I wouldn't have imagined. I suppose homes are always a reflection of whoever lives there. I'd just never experienced it so strongly before.

I walked through his condo and I saw him there, felt him there, swore I could even smell him there. When a voice spoke from a distant room, I spun, for a moment thinking I was hearing him, too.

The voice was Diaz's, of course. I hadn't wanted him here. Hadn't even wanted him in Virginia with me. As a cop, I'd been accustomed to new partnerships, but I've grown spoiled, and if it's not Jack or Quinn at my side, I'd rather work alone. Yet Diaz wasn't just some random guy tagging along. He was a professional. A professional what? No idea. Contrapasso agents don't share their backgrounds. Hell, I don't even dare ask his first name. I did know he was a skilled investigator, like all their agents. Which meant I couldn't afford to refuse his help. I'm not sure that was even an option.

Our search centered on Quinn's desktop computer. He had a laptop, but that was for his work—his legit work—so anything he'd kept on this job would be on the desktop. His security was set up by Contrapasso, another condition of employment. They said it was to guarantee he had the best security possible, but he knew it was so they had access. It was one of the things that had kept me from signing up. Today, I was glad they'd done it.

Their security didn't make the computer accessible remotely. Quinn's data was completely fire-walled. That left him safe from cyber attacks. It also explained why we were in his condo, rather than connecting to his home network from some safer location.

Quinn's search history showed he'd definitely been doing research on his target. Hours of prep work, digging through every news article and cross referencing wherever possible. He'd found a home address, vacation home address, work address, cell numbers, car license and registration.

"One thing I'm not finding?" I said. "Any record of that plane ticket."

"Here," Diaz said. "Let me try."

He ran a few things across the screen, his fingers flying as fast as Evelyn's when she was working her

Internet magic. He pulled up some piece of software I'd never seen, one that apparently hunted for deleted data on the hard drive.

"Nothing," he said. "I'll get someone on that. We confirmed the ticket existed and was in his name, but we didn't dig deeper. I'll find out how it was purchased and from where. Good catch."

That was the advantage to working with Contrapasso—as good as Evelyn was, they had access even she couldn't match. That's what happens when you have attorneys, judges, FBI agents, CIA agents and more on the payroll. Part of the price for those members joining is providing that access, even if it risks their jobs. Contrapasso isn't about furthering a career or padding one's income. It's an ideological choice. Which is why I struggle with *not* joining. I share their ideology. I'm just not ready to take the leap and risk the rest.

We finished the search, and I compiled my notes, checking for any gaps.

"Okay," I said, straightening as I turned to Diaz. "Show me the last place your GPS picked him up."

I was in a coffee shop, sitting by the window, watching the building where Contrapasso had lost contact with Quinn. I'd told Diaz I needed to do this alone, to focus on my thoughts, but that was bullshit. Even if he'd have sat and said nothing, I'd have felt obligated to talk to him, to hash this through with him. And he wasn't the person I wanted to hash it through with.

I checked my phone. No call from Jack, which I expected but still . . .

I fingered the numbers on my cell. Maybe a quick call?

Except this wouldn't be quick. Nor was it important enough to break the rules for. I just wanted to talk to him.

I pocketed the phone and sipped my coffee as I gazed at the building. It housed the office of a private investigator the family of Quinn's target had hired when the daughter took her own life. It made sense that Quinn would have gone there. It also made sense the GPS tracker stopped working late at night. This wasn't a Marshal case—Quinn wasn't going to walk in, flash his badge and question the investigator. He'd have been breaking in to copy the files. Quinn needed to be absolutely sure his target was guilty before he began figuring out how and where to pull the hit.

So all that made sense. But the rest . . .

Damn it, Jack. I wish you were here. I really need someone to talk to.

No, I need you *to talk to.*

Then talk.

I heard his voice, that laconic tone, as if even those two words had to be pulled out by force. I looked up at the chair across from me. Of course he wasn't there. But I could picture him. He'd sit with his back to the building because that didn't concern him. This was my job. He'd do what I asked, but otherwise he'd be there only as a sounding board. He'd drink his coffee, comfortable in the silence, waiting for me to break it.

I checked the phone.

Nope, gotta do it this way. Just don't talk out loud. Makes people wonder.

I smiled and shook my head.

What doesn't make sense? The job?

No, it was exactly the kind of opportunity Quinn would jump at.

Yep.

That's all he'd say, but even in my imagination, I heard more in that word. Enough that it made me stop and think.

It seemed tailor-made for Quinn, didn't it?

Yep.

And what about the airline ticket? I can't say Quinn would never pull a stunt like that...

Jack snorted.

Yes, he might. But there was no reason to do it *now*. He didn't know Jack was away. I hadn't hinted we were having problems.

Yeah. Why now? No point.

If Quinn hadn't bought that ticket, who had? The

obvious answer? The people who'd "discovered" it. Contrapasso.

According to them, Quinn had been wearing a GPS tracker that his attackers somehow found and disabled the moment they grabbed him.

Either way, suggests one thing.

That if that tracker really had been disabled, whoever took him knew it would be there.

My cousin's killer had turned out to be the lawyer who helped get a "not guilty" verdict for her alleged killer. A lawyer who'd turned his attention to activism, which got him recruited by none other than the Contrapasso Fellowship. He turned out to be only one of a handful of rotten apples. One of his confederates who'd walked away clear of the whole mess? The same guy who came to visit me just before my missed call from Jack. Diaz.

Chapter Eight
Jack

Jack stepped off the plane in Baltimore and turned on Cillian's phone, holding his breath until he confirmed he hadn't missed any texts or calls. In other words, the goons hadn't grabbed Nadia yet.

With some trepidation he switched on his own phone. Part of him wanted to see a message from Nadia. But part of him feared that, too—if she found a way to make contact, it might attract the attention of her pursuers.

There were no messages from Nadia.

He did, however, have a voice mail and two texts from Evelyn. Nothing more than, "Call me," and maybe the frequency of those made it seem urgent, but that was just Evelyn. If she wanted to speak to him, goddamn it, he should be available to speak.

He sent back, "Busy," and headed to the car rental area, his carryon slung over his shoulder. His bag held nothing suspicious—he kept his work gear in storage or purchased it on-site.

He was in the car rental line when Evelyn called. He let it ring three times, enough to earn him, "Aren't you going to get that?" glares from the others waiting to be served. Then he answered, grunting a hello.

"Good to hear you too, Jack-o."

"Busy."

"Yes, I got the message. Minimalist, even for you. I know you're working, but I want to talk to you about Dee."

He stiffened. Before he could speak, Evelyn said, "I'm concerned about her going after Quinn. I understand she's worried but—"

"Fuck this phone."

"What—?"

"Damn tech. Never fucking works. You still there?"

"Yes, I'm right—"

"Hello?"

"I said—"

"Can't hear a fucking thing. Goddamn it. Look, I'm busy, okay? Working. You got a problem with Dee? Call Dee."

He hung up. Then he switched his phone off and headed back into the terminal. He found a payphone, turned on his cell, and sent Evelyn the number. It was encrypted, of course. Some code she'd made him memorize years ago. He could still remember bitching about that. *Fucking codes, Evelyn? I'm a hitman, not MI6.*

Like the tech, the codes seemed like overkill and most of the time they *were*. Nadia got a laugh out of hitmen in books and movies—top-notch assassins trained in every imaginable martial art, Olympic-level marksmen who carried the kind of tech found only in sci-fi movies. They could kill anyone, anywhere, and leave no trace.

The truth was that your average hitman killed by walking up to a target and shooting him. That was getting tougher these days, with cell phone and street security cameras. But that was still the most common kind of hitman. Jack wasn't that kind. He was a helluva long way from the Hollywood version, though. Today, he was damned happy for that code.

It was twenty minutes before the phone rang, which told him Evelyn had driven to a payphone herself. Meaning she understood the seriousness of the situation.

"I fucked up," he said when he answered the phone.

"I'm not your damn priest, Jack. What the hell is going on?"

"Just told you."

"Just confessed, you mean, which means Dee is in trouble, because that's the only person you're going to feel guilty over. But unless you're the one who took out Quinn—and some days, I wouldn't blame you—I have no damn idea what's going on."

"It was a trap."

"For him? Her? You? Can you use a few more words, Jack? If Dee's in trouble—"

"It was all a trap. My job in Ireland. Taking Quinn. Getting Dee to go after him. It's connected. I'm overseas. Kidnap Quinn. Lure Dee out. Grab her. Get me to take a job."

A moment's pause as she pieced that together. "All that to hire you? Whatever happened to picking up the phone? Oh, wait. I know. *Someone* is inching toward retirement, shutting down all avenues of contact so he can play Grizzly Adams in the middle of nowhere with Jane."

"Tarzan."

"What?"

"It's Tarzan and Jane. Not Grizzly Adams."

"Do you actually want my help or do you want to test my pop culture knowledge first?"

"Getting old. Gotta check."

"Fuck off, Jack. The point is—"

"Point is you're wasting time. Giving me shit. Yeah, that's always fun. But save it. This job? Wouldn't have taken it. Even before Dee. Cillian says it's cartel shit."

Evelyn let loose a few creative curses. She also stopped hassling him. She was the one who'd counseled him to keep his distance from cartels. The mob had rules and codes of conduct. Sometimes fucking stupid rules and codes of conduct. But they had honor. If the cartels had honor, it didn't extend to people like Evelyn and Jack.

"Need you to call Dee," he said. "Tell her—"

"No."

"Don't pull your shit. Not now. Call Dee. Warn her. Find out where she is—"

"So you can run to her rescue?"

"Doesn't need rescue."

"Exactly, which is why you are going to stay the hell away from her. You want to blame yourself for this? Fine, but don't compound the problem by running to her side. She's a helluva lot more careful than Quinn. That's the advantage to being a woman. We don't go striding into danger, King Shit, thinking we can handle all comers."

Jack snorted a laugh.

"You got something to say, Jack-o?"

He didn't answer. She was right about Dee and Quinn. However, as a generalization, the rest was bullshit. Evelyn herself was the one who'd stride in, guns blazing, while Jack hung back and assessed. Not as much a gender disparity as a difference in personality.

"You're right," he said. "About Dee."

"Good. So she'll make it tough on them, which means they'll need to keep her under surveillance, which means you cannot show up or, being a cartel, they're liable to get pissy and just shoot her to punish you for screwing up their plan."

"Fuck."

"Yes, *fuck*, Jack. At the very least, they'll realize their scheme is ruined and Quinn will have outlived his usefulness. Maybe you wouldn't be too broken up by that, but you wouldn't be dancing on his grave either. More importantly, Dee would blame herself. Because she's good at that, kind of like someone else I know. Dee won't want Quinn dead, so it's best not to let Quinn die, right?"

"Yeah."

"Slow down and think. I know you aren't being reckless—otherwise, you'd have called me from Ireland or, worse, called her. But for you, this is panic. Just stop and think it through. *All* the way through."

He shifted the receiver from one hand to the other, trying to squelch that roiling in his gut that said he was already moving too slowly, that Nadia was in danger and goddamn it, he was only a couple hundred miles away and—

He inhaled sharply. Panic. That's what he was feeling. The last time he'd even come close . . .

He squeezed his eyes shut and swore he could still smell the smoke.

He'd gone to get cigarettes. His shift at the mechanic's had ended, and he'd walked halfway home before remembering the cigarettes. His brother, Tommy, was out, and he didn't like Jack's brand, and it wasn't like he could run and grab a pack himself. Not after he'd nearly lost his leg in the mission that got their two other brothers killed. The mission that made Jack tell the guys in charge to go fuck themselves. He'd warned them their plan wasn't safe but who the fuck was he? Some kid whose only fucking talent was killing people. He'd quit the group and refused to go back, and all he'd wanted that day was to get cigarettes for Tommy. So he'd gone back for them, and when he returned to that same spot, a mile from home, he saw the smoke. He dropped the cigarettes and he ran because it didn't matter if he couldn't see where that smoke came from. He knew. He just knew.

"Jack?"

"Yeah." He pinched the bridge of his nose. "Okay. You're right. But I gotta let her know. Gotta figure out a way—"

"I'll tell her."

He shook his head. "Can't use her phone—"

"I have a plan."

Chapter Nine
Nadia

"I'm going home," I told Diaz as I met up with him in the parking lot.

"What?"

"My caretaker called. There's a power-supply problem at the lodge and if we don't get it fixed by Thursday—when we're fully booked with a corporate retreat—we're screwed."

"Okay . . ." he said slowly. He was at his car, talking over it, his hands on the roof where I could see them.

"I wanted to help," I said. "I still do, and if I can, I'll come back, but really, you guys can handle this. You have actual investigators. I'm just an ex-cop who never even made detective."

"But you're good. Damned good. We could really use—"

"I can't, and I feel like shit about that. But my real-life job comes first. I understand that's an inconvenience, me coming here and then cutting out on you . . ."

He shook his head. "I'm glad you came, and of course I wish you could stay, but you're right about the lodge. It's important for all our agents—and potential recruits—to have an outside life." He stepped back. "Can I give you a lift to the airport?"

"I have my rental," I said, pointing at it.

"I know. But I'm guessing you're flying out of DC and traffic's a bitch this time of day. With two of us, we can take the commuter lane. I can have the rental agency pick up your car."

I shook my head. "I'll be fine, thanks."

"Let me write down some alternate directions for you. Back roads. They'll take you a bit out of the way, but at this time of day, it'll be worth it. I'd suggest not booking a flight until you're there, to be safe. They run frequently enough that you'll have no problem getting one."

I thanked him as he wrote out directions. Then headed for my car. As I was getting in, Diaz called to me, "Wait! That gun I lent you—"

I shut the door, fired up the car and, with a friendly wave—pretending I couldn't understand what he was mouthing—I drove from the lot.

Diaz was tailing me. I couldn't see him, but I knew he was there. Because the chances he'd sent me on these back roads to the airport just to be helpful? About zero.

I was now on a truly back road—a dirt one. It was empty, which at least made it tough to tail. As I drove down a dip, I spotted a car in the distance behind me, its running lights off. It looked gray or silver, nearly invisible in the daylight. Diaz's car had been dark. Was he behind that one? Or had he switched vehicles?

My work phone rang. I grabbed it so fast I nearly dropped it.

"Hello?" I said. *Please, Jack. Please be—*

"Where the hell are you?" Evelyn said.

Damn it. "This really isn't the time, Evelyn. Can I call you—?"

"Everyone's so busy today. A woman tries to be helpful, and that's all she hears. I don't know why I bother."

"Because if we're busy, it probably means we're doing something interesting, and you're bored. Like those nosy old ladies who sit on the front porch and yell at the neighborhood kids."

"I wouldn't yell at them. I'd shoot them."

I smiled. "Look, I can't talk but . . . you said everyone's busy, does that mean you were talking to Jack?"

"No. Bastard gives me shit if I call him on a job. Says I'm *interrupting* him. Like he'd even have those jobs if it wasn't for me. I suppose he talks to *you*."

"Not this trip. He's having phone problems. I was hoping maybe he'd resolved the issue."

"So that's why you answered so fast. Well, I'm sure he's fine. About you, though . . ."

I glanced in the rearview mirror to see the other car zooming up in a cloud of dust.

"I really have to—" I began.

"You went after Quinn, didn't you? Weekend's over so you can leave that damned shack of yours and go chasing after the Boy Scout who obviously was *not* prepared."

The car was fast closing the gap between us.

"Can we talk about this later?" I said. "I'm—"

"I'm coming to help," she said.

"What? No. I—"

"I'm bored. You want me to admit it? Fine, I just did. I'm bored and you're out there alone, with no backup, Jack having fucked off to Ireland."

"I worked alone for years, remember? I'm fine. Really."

"Are you in Virginia?"

"Yes, but I honestly don't need your help."

"I'll call when I get there."

She hung up. I glanced in my mirror. The car was still coming fast. I shoved the phone into my pocket, took out the gun and wedged it under my thigh.

When the car drew close enough, it turned on its

signal. *See? I'm just an ordinary citizen, signaling my pass. No need for panic.*

I could see two men in the car—driver and passenger. Dark hair, brown skin, clean shaven . . . which also matched Diaz's description.

The car veered out. I slammed on my brakes, and it shot past. The driver started to swerve at my car before he realized it wasn't beside him. He hit the brakes, and his car went into a fishtail. I geared into reverse, punched the gas and zoomed backwards to what looked like a laneway heading into the forest. The other driver had come out of his fishtail and was getting turned around. I steered into the laneway, car rocketing over the rough dirt road, which I quickly realized was not a driveway so much as a turnoff spot for hunters or hikers to park.

The trail narrowed as it headed farther into the woods, and I kept going, totally violating my rental agreement. Another good reason never to use my real credit card.

The 4x4ing would have been easier had I been driving an actual 4x4. But one advantage to the compact car was its size. The driver of the other vehicle—possibly accustomed to smaller vehicles—hit the gas and made a valiant effort to follow me down the narrowing trail, plowing down small saplings before getting wedged between two trees. I'd have found that far more amusing if I did not, at that moment, reach the end of my own trail, which soared up the side of an embankment that only an ATV could scale.

I braked hard. Then I snapped off my seatbelt and, gun in hand, peered around the headrest. The other guys were already getting out of their vehicle. Shit.

I cracked opened the driver's door, then inched over to the passenger seat and kicked the driver's door wide. I fired a shot through it. As they took cover to return fire, I threw open the passenger door and rolled out.

I ran into the forest. It didn't matter that I made a racket—what counted now was getting as far from these two as possible. When I was out of reasonable firing range, I hit the ground. Then I rose on all fours and crawled quietly to my left.

I could hear them speaking Spanish, which wasn't helpful, my vocabulary limited to please, thank you and, "Where's the restroom." I could, however, track their voices. One was coming my way while his partner circled around.

I surveyed the playing field. Further to my left was a hunting blind. It was in rough shape, likely a decade since anyone used it. But it gave me something to aim for, and I crawled that way while periodically turning to throw rocks or sticks in the other direction. My pursuer fell for the trick while I continued to the blind and hunkered behind it.

A hunting blind is made for rifles. Also for deer, who aren't the smartest beasts in the forest. This provided temporary shelter, nothing more. What I needed was . . .

I looked up. The tree was climbable above about ten feet. That meant if I could use the blind as a ladder, I could get up there. I would, however, be exposed while climbing.

I checked my options again. I'd lost sight of the guy circling around. His partner was about twenty feet away—too far for a decent shot through dense forest.

I threw another rock, but now that he was closer, he only looked around instead of following the sound. I crouched motionless behind the blind until I heard the tramp of his feet again.

When his footfalls stopped, I peered through a hole in the blind to see he was looking in the opposite direction, bobbing and weaving as he tried to see something he thought was me.

While he walked toward the stump, I scaled the blind. I was putting my foot on my third and last piece of frame when the rotted wood gave way. I grabbed a branch overhead before I fell, but my foot knocked hard against the blind, the sound as loud as a shot.

The guy spun. I swung into the tree, getting up among the leaves. They hid me, but the guy now knew roughly where I was.

He lifted his gun. He didn't fire. A handgun isn't an MK-47—you can't just spray wide and hope to hit your target. As good as that leafy cover was, some part of me must have showed, because his head swung up, his gaze and gun lifting and—

He dropped with a bullet between his eyes. I exhaled and allowed myself a smile as I lowered my gun. While a handgun is less than ideal for sniping, it'll do the job if you can get into a clear position . . . like up a tree looking down on your target.

The gun was a Smith & Wesson 9mm, which meant I had ten rounds and no backup ammo. Not ideal, but at the risk of sounding cocky, with one remaining target and nine shots, I felt okay about it.

Now all I had to do was figure out where the other guy—

A twig crackled underfoot. *Behind* me. The guy was right there, ten feet away, his gun rising. I fired but I wasn't ready. My bullet hit him in the shoulder and I didn't have time for another. I jumped from the tree. He fired just as I leaped—three rapid-fire shots, the first flying over my head, the second whipping past me and the third . . .

I tried to twist in mid-flight, get out of whatever path he expected me to fall. I twisted too blindly and while the bullet only hit my arm, my head struck the blind, cracking against the frame as I went down. A moment of gray. Then a very hard landing jolted me awake.

I tried to scramble up but nearly blacked out. I crouched on the far side of the blind and blinked hard.

Damn it, focus!

Gun. Where was my gun?

I must have dropped it when I grayed out.

I looked around. I could hear my assailant tromping toward me, breathing hard, obviously injured worse than I'd thought. Good. Yet he was still coming and my damn gun must be on the other side of the blind.

I pulled out the knife I'd picked up while following Quinn's trail. Jack's rule: Never leave home with only one weapon. I just needed to get in a position to use it.

I pushed to all fours, gritting my teeth against my throbbing head as I crawled. I peeked around the blind while keeping my head as low to the ground as possible. The guy was headed my way with his gaze fixed on the blind. My gun lay three feet away, just out of reach.

My fingers clenched the knife, but I couldn't stop eying the 9mm. It was the safer bet. Getting to it, however, was not a safe bet. Nor could I leap up and charge him with my knife before he could turn and shoot. Hell, I might not be *able* to leap up. Blood ran down my arm. My head swam. My eyes kept losing focus.

Only one option, really, as imperfect as it was. I shifted into a sprinter's start and the world swayed.

Focus, just focus.

The thug started moving around the blind. My muscles tensed, but I held still, waiting until he was completely out of sight and then—

I dashed to my gun and swung it up as he cursed in Spanish and raced around the blind and—

A shot. *As* I was still squeezing my trigger. I fired and dropped. Not that it would do much good. Bullets don't move in slow motion. But then—two seconds later—I saw the thug's muzzle blast, his gun pointing up, shot going wide as he fell.

My shot had hit him in the chest. As he fell, I saw blood on his face. There *had* been another shot. Another shooter.

That shooter may have killed my opponent, but I wasn't lowering my weapon to high-five him, whoever he was. I ran deeper into the forest and hit the ground in a roll. I did not intentionally hit the ground in a roll. Nor did I intentionally stop running. My brain betrayed me, dipping into unconsciousness just long enough for me to stumble.

I came to on the ground and scrambled up on all fours.

"Dee?"

It was Diaz's voice. I went still and carefully shifted to sit, facing him, my gun ready.

"Obviously, I'm not here to shoot you," he called. "I just killed the guy who was trying to."

I said nothing.

"Okay, I know you're not going to take my word for it," he continued. "Even if I *did* just save your life."

I tried not to snort at that. He grunted, and I could see a shadowy figure near the blind. Another grunt and a thump, as he moved the thug's body.

"I see you didn't actually need my help. Nice shooting."

I shifted position, squeezing my injured arm with my free hand to stop the bleeding.

He continued. "I knew something was up. We did—Contrapasso. The plane ticket was purchased in Mexico, with a card number Quinn no longer uses. I knew all that *before* I came to see you."

He took a few steps, looking around. "Contrapasso thinks you might have been involved in whatever happened to Quinn. That's why they sent me. I disagreed—I don't see a motive. But that ticket meant someone was linking you to Quinn's disappearance, which bore investigating. When you wanted to come back and hunt for him, I realized *that* might have been the point of letting us find the ticket—*getting* you involved. Luring you out. They knew you flew into Buffalo, so they bought Quinn a ticket there. But they didn't actually know where to find you."

I still said nothing.

He continued. "I suspected you'd pick up a tail as soon as you went to check out Quinn's last known location. You did. They probably hoped you'd go into the building, where they could grab you. When that failed, they followed your car. That's why I sent you down these back roads. To give them a quiet spot to cut you off. I was behind them. That's also why I didn't come after you to get back the gun."

He went quiet, looked around, and then sighed. "Tell me what else you need, Dee. You suspected something was up—that's why you cut out early. You obviously thought *I'd* set you up. I didn't. Let's figure out who did. Together."

I waited.

"Listen," he said. "I'm putting my hands up. My gun is holstered. Tell me what else you need."

I waited until he had his hands raised and I could see they were empty. Then I rose just enough to peer around the area, looking for any sign he wasn't alone. The forest was still and quiet. I opened my mouth . . . and caught a movement to Diaz's right, a dark shape slipping through the trees.

Son of a bitch! Double-crossing—

Sunlight glinted off a gun. A sawed-off shotgun. Very clearly *not* pointed at me.

"Diaz!" I shouted. "Get—!"

The shotgun fired. Diaz went down. I was halfway to my feet. I froze and had to lock my knees to keep from dropping so fast I'd be spotted. Gaze fixed on that shotgun, I lowered myself slowly back to a crouch. I almost fell doing it, my head swimming, as if in delayed reaction to jumping up. I blinked hard and rubbed my face with my free hand. Then I hunkered there, my gun poised, trying to get a clear shot, but the guy was on the move, walking toward Diaz, who lay moaning on the ground. The gunman walked right up to Diaz, aimed the shotgun and—

I fired. Even as I pulled the trigger, I knew my angle wasn't good enough. The gunman staggered back, the shot catching him in the side. He swung the shotgun in my direction. He fired. I hit the ground hard. A couple of pellets ripped into my shoulder and side. I raised my gun. A blur of movement as Diaz grabbed the guy's leg.

Damn it, no, Diaz. Don't—

I fired mid-thought. So did the guy with the shotgun. He swung it on Diaz and fired and my bullet hit him a split-second later, catching him square in the chest and he went down.

I pushed up—too fast—and nearly passed out. Teeth gritted, I stood and staggered toward them, my gun ready, my gaze on that shotgun, still in the guy's hand. The barrel lifted, barely half an inch, shaking hard. I was about to squeeze my trigger when the shotgun fell and the guy let out a long hiss and went still.

I continued toward them, slowly and carefully, still aiming in case the shooter was faking. When I was close enough, I kicked the shotgun. It fell out of his hands. I checked for a pulse. None. Then I turned to Diaz.

There wasn't any need to check for Diaz's pulse. The guy had aimed that shotgun at his head, point-blank range. I swallowed and turned away. Even that movement seemed too much, as if my body had hit its limit. I tried to lower myself to the ground and got halfway down before collapsing.

I blacked out for a second. When I came to, it took a few more seconds to orient myself. Then I saw Diaz and remembered what was happening. I needed to get out of here. Those three guys weren't working on their own— they were very obviously hired thugs, and their handler would be tracking them by GPS. When they didn't call in an update—

As if on cue, a phone vibrated from the pocket of the guy with the shotgun. I fished the cell out. The caller ID only said "Juan," but I knew it wasn't a buddy calling to see if he wanted to come over and watch the game.

I pocketed the phone. I needed to get out of here. Just get up and . . .

Halfway to my feet, I swayed, the world dipping and darkening. I quickly lowered myself again.

I might be able to get as far as the cars, but neither vehicle was in any condition to get me out of here, and I didn't know where Diaz left his.

I just needed to get someplace temporarily safe. Someplace I could rest and assess my injuries.

I took the guy's belt to use as a tourniquet and

checked his pockets for anything else I could use. A wallet—probably fake ID, but I grabbed that. A pocket knife. Might as well take it, too.

I put the small stuff into my pockets and crawled to Diaz and the other guys. I emptied their pockets, taking cell phones, wallets, car keys and weapons. That's a lot to carry, but if I had to hunker down in rough shape, preparing to fend off more attackers, I was building an arsenal.

With everything stashed and the shotgun in hand, I rose at the rate of a ninety-nine-year-old with bad knees. At least the slow movement kept my head from swimming. I got upright and then continued at that pace, cutting a careful path, not leaving footprints on open ground or mowing down undergrowth to betray my route. Focusing on that task seemed to help, and my head remained clear for about fifty paces. Then I started to sway. By that point, I was almost where I wanted to be—a particularly thick stand of trees with lots of bushes. I got in there and huddled down like a rabbit in a thicket.

And then I just cut out, as if I'd expended every last bit of energy. I had to grit my teeth and struggle to stay conscious as I bound my arm. I'd lost blood. I was afraid to even calculate how much, but I suspected it contributed to that light-headedness.

I got the belt on for a tourniquet. The wound didn't seem bad. Just messy. I was trying to get a better look, twisting to see it on the back of my biceps, when my phone rang. As proof of how out of it I was, it took at least five rings before I realized what I was hearing. Then another two rings as I thought, "That's right, Evelyn's coming. I should have called her for help." And yet another ring before I grabbed it, thinking, "Shit! My phone is ringing. *Loudly.*"

In my confusion, instead of answering, I solved the latter problem by turning my phone to vibrate mode. Of course, by that time, Evelyn had hung up.

I went to call her back and . . . And I couldn't. It was as if I truly had drained even the last dregs of strength, and I sat there, staring at the phone, thinking, "What was I doing?" as the world grayed and then came back . . . grayed and then came back.

Call Evelyn.

Yes, I needed to call . . .

How did I call . . .?

Redial. Hit—

The phone buzzed softly in my hand. I stared at it.

Focus, Nadia. Answer the phone.

I hit the button and as I did, everything dimmed, just for a second. But I came back, hearing Evelyn saying, "Dee? Are you there? Dee!"

"Yes." I slurred the word and struggled to focus. "I need . . ."

That graying again, as if someone was fiddling with

the world's brightness dial.

"Dee? Where are you?"

"Shot . . . I got . . ."

"Dee? Where *are* you?"

I tried to blink back the mental fog, but the world kept dimming as I struggled to remember the name of the road. *Just give her the name of the . . .*

Darkness.

Chapter Ten

Jack

Jack was still in DC. Well, technically, he'd crossed the Virginia state line, but only because finding a roadside motel in Washington had proved to be a pain in the ass. Or that made a good excuse. Of course, when Evelyn landed, she'd given him shit, saying she was sure he could have found a place between Baltimore and Washington. She didn't push the matter. She knew he had to get closer to Nadia, to feel he could swoop in if something went wrong. The fact that he was holed up in a motel and not at Quinn's condo, searching for clues, was really as much as she could expect under the circumstances.

It took over an hour after she landed at Dulles, though, before she was at his door. He'd been checking out the window at every car door slam, and he had the door open before she could knock. He expected a sarcastic comment. She just walked in and handed him a pack of cigarettes.

"What the fuck?"

"You're welcome, Jack. Really, you are. And we won't even mention what a pain in the ass it was for me to find your damned brand without detouring over half the city."

"I was just in Ireland. Brought back a carton."

"Which I'm sure you left in your locker when you picked up your supplies. You're going to need them to get through the next few hours. In fact, I suggest you have one right now."

He shook his head and tossed the pack on the bed. "I'm fine. You called Nadia? Got an address?"

Evelyn walked over, picked up the cigarettes, took one out and handed it to him. "Smoke. I'll pay the cleaning fee."

He loomed over her. "You did talk to her. Right?"

"Yes."

He exhaled. She tried to pass him the cigarette again. He shoved it back into the package. "Where is she?"

Silence. He turned to Evelyn. "You talked to her . . ."

"I think so."

"What? How can you *fucking* think—?"

"I called her and someone answered, and I'm ninety percent sure it was her. But she was . . . in rough shape. I don't know what exactly happened, but she was trying to answer me and then she just couldn't. I kept trying to talk to her, but there was no answer."

Jack grabbed his jacket and strode to the door. Evelyn

caught his arm, releasing it before he could throw her off. She sidestepped in front of him, blocking the door.

"What exactly are you going to do, Jack?"

"Find her."

"How? You have no idea—"

"Felix," he said and reached for the doorknob, but she slammed her hip against it, wincing slightly, the move not quite as easy as it would have been fifty years ago.

"Fine," she said. "You're going to call Felix and hope he can help. So call him. From here."

Jack shook his head. "On the road."

"Slow down."

He met her gaze. "No."

She returned the look. "*Yes*, Jack, because as guilty as you feel now, you're going to feel a helluva lot worse if you get her killed by wasting time running off half-cocked to find her."

"Wouldn't do that. I'll be careful. Just—"

"Do you even have your weapons?"

He had his main gun holstered, as usual, but hadn't taken his backups. He glanced over his shoulder at the duffel bag from his Washington locker. When he turned back, Evelyn had her own gun pointed at him.

"Slow the hell down, Jack," she said. "Or I swear, I'll put a bullet through your leg."

"That's not my leg."

"Close enough. Now call Felix and see what he can

do."

Jack glowered at her, but the truth was he'd only been heading to his rental car so he could feel like he was taking action. So he could drive farther into Virginia and get closer to wherever Nadia was. It wouldn't make much difference. It would just make him feel better. Wouldn't do any harm, either, but he knew better than to call Evelyn's bluff. She'd shot him before.

He called Felix. "Dee's phone," he said when Felix answered. "I need to track it."

"I'd make some smart comment about the lack of pleasantries," Felix said in his perfectly-articulated English, "But I know you're not asking because you forgot where you're supposed to meet her for lunch. I presume there's a problem?"

"Yes."

"And you need to know where she is. But the thing about making a phone that doesn't register on GPS, Jack? It doesn't register on GPS."

"There's a back door."

"I don't believe I ever said—"

"There is. You have the key. Open it."

"It's not that simple. If it was, anyone with a little knowhow could do it."

"Just open that door. Whatever it costs. Bill me."

"I'm not trying to justify a higher price, Jack. I'd hope you'd realize that. Nor am I stalling. I'm at my computer working on it as we speak. But it's going to take time, and if Dee's in trouble and you have any other way of locating her . . ."

"I don't."

"Then let me do this, and I'll phone you back."

Jack grunted his thanks and hung up. Evelyn waved him back toward the bed, her gun still trained on him.

"Put that away," he said.

"Not until I'm convinced you won't run out the door."

He snorted and backed onto the bed. "Wouldn't run. Just knock you out of the way. You're old."

"Fuck you, too, Jack." She holstered her gun but kept her tailored suit jacket open for easy access. "My role here is to make sure you keep it together, and if that means putting a bullet in you, I will, because I sure as hell don't want to deal with you if you lose her."

He shifted on the bed as he tried to shove that thought from his head. Really not the way to calm him down.

"*This* is what you need to fix," she said. "Not making sure she's safer. You've done everything you can short of locking her up at that damned lodge of hers, which, by the way, I don't suggest you try, however tempting it might be."

He gave her a look.

She continued. "You don't need to make her safer.

You just need to calm down. You love her. Which is a pain in the ass, as you're about to discover. Life's a whole lot easier when you don't give a shit about anyone. But this is your choice. So deal with it. Get off that hamster wheel of this-is-all-my-fault-and-I-have-to-save-her. She'll save herself."

"She's *hurt*."

"We have no idea what happened, and as frustrating as it is to sit on our asses and wait for Felix to give us her location, that's what we have to do."

Before Jack could answer, a phone rang. He grabbed his only to see that the screen was dark. It was Cillian's, over on the nightstand. He started to scramble for it. Then he stopped, inhaled and closed his eyes for a split second before answering.

"Yeah," he said.

"We have her," a voice said in a thick Spanish accent.

Jack ramped up his own accent as he said, "Wha?"

The man spoke slower, as if communication was an issue. "We have his girl. Dee. She took the bait. We grabbed her."

Jack's heart pounded, but he only grunted. "Now what?"

"Where is he?"

Jack resisted the urge to give another short answer. Cillian liked to talk. So he said, "He's doing the job I set him on, like we agreed. I've been having a fuck of a time with it. He's not a fucking amateur. He wants to get done and get home, and I keep having to find new fucking things for him to do to keep him here."

"We are paying you very well for any inconvenience, so do not whine to me, old man. Your part is almost over. Call him in. Have your men disarm and disable him. I will call in two hours to speak to him."

"Two hours? I'll be lucky if I can even get hold of him in—"

"That is your problem, and I would not advise you to make it ours. Two hours."

"Make sure you have the girl."

"What?" the man said, his voice sharp.

"He's going to want to speak to his girl before he believes you have her."

"Do not tell us how to do our job."

"I'm just warning you. I know Jack and—"

"And you will control him and convince him to do as we ask. He will speak to his girl when we are ready. We have much experience in these things and we do not appreciate some drunk mick thug—"

"Hey! I'm—"

"A thug. A blunt instrument. Do not attempt to think. You will only strain yourself. Two hours."

The line went dead. Jack stood there, holding the phone, eyes closed.

"So they have—" Evelyn began.

He raised his finger, asking for a moment. To his surprise, she actually stopped talking.

"All right," he said when he opened his eyes. "They seem to have her. But she's okay. Alive. They won't hurt her. Not unless I refuse their job. I have two hours."

"They won't have left her cell phone on, Jack," Evelyn said, her voice uncharacteristically soft. "They probably wouldn't even take it with her."

"Yeah, but it'll tell us where she was last. That's my only clue. I'll take it. I just need to set an alarm." He took out his phone and did so. "Two hours. Gotta make sure there's no background noise." He pocketed it. "Now can we drive? Get into Virginia?"

Evelyn nodded, and Jack retrieved his backup weapons and kit.

Twenty minutes after they left the motel, Felix called with a GPS location. The *current* one. Her phone was still on. Felix had tried calling but gotten no answer. That was troubling—both the lack of an answer and the fact that the phone was still active. In the meantime, Felix wanted to know what was going on. Jack was driving . . . and feeling even less talkative than usual.

"Put Evelyn on," Felix said. "I'm trying to help, Jack, not merely satisfy my curiosity. I can tell by the number you used that you're on a backup phone from one of your lockers. It's a safe connection, yes?"

It was. Jack had disabled the phone he'd used in Ireland. He hated doing that to his only possible connection to Nadia, but it was the safe move. He passed his phone to Evelyn. She left out the details of where Jack had been and who he'd been working for—most of which Jack hadn't shared himself. Then she put Felix on speaker.

"So the client who brought you overseas, Jack," Felix said. "You knew him?"

"From years back. Owed him a favor. Open chit."

"And he conveniently chose to close it at a time when you're trying to cash all those in."

"Yeah. Guaranteed I'd come."

"Where's he now?"

"Tied to a bed."

Felix chuckled. "Did you leave him a bowl of dog food and water? I've heard that's a specialty of yours."

"Something like that. He's fine. Not going anywhere. Gotta figure out how to handle it. What to do with him."

Evelyn made a noise that said the answer was clear. Cillian had to die.

"If you need someone to handle it for you . . ." Felix said.

"If it needs doing, I'll do it. Only right. Anyway, he's alive. Needed that. Just in case."

"Agreed, but you've made sure he can't tell this cartel

you're coming for Dee and that's the important thing right now—that he is incapacitated. As for the cartel . . . Evelyn is right, this scheme is a lot of effort to hire a pro. That means they need the best. No substitutes possible. I'm going to guess it's political. That is, sadly, becoming more common for the cartels. If they can't bribe a politician, they take him out of office—permanently. To need you on the job suggests it isn't some village mayor they want killed. We're talking serious political assassination."

"Doesn't matter. Not doing it."

"No, but the point, Jack, is that it will help if I can find out what they want you to do. That will tell us who's pulling the strings, and then Evelyn and I can scour our contact lists for someone who can get inside information. Go through the back door."

"Right," Jack said. "Okay. Good. Appreciate it."

"I know you do, and while I won't turn down a return favor, this is mostly for Dee and Quinn. Yes, I know you aren't a fan of Quinn's, but he's saved my skin a few times. I owe him. Let me see what the news is on the grapevine for cartels and political assassination jobs."

"Thanks."

"You're welcome. Evelyn? Let's put our heads together on this while Jack drives."

* * * * *

As soon as they neared the GPS spot, Jack knew what had happened. It didn't take Sherlock Holmes to read the signs. Skid marks suggested a hard braking on the road. Then tire treads led into a partly overgrown laneway, the undergrowth mowed down. When Jack slowed driving past, he could peer down that lane and see the rear bumper of a car.

"They ran her off the road," Evelyn said.

Jack kept driving. "No. She led them off. That's not her car. Too big. Not a rental either. She made them. Braked. Drove down there. They got stuck."

"And you're doubting that she can handle herself?"

"Never said that. Everyone can use help."

He found another pull-in farther down and drove the rental in as far as he could and then pulled off to the side, rolling over the rough ground until he was sure the car couldn't be spotted from the road.

"We need to be ready for a trap, Jack," Evelyn said as he opened the door.

"Know that. But her phone's on. Gotta be a reason."

The reason he hoped was that Nadia had known she was about to be taken and ditched the phone so Evelyn would contact Felix and unlock the GPS. But there was also a good chance that whoever took her had left that phone on intentionally, to see who might come looking.

Jack checked his watch. Just under ninety minutes until the cartel goons would call "Cillian" again.

He got out and looked around. Everything seemed quiet, but that didn't mean shit. He started in the direction of the GPS signal, his own phone out, using a tracker Felix had installed remotely. Evelyn followed. They were about five hundred feet out from the signal now.

They'd barely gone another dozen paces before voices floated over, men speaking Spanish. Evelyn tried to catch his eye, but he ignored her. The men weren't whispering so it wasn't a trap. Maybe they'd come back for Nadia's missing cell phone. Or a missing comrade she'd killed. Trap or not, Jack would still approach with care.

He covered half the distance to the voices. He'd picked up some Spanish over the years—couldn't really avoid it, living in the States—but fuck, it wasn't like he'd studied it or anything. He wasn't like Nadia, who learned new things just because she found them interesting. While he was more likely to pick up a novel than turn on the TV, he'd never been good at school. He'd dropped out to become a mechanic. That's what he was good at— figuring out stuff like engines. Or how to kill people without them knowing they were about to be killed.

From what he could pick up, the men were hunting for something or someone, which he'd already guessed. He looked at Evelyn. She knew more Spanish, but she was frowning, head tilted, and he suspected it wasn't so much a language barrier as the fact she couldn't hear the voices as well as he could. She was too vain to wear a hearing aid until her doctor recommended one. Which meant she got along fine in day-to-day conversation. But ask her to decipher one a few hundred feet away and she struggled.

Jack hunkered down. Evelyn motioned to say she wanted to get closer. He raised his hand, telling her to hold on. He picked apart the voices and the sounds of movement. Two men talking. What sounded like a third searching without adding to the dialogue.

He lifted three fingers and then pointed in each direction. Moving to the side, he scanned the best view of the playing field. Then he indicated a route they'd take. Evelyn didn't argue, which was as sure a sign as any that she needed to rely on him to hear from this distance.

Jack aimed for the silent guy first. When he drew close enough, he motioned for Evelyn to continue toward the other two, in hopes she'd overhear their conversation better, though he knew not to say so. Pointing out Evelyn's weaknesses was like intentionally stepping on a tiger's tail.

He slipped through the woods until he could see the third man. It was a young guy, maybe mid-twenties. Not Hispanic, which may have explained why he wasn't joining the conversation—most likely local hired help, not considered a real part of the team. He was clearly hunting for something, doubled over and pulling back shrubs and undergrowth. Paying absolutely no attention to his surrounding. That preoccupation meant Jack could get within ten feet. He lined up his shot and put a bullet through the back of the guy's head, dropping him to the ground with a thump no louder than the suppressed shot. His two comrades continued talking, oblivious.

Jack pulled brush over the dead man's head to hide his light hair. As for the guy himself, the only thought Jack spared him was to wonder, for a moment, whether he *ought* to spare him a thought. Whether Nadia would. You couldn't be a philosopher in this job. Or much of a humanist, for that matter. Only now that he was with Nadia did he pause to contemplate what *she'd* think. Because that was still the only criterion that mattered. Not whether it was right or wrong, but whether it might bother her. This wouldn't. Yeah, the guy was young, but he wasn't a child. He knew what he was getting into, and if he didn't believe it could cost him his life, that was just stupidity. No cure for that.

Jack remembered the first time he'd really understood the risks himself. He'd been sixteen when the group recruited him, and all he'd cared about was showing his brothers he wasn't a little kid. Second mission, he took out his mark with ease and then realized one of the other recruits had been made. Jack killed the guy who made him, but not before the guy popped off a shot. Wasn't fatal, and Jack dragged his comrade into an empty building. That's when his handler came along, decided the guy needed serious medical care and popped him two in the head.

The kid had been six months older than Jack. Signed up because his infant daughter was sick and he needed money for medicine.

"Too fucking bad," his handler said when Jack protested. "He wanted safe? Shoulda stayed on the farm."

That was when Jack realized that not only could he die, but if he fucked up, his termination papers would be the permanent variety. And all he'd taken from that lesson? That he had to make himself less disposable. Had to be so fucking good that if he'd been shot, they'd have gotten him to a fucking hospital.

As for the rest? Well, if he wanted safe, he could go back to being a mechanic's apprentice, making a couple bucks an hour and praying the boss's rusted hoist didn't drop a car on him. You make your choices. You live with them. Or die with them.

Jack was on the move again, sliding through the forest as he made his way to Evelyn. When he reached her, she typed out a note for him on her phone to avoid speaking.

They're looking for something. That's all I know. Chatter is just macho bullshit about sisters they want to screw. Seems the gals are holding out for wedding rings.

Jack grunted. Picking off one of these two would be tougher, given how much they were talking and how close together they walked. Jack surveyed the situation. Then he took Evelyn's phone and tapped out his plan. She adjusted it, of course, not because it needed adjusting but because she had to put her fingerprints on it. Jack let her. He didn't play the pissing game with Evelyn—or with anyone else. No fucking time or energy for that bullshit. As long as the core plan hadn't changed, she could have her tweaks.

Jack slipped off. He'd take the long route around. The tougher route. The one better suited to the younger guy, which was a bit of a laugh, all things considered but, hell, kinda nice to be "the younger guy" once in a while.

He had to dart across open patches without being seen or heard. He managed it easily enough, and gave Nadia credit for that. In the early days, he'd meet her out in the forest and sneak up on her. He'd pretended, of course, that the subterfuge was accidental—that's just how he moved. And it was, in a way, but part of it had been a game, too, surprising Nadia in her own element, the forest. Also, yeah, some ego there too. Showing off, though he'd never admit it.

It'd taught him how to move better in the woods, which stood him in good stead now. He was about to cross the last patch of open ground, near what looked like a broken-down hunting blind, when one of the men turned and Jack ducked fast. His hand shot out to steady himself against a tree and it touched something slick. He looked to see blood spray and flecks of a substance that would make most people look closer, wondering what it could be. But no one who made a living shooting people in the head would ever ask that. It was brain matter.

Jack saw the sheer fucking quantity of the shit—on the tree, on the undergrowth. That much didn't come from a normal bullet to the head. This was from a shotgun.

Shotguns were for thugs who enjoyed their work, liked to make a fucking mess. Jack might not be one to claim he had standards, but using a shotgun was just fucking disrespectful. It didn't only make a mess—it killed slower and . . .

And Nadia did not use a shotgun.

He grabbed the tree again to keep himself steady because *Nadia did not use a shotgun.* Which meant . . .

It meant nothing. Maybe she took it from the thugs chasing her.

That's when he saw the body. An outstretched hand on the ground. A man's hand with a wedding band. His gaze traveled from that wedding band to the perfectly manicured fingernails to the Bulova watch to the suit jacket cuffs.

Jack eased to the side to get a better look. It didn't help much—the guy had been shot in the face and, fuck yeah, that was just not the way to do it. Really wasn't. From what Jack could see, the guy seemed Hispanic, but the thug kid Jack shot had been in jeans and a leather jacket. From the glimpses he'd caught of the other two, they were similarly dressed. What was with the suit?

If he had to hazard a guess, he'd say the guy had been shot by the thugs. Nadia wouldn't do this.

But who the hell would the thugs have shot if not Nadia? The suit screamed "Federal Agent." Someone from the Marshals office tailing Quinn? Fuck, they really didn't need that.

Jack continued to close in on his target, pausing only to text Evelyn a warning.

Body. Looks fed. Marshals?

He'd never known Feds to travel solo, and he considered changing his plan in light of that, but the woods were silent. If that was indeed a dead agent, his partner would have been on the phone the moment the shot pellets hit and by now the woods would be crawling with Feds. More likely Jack just had to worry about stumbling over a second agent's body.

He moved in behind his target and waited for Evelyn's signal. It came as a shot as the second of the thugs went down and Jack's target wheeled toward the noise, his gun rising.

"Stop," Jack said.

The thug, of course, did *not* stop. Not until Jack put a bullet through his knee. He went down screaming, the pain apparently enough to make him temporarily forget he was armed. Jack fixed that by knocking the guy's gun from his hand. Then he kicked the injured knee, setting the guy both screaming and falling. Another kick convinced him to stay down.

Evelyn showed up a moment later. The guy lifted his head, saw her and seemed to decide that the sight of a little old lady meant he really shouldn't be giving up so easily. He started to rise. Evelyn shot him in the side.

"By the way," she said as he writhed in pain. "I didn't *miss* your heart. That comes next. Unless you tell us what we need to know."

The thug swore in Spanish. Evelyn waited him out and then replied in the same language. Jack focused on the guy's body, watching for any sign he was going to bolt and ignoring the urge to try to figure out what they were saying, even when he heard the words for "woman" and "brown hair," meaning they were talking about Nadia.

He kept his ears attuned to the sounds from the surrounding forest. When he heard a soft groan, it came from his left, past the old hunting blind. The undergrowth rustled. Evelyn didn't hear it and kept questioning their captive, her voice sharp. Jack motioned that he'd heard someone and backed off in the direction of the noises.

As he approached, the noises stopped. He could make out a figure nestled in a thick patch of undergrowth and bushes. The figure half rose, carefully and quietly, and said, "Stop right there."

When he heard the voice, he did the exact opposite, jogging forward, his gun lowered.

He could see more of her then—the auburn curls, the heart-shaped face, the stubborn chin, and even if he couldn't see the rest, his memory imprinted it. Hazel eyes. Freckles over her nose. Thin scar on her neck. And dimples, though she definitely wasn't smiling. *He* was. He was grinning like an idiot and—

"I said stop," Nadia said. "One more step, and I'll—"

"It's me," he said. Then added, because it seemed prudent, "Jack."

He moved around the bushes to see her crouched in the undergrowth, and he wanted to rush forward, drop his gun, scoop her up and hug her, as tight as he could. Like some movie reunion scene. Crush her against him and say, *Thank God. I was so worried.* Instead, his grin fell away and he stood there, awkwardly holding his gun at his side, as he said gruffly, "You okay?"

"I think so." She started to straighten, swaying, and he could see blood on her arm, which was bound with a makeshift tourniquet. He said, "Slow down," but she was already up . . . and that sway turned into a topple. He rushed forward, his gun shoved in his pocket as he caught her.

"Or maybe not . . ." she said with a chuckle, and he heard that laugh, as wry as it was, and he gave her that fierce hug he'd imagined, her face against his chest until he heard a stifled hiss of pain and quickly moved back, saying, "Fuck. Sorry. Fuck," but she drew him into a hug as tight as his own and said, "Thanks for coming," and he had to chuckle at the way she said it, as if he'd done her a favor, possibly inconveniencing himself in the process. *Hey, thanks for coming by. Sorry about all the trouble.*

"Gonna get you—" he began, and then heard Evelyn's "Goddamn it!" followed by a shot. Nadia grabbed the nearest tree for support and pushed him off, saying, "Go." He cast a quick glance around, making sure the area was clear. Then he ran back to find Evelyn standing over their hostage, blood pumping from his chest.

"Fuck," Jack said.

"He's still alive," Evelyn said.

Barely. Jack glanced at Evelyn. She didn't explain what had happened, just kept her gaze on the downed man, and that was all he needed to see. That she wouldn't meet his eyes. He also noted dirt on her left knee and mentally filled in the rest of the story.

She'd lost control of her captive. Maybe she'd heard Nadia's voice. Maybe she'd just turned to see where Jack had gone. In years past, that wouldn't have made a difference. But these days, a quick shove was all it took to put her down. She'd had to shoot fast and blind. Which meant they now had a dying hostage.

"Shit," a voice said behind him. He turned to see

Nadia making her way toward them, moving from tree to tree. He strode over, but she waved him off. "I've got it. Just a little woozy. Good thing you guys got here, or I might have staggered right into their path."

Jack doubted that, but he only said, "Fill me in?" as he walked to the dying man.

Chapter Eleven
Nadia

I watched Jack take control of the hostage as I struggled to keep my brain on track. It was still fuzzy, like I'd woken from a deep sleep. I kept staring at Jack, thinking I was imagining this, I had to be, that I'd fallen unconscious and was dreaming he'd arrived.

He glanced over. I got the message. *Talk.* He had a hostage living on borrowed time.

"Not sure how much you know already," I said. "Quinn was kidnapped. Diaz came to tell me."

"Diaz?"

"The Contrapasso guy. Who is . . ." It took a moment for me to remember. Then I turned, seeing an arm on the ground through the trees. "Over there."

"Fuck," Jack said. "Turned on you? Or helping you?"

"Honestly, I'm not sure. I thought the former, but I think it was the latter. He knew something was amiss with Quinn's disappearance, so he let me take off as bait. That trap caught three guys, who are now dead."

Jack grunted, as if this didn't need to be clarified—of course they'd be dead if they came after me.

"Hispanic?" he said.

I nodded. "But I'm not sure if that's significant."

"Yeah. It is." Jack kicked the man on the ground. "Isn't it?"

The guy only groaned.

Jack hunkered down. "You want us to help you?"

The guy nodded. I started toward him. Jack saw that and said, "Evelyn?"

It took a moment before she blinked and then patted the guy down and removed his weapons, which was indeed what I'd been going to do. The fact that Jack had to prod her meant she wasn't quite herself either. Evelyn rarely ventured into the field these days and she says that's because she's retired, which is true, but I'm sure she also doesn't appreciate any reminder of her age. She must have been holding the hostage when she'd been forced to shoot him, which had thrown her off her game.

I watched that pat-down carefully, in case she was too distracted to do it right. She wasn't, of course. She removed a knife, gun, wallet, cell phone and then did a second pat before backing away.

"You want help," Jack said. "We want answers. Which cartel?"

The man said nothing.

"Let's try that with more words," Evelyn said. "Which cartel do you work for?" When he still said nothing, she switched to Spanish. Jack gave him about two seconds to reply before a kick had the guy whimpering in pain.

"I—I do not know," the man said, his voice halting and heavily accented. "I was hired. Me and my . . ." He weakly turned his head. "My brother. He is dead?"

I would have pretended that his brother may have survived his injuries, but Jack said, "Yeah. So you were hired. By who?"

"I do not know. They went through my brother. He took the orders. Go there. Do this. Come here. Do that." The man let out a slow hiss. "I need help. Now. Or I will—"

"Help's coming," Jack said. "They told you to come here. And do what?"

"Find the woman. Others had followed her. They did not report back, and so we were to come and see what had happened. See if she was still here." He glanced my way and his eyes narrowed as he said, "She was," as if I'd caused his brother's death by not jumping up sooner to announce my presence.

"They're holding someone else hostage," I said. "A man. He's around my age, about six-two, big guy." I didn't add more, not knowing what disguise Quinn might have been wearing. "Do you know anything about that?"

Jack's hands flexed on his gun. He eased back, just a half inch, but I got the message. He didn't really care where they were holding Quinn. Well, yes, he'd have gotten to that part eventually, but right now, knowing what these guys had in store for me was more important to him. I understood that. I appreciated that. But I wasn't in danger right now. Quinn was.

"Answer," Jack said, in a quasi-reluctant growl when the guy glanced up, as if checking for the go-ahead to respond, because, you know, it was just the chick asking, so it probably wasn't important.

"He is in a building," the man said.

"Really?" Evelyn said. "I thought they'd hold him hostage in the middle of the damned highway. Do better."

Again, he glanced at Jack, ignoring the fact that the old lady asking was the one who'd shot him in the chest.

"He is alive," the man said. "I had to take him food. He did not eat. He talked to me. *En Español.* My brother heard and he was angry, said the man was trying to get information about our employer, but he was not. He only talked, asking about me."

Getting to know the low man on the totem pole. Forming a relationship. Which meant Quinn was fine, just sitting tight and trying to figure a way out. Exactly as I'd expect.

The man grimaced. "I really need—"

"It's coming," Jack said. "This building. Where is it?"

The guy didn't know—they'd been taken to and from it in the back of a van. They really were only hired muscle. Jack did manage to get details about the building and the immediate vicinity. That was as far as he got before the guy started going into shock and when he did speak, it was incoherent babble about his mother and his brother and his girlfriend.

"Dee?" Jack said. "Can you head out? See if any help's arrived?"

Evelyn frowned, not comprehending. I nodded and turned away. I'd gone about a half-dozen steps when a suppressed shot fired behind me. One through the side of the head. An instant kill.

Jack didn't send me away so the guy would think I was bringing help. I'm sure the guy had thought I was, which was good—one last moment of hope before everything went dark.

Having me turn away was partly Jack saying, "I don't want you to watch me do this." But it was also, by projection, "I'd rather not do this." He couldn't turn away, so he asked me to. Jack didn't promise the guy would be fine. He didn't promise we'd save him. He said he'd help. Which he had—in the only way he could, by administering a merciful and quick death.

When the shot came, I turned back quickly, because hesitating would say that I needed a moment to collect myself and slap on an "it's okay" face. I didn't. I said, "We should get going. They'll send more as soon as these guys don't call in."

Jack nodded. Then he looked around, saying, "The other guys . . ."

"I've cleaned them out."

Another nod. "Good." He walked over and put his arm around my waist, supporting me. I said, "I'm fine," but he said, "Humor me," so I did, leaning on him.

As I turned, I caught a blur in the forest. Jack did too, at the same moment, his hand going to my back, shoving me down. I stumbled, caught off guard, but his mouth opened in an oath, and there was a near-comical moment of Jack trying to steady me and then remembering why he'd pushed me down and mouthing another "Fuck!" By that time, I was already halfway to the ground of my own accord—and yanking the leg of his jeans to get him down beside me.

That's when I remembered Evelyn, who could not drop nearly so easily. I saw she'd swung against a tree, her gun out. I looked at Jack. He nodded, saying she was fine. Through the trees we could make out two men heading toward us. Two men in suits.

I whispered "Contrapasso," to Jack, who nodded. Like the cartel thugs, when Diaz didn't check in, his boss would have sent reinforcements to his last known location.

The two men continued forward, guns leveled in our general direction, but well over our heads. They'd seen or heard something but been too far out to actually spot us.

"Stop," Jack said.

The man in the lead slowed, his head tilting as if not sure he'd actually heard a spoken word, which is one problem with Jack being so terse.

"Stop right there," I said.

"Dee?"

"Identify yourself, please."

Jack's lips twitched at the *please*.

"There are three guns trained on two of you," I said when the man didn't respond. "There are also seven bodies on the ground around you, which means we're a little tired of being chased and ambushed. Two more won't matter, but if you are who I think you are, I'm not eager to add yours to the count."

"Haskell," the first man said. "Contrapasso. We're here for Agent Diaz. We know he tailed you to this location, and he'd damned well better not be one of those seven bodies."

"He is," I said. "I'm sorry. I came in here to avoid being run off the road. Two guys pursued. Diaz followed them. We took out the pair, but apparently there was a third party we hadn't seen. He got Diaz. I finished him. Then three more came looking for me. And I'm going to guess they won't be the last, so if you two will drop your weapons and raise your hands . . ."

Haskell snorted. "Not a chance. You've accounted for the seven bodies, but not the two other guns you say are trained on us."

"That'd be me," Jack said.

"And you are . . .?"

"Take a fucking guess."

Haskell's partner eased to the side, trying to get cover as he moved slowly.

"Jack," Haskell said. "Diaz's report said you were abroad."

"I'm back."

"Conveniently."

"Meaning?" Jack said.

"Quinn disappears with clues leading us to Dee, who jumps at the chance to come find him. And then you suddenly reappear."

"Yeah," Jack said. "We kidnapped Quinn. Then came to rescue him. Got bored. Needed action. Can't find it? Make my own."

"If you're suggesting you two lack motivation for kidnapping Quinn—"

Jack cut him off with a snort.

"Diaz told me Contrapasso suspected me," I said. "But unless there's some motive I can't see, Jack's right—it makes absolutely no sense for us to take Quinn and even less to come hunting for him if we did."

"We don't know what your game is, but there's obviously a game."

"Obviously," Jack said.

Haskell's face mottled. "Just because we can't see your motivation—"

"Not the point. You don't know *exactly* why? Fine. But no fucking *clue*?" Jack shook his head.

"We have ideas."

"Name one."

Haskell started to bluster. No one paid him any attention, because we were watching his partner creep around the side. Not watching him directly, of course, but aware of him. Waiting while Haskell thought he had us distracted.

I considered the options, relying on what I knew of Contrapasso. Then I walked to Evelyn, leaving Jack on his own. Sure enough, the partner headed to Jack. A thug would grab the old lady mentor or the girlfriend and use us to threaten Jack. Whatever Contrapasso's faults, they weren't going to even pretend they'd hurt Evelyn or me. And they were bright enough to go straight for the biggest threat.

Jack pretended not to notice and kept goading Haskell. I feigned boredom with the proceedings—a pissing match between alpha males—and started whispering to Evelyn, asking her when they'd arrived, how they'd found me. Pointless crap that did have a point, in that it gave Haskell's partner the confidence he needed to get right up behind Jack.

Jack's gaze flicked my way. I hesitated. I thought I knew what he meant. But I wasn't entirely sure he'd put that much faith in me until—

The partner took two final steps, bringing him right up behind Jack.

I spun, gun up, snarling, "Stop!" It startled the guy enough that he did exactly that, as Jack wheeled and slammed his fist into the guy's gun arm, knocking the weapon to the ground. I was there in a few running paces, kicking the gun away. The guy danced back as he went for a secondary weapon.

I was already turning on Haskell, who'd been caught off guard. Evelyn turned, too, and stumbled, dropping again to one knee. I started after her, but Haskell was faster. He lunged after the easy hostage . . . and found himself with a gun pointed at his groin as Evelyn recovered from the pratfall.

"Drop it," she said.

He hesitated. She fired a shot between his legs. He lowered his weapon.

"Drop the gun and put your hands behind your back."

He did. In the meantime, Jack had the partner down and was relieving him of his weapons and cell phone as I stood guard.

Once they'd patted down the two and eased back, I

said, "We have no reason to take Quinn, and Quinn has no reason to fake being taken. You seem to think we lured Contrapasso in, but that's just paranoid bullshit. Diaz knew it. He still did as he was told, testing me. I passed. While he's not alive to confirm that, unfortunately, the battleground should speak for itself. Unless you guys are hooking up with cartels, we're both caught in a trap. I have no idea what the purpose of that trap is . . ."

I trailed off as I saw Jack's expression. I turned to him. "You do."

"Yeah. Hiring me."

"Kidnapping Quinn is about hiring you?"

"Daisy chain," he said. "Take Quinn. Lure you. Take you. Get me."

"Grab Quinn to lure me away from home and then take me hostage to convince you to do a job. Cartel work, I'm guessing. Because you don't take those jobs."

"Yeah."

"Isn't that a little complicated?" Haskell said.

"Not if you want Jack badly enough," Evelyn said. "Obviously it's a big job. Important enough to go through the hassle."

"Political?" I said.

"That's our guess," she said.

I turned to Haskell. "The fact it seems so damned complicated should suggest it's true. We'd make up something a lot simpler. And if you know anything about Jack's work history, you know that's not his line of work—cartel or political assassinations. Meaning he'd need a very big carrot to do it. But you two are just Contrapasso lackeys, so since we have some idea what's going on here, we're going to leapfrog over your heads."

Evelyn took out Haskell's cell phone. I reached for it, but she pretended not to notice and placed the call herself. She did have more contact with them, and where I'd have dialed a number in Haskell's recent call list, she dialed one from memory.

"Edgar?" she said. "Evelyn. I'm with Dee and Jack. I'm sure you know what's going on, so I'll skip to the update. Diaz is dead at the hands of the people who took Quinn. We have Haskell and his partner. If you want them back, you'll give us everything you know about Quinn's kidnapping, and then back the fuck off before you lose more agents. Understood?"

She listened for a few moments and then said, "You do that. We'll call in two hours for an exchange: your agents for your intel."

Jack had the hostages sit back-to-back while Evelyn and I watched him. Then he jogged off, presumably to get bindings. And, yes, he did return with those, but he secured the men as fast as possible and then opened the first aid kit he'd brought back.

He didn't ask me to remove my jacket and shirt.

Didn't tell me to either. That was implicit. I did, and he cleaned my wound and dug out the shotgun pellets. Evelyn grumbled that I was obviously in no danger of bleeding out and we really needed to move before more thugs arrived. It was a half-hearted complaint, stopped by a single look from Jack.

I added my protest, more fervently. My injuries, far from life-threatening, should not take precedence over a speedy escape. But, well, having someone care enough to make sure I was okay before we went another step? It meant something. I'd spent a lot of years being that person for others—strangers even, at the lodge—while feeling as if I didn't deserve the same in return. So I appreciated it . . . though I still did hurry the process along, well aware that I didn't want us facing *more* danger because I enjoyed being fussed over.

The bullet wound was tissue damage, nothing serious, as gunshots went. Jack had Evelyn take a look to confirm his diagnosis. Then he bound it and tried to check my head, but I insisted that was fine and we got our hostages up and moving. That's when his phone vibrated. He cursed and waved for us to watch the hostages while he took a phone from his pocket. Someone else's phone.

"No," he said when he answered. "I don't fucking have him, all right? I told you I couldn't do it in two hours. I left a message through his answering service, and I'm expecting a call back any minute now. If you give me a number—"

Pause.

"Yeah, yeah," he muttered. "Fucking paranoid bastards. Fine. Have it your way. Call me back in an hour."

Pause.

"Two hours then. Fine by me."

Pause.

"Yeah, yeah. If I don't have him, you'll kill me and my dog. Too bad I don't have a dog. I'll have him by then, okay? He might be busy, but he's not going to ignore my message."

I didn't look to Evelyn for an explanation. Jack was using full sentences and had dialed his faint Irish accent up to eleven, which meant he was impersonating someone. Likely connected to the job he'd been doing overseas. He'd explain later.

We relocated Haskell and his partner about a kilometer deeper into the forest. They'd be safe there—any thugs wouldn't hunt that far past the bodies. When they glowered over their gags, I reminded them that we'd tried to play fair and they blew it. They would suffer some discomfort for a few hours. They'd survive. Probably.

We got my overnight bag from my rental and wiped down the steering wheel and doors, though it's not as if that's a serious issue with a rental car. If it was, I'd have worn gloves. Then we left the car where it was. Wouldn't be the first time, which is why we use credit cards that aren't linked to our aliases.

Next we headed to Jack's rental. He said he had a motel room closer to Washington but declared that too far and unsafe.

"Got our stuff," he said. "No reason to go back."

Evelyn argued—it wasn't that much further and as long as the room was paid for . . . Jack said nothing, which was his usual way of winning a fight with Evelyn. He just didn't acknowledge the dispute.

I cleaned up in the car as he drove to the first gas station and bought me two bottles of root beer and a bag of Skittles.

"I'm hungry too, Jack," Evelyn said.

"You didn't pass out from blood loss."

"I think it was more the blow to the head," I said as he climbed into the car.

"Combination. Eat. Drink."

I smiled. "Be merry?"

"Sure." A half-smile my way. Then he glanced at Evelyn. "Can ask her to share. Be nice, though."

She flashed him the finger.

Jack drove us to a hotel off the highway and checked in while we waited in the lobby. Then he walked over and handed Evelyn the key.

"Getting food," he said. "Dee's hungry."

"I don't believe that's possible," Evelyn said. "Given the sheer quantity of sugar she just consumed."

"She is."

"Which she communicated to you telepathically?"

He turned to me. "When'd you last eat? Proper meal?"

"You know, Jack," Evelyn said. "Women don't really like it when you make presumptions about what they do and don't want."

I shook my head. "He knows that if I'm *not* hungry, I'll say so. We'll go eat. I'd offer to bring you back something, but McDonald's isn't really your style."

She looked around the chain hotel, nose wrinkling. "Nor is any room service this place provides. Why don't we drive—?"

"You can," Jack said, and he steered me away before she could continue. We'd gone about halfway across the lobby when he said, "How hungry are you?"

"I could do with that"—I nodded at the vending machines—"and a quiet corner to talk."

He pulled a key card from his pocket. "Got a second room. Talk there? Or . . . whatever."

Jack didn't even give a suggestive brow raise at the "whatever." He only accompanied it with a laconic shrug, as if he meant I could nap or take a shower. I knew better, though.

"I'll take *whatever*," I said.

His "Good" hardly rang with enthusiasm, but I

grinned, as if he'd accompanied it with the smuttiest suggestion imaginable. We walked to the vending machines. He took his time making selections and feeding in the money. One root beer. One Coke. Two packets of Skittles, one of Starburst chews and a bag of licorice. He handed me all of it.

"What are *you* eating?" I said.

"Whatever you don't finish."

I shook my head and fed in a five, getting peanuts and a Snickers bar for him. I handed them over. "Energy," I said. "You'll need it."

Without the barest hint of a reaction, he put the snacks in his pocket, and we headed for the elevator. Silence as we waited for it to arrive. More silence as we got on. He hit the floor and then the Close Door button and only then did he glance my way, just for a split second.

"Hold the elevator!" someone called.

Jack reached out and jabbed the Close Door button again. A middle-aged businessman rushed over as I feigned checking my phone and prayed for the doors to shut faster. He managed to grab the door, and Jack's eyes narrowed, almost imperceptibly. He glanced at me and then back, and shifted his weight, as clear a sign of annoyance as if he'd cursed.

I stood on the right side of the elevator car. Jack was at the left, near the front. When the guy walked on, he was looking at me, and he hit his floor without noticing Jack, too busy checking me out. And I was busy checking out my arm, making sure there wasn't blood showing, presuming that was what caught his attention.

"Here on business?" he asked.

I was wearing jeans—muddied at the knees—a denim jacket, a T-shirt and my sneakers were even more mud-caked than my jeans.

"Uhhh . . ." I said.

"We are," Jack said, and the guy jumped about a foot.

Jack didn't do anything except say those two words and turn a completely expressionless stare on the guy. But there's an edge Jack can flip, like a switch, and I have no idea even what it entails—stance, expression, eye contact or just a combination of all of the above. But the guy took one look at Jack and decided standing at the back of the elevator seemed a whole lot more comfortable. The far back, in the corner, putting the maximum distance between me and him.

I quirked a half-smile at Jack. He gave just the faintest roll of his eyes. The elevator stopped. He waited for me to get out first and then walked beside me down the hall. We reached the room. He put in the card, still taking his time.

He opened the door. Held it for me. Followed me in and fastened the locks. Keycard placed on the entry table. Then he glanced at me. It was a careful glance, a cautious check, because, you know, despite my signals, I might really have just wanted to come up here and talk and eat candy.

I shrugged off my jacket and laid it aside. My shoes followed. He just stood there watching, the kernel of doubt and, yes, disappointment shadowing his eyes, blinked back quickly because he was going to be a gentleman about this. I'd had a hellish day—chased, shot, hit my head . . .

Even when I walked over, coming within an inch of him and looking up, he held himself very still. I put my arms around his neck and said, "Missed you," and then I smiled and that was what he'd been waiting for—that smile.

His arms went around me, pulling me to him so fast I gasped, that gasp cut short as his mouth met mine in a kiss that knocked every other thought from my brain, knocked every worry from my brain. There was always that moment, when he came home, when he didn't immediately drag me off to bed, when he acted like it was the last thing on his mind, that moment when I wondered if the separation had given him time to reconsider, time to think this wasn't what he really wanted. I knew better. I knew him, and I knew this was just him, that perfect control waiting, teasing even, drawing out that reunion. Still, I worry every damn time that this time might be different. And then he kisses me.

He kissed me and it really was no exaggeration to say I forgot everything else, from the events of the day to the pain my arm. Hell, I wasn't even sure what was going on at that moment, just that kiss, that deep and hungry kiss and the next thing I knew, I was falling back onto the bed, without even realizing we'd moved from the front door. I was on the bed, and his shirt was off and then mine was, and I did notice that, kinda hard not to, with his hands on me, his touch making me gasp again.

Then jeans off and me pushed back on the bed, up to the pillows, and he was over me, still kissing me, hands everywhere they needed to be, and I wrapped my fingers in his hair and pulled back enough to say, "I really, really missed you," and he said, "Yes," and I could laugh at that. I would, later. Shake my head and laugh. But I knew what he meant, and I knew that was all he could give, maybe all he could ever give, and I was fine with it. Even if he could never tell me how he felt, he showed me, and that was what counted, and when he said, "Yes," he kissed me again and pushed into me and showed me, as best he could.

We lay in bed afterward. Jack was on his back, his arm around me, eyes closed. Not asleep. For Jack there are about ten levels of relaxation. This was the stage right before sleep, though, when he was chill enough to close his eyes, his muscles not quite slack. Chill enough, too, that I could prop up and watch him and not make him feel as if an enemy loomed. I could even brush sweat-soaked hair from his forehead and he didn't tense, his eyes didn't open.

I looked at him. The angular face that wasn't quite handsome. The crow's feet at the corners of his eyes. The shallow lines around his mouth. Gray cautiously invading his black hair. He grumbles about his age, but most of that discomfort can be chalked up to his career, which isn't that different from a star athlete, where retirement comes so much sooner than it does for everyone else. He's still nowhere near ready to be put out to pasture. He knows it; he just likes to grumble. Professional concerns aside, he looks damned fine for fifty, and I'll admit how much I enjoy this part, just watching him, running my fingers over his biceps, his stomach, his chest.

There's a surgically erased tattoo on his biceps. That's from those early days in Ireland, when he signed up to fight for what others believed in, because his brothers did and because, at sixteen, sometimes you're desperate enough for change and adventure and validation that you don't give a damn about the rest.

He'd spent his first big paycheck post-Ireland getting that tattoo removed. He'd eaten canned food and slept in parks because the check barely covered the surgery and he wasn't living with that tattoo a moment longer. I can still see the ghost of it. I once told him it can be more thoroughly removed now, but he only shrugged and said it was fine. Which meant he didn't want that ghost taken away. Didn't want the memory erased completely.

There were other marks. Scars and old cigarette burns. When I asked him about the burns, he just shrugged and said, "Part of the job." Just work. It happens. No big deal. Not to him, anyway, not beyond the fact that they too would signify mistakes he'd made. He'd survived. Survived and learned and improved and that, he'd say, was all that mattered.

He opened one eye and said, "I'm sorry. What happened. Targeting you. I'm really, really—"

I put my finger to his lips. He made a face and said, "Just wanted you to know—"

"Do you honestly think I don't? I understood the risks before we got together. How many times have people tried to hire us for the same thing? If you need to make a statement to a man, go after his wife, girlfriend, lover. We've discussed this. And discussed it . . . and discussed it . . . and discussed it, which mostly consists of you telling me and me saying, 'I get it.'"

He made that face again, the one that said he'd like to say it again. Apologize again. Deeply and profusely apologize because he wasn't sure how else to deal with it. But it's not as if it'll make him feel better. Self-recrimination only drags you down into the tar pit of self-blame. I know that as well as anyone. So does he, which was why, after a moment, he nodded and reached for his Snickers bar. He couldn't quite reach it on my side of the bed, so I opened it, and then gave him the Coke.

"Recharging my batteries?" he said.

I smiled. "I don't think we'll have time for that."

"Make time."

He took a bite of the bar, chewed and then settled in.

"You want to know?" he said. "Details? What happened over there?"

"I always *want* to know, Jack. It's a question of whether you're okay with telling me and if not, I understand. Since you're offering, though, I'm guessing you are. So, yes, tell me what happened."

He did. Until now, I'd only known that he had gone to do a job as repayment for a debt owed to someone who'd helped him get his start. It was no coincidence that Jack had been in Ireland when this all went down. His old colleague had double-crossed him.

Jack told me exactly who Cillian was and what he'd done for Jack in the old days. Then what he'd done *to* Jack now. He told the story matter-of-factly. Just business. But I knew this hurt. Jack was a man of his word, treating his colleagues and clients fairly. And I got the sense Jack had really looked up to Cillian, that thirty years ago he had hoped for a relationship that might mellow into friendship, and that hadn't quite happened—

Jack had permanently relocated stateside—but he'd still felt a nostalgic bond there. Which Cillian had blown to hell.

Worse, while Jack never said it, I knew he'd have to kill Cillian. I would gladly do it for him, but I knew enough not to even offer. Instead, I leaned over and kissed him and he pulled me on top, and I set about doing what he would allow—showing him that I understood and I cared.

Chapter Twelve
Jack

Nadia was sitting up in bed, munching on Skittles, occasionally tossing one his way, grinning when he caught it, which he always did. Before he met her, Jack couldn't even remember the last time he'd eaten candy. Real candy—the kind that's pure sugar and chemicals. It was a reflection of the side of Nadia that first made him fall in love with her. The vulnerable side. The innocent side. The genuine side. Not childlike, but open in a way he hadn't been himself in so many years.

Nadia never had any shame in admitting her love for candy, and she'd light up when he bought it for her, the way other women might light up over diamond rings. He'd get that same look every time, no matter how often he showed up with candy in his pockets. A grin that wasn't so much for the candy itself as for the gesture—genuine surprise and joy that he'd gone out of his way to get her something, even if it entailed no more than stopping at a shop. Such a small thing, one that explained so much about Nadia.

He watched her, sitting naked in bed as she talked between candies, and he knew he loved her. He hadn't said the words. He wasn't sure how to, because he never had, not even when he'd been fifteen and dating a girl whose name he'd long since forgotten and when he'd try to slide his hand up her shirt, she'd stop him and say, "I need to be sure," and he'd known she hadn't meant she needed to be sure she wanted sex, but that she needed to be sure he loved her. Except he hadn't. She was just a girl he liked, and he wouldn't lie about that, even if it meant getting sex before his sixteenth birthday.

But now he *did* feel that way, and he had no fucking idea how to say it. He'd started to, many times, after they made love, but that seemed the wrong moment, like she'd think it was just part of the afterglow. He'd considered saying it *before* sex, but what if she didn't say it back? He didn't care—it wasn't a test. But if he said it and she wasn't ready, she'd panic and then feel bad and . . . yeah, definitely gonna spoil the mood. But when the hell do you say it? And why the fuck was it so hard to figure this out? He wasn't fifteen anymore.

Just do it. Say it and then say something else, fast, so it doesn't hang there, waiting for a response. Say it and then . . .

And then say more. Not just, "I love you," but more

about how he felt, which would take away any obligation because it would have moved past a response, and he'd get the chance to say more, because he had more to say, and that would be the opportunity. Get the words out. All of them.

"Hey," he said, and she gave him that breath-taking grin that made him understand the meaning of that overused phrase because that one really did take his breath away.

"Hey," she said back.

Okay, keep going. You've got her attention. Just go. Three, two, one—

"I—" he began.

"I've been—" she said at the same time and then stopped. "Sorry. Go ahead."

"Nah, go on."

She hesitated, but he motioned for her to continue, and she said, "I've been thinking about Cillian and the cartel and this whole setup. Besides being hellishly complicated, does it bug you at all? Any of it?"

"Yeah," he said, and he exhaled the word on a breath of relief, almost as great as if he'd actually gotten those other words out. He'd been thinking this himself—that it bothered him—but he'd pushed it aside, feeling like he was just being paranoid.

"Yeah," he repeated. "It does."

"Good," she said. "So I'm not overthinking it." She

lowered herself to lie facing him. "Okay, tell me what's bugging *you*."

He did.

An hour later, they were in Evelyn's hotel room, looking at an image on her laptop. An image of the building where they thought Quinn was being held. And they'd been able to find it online. Just sitting there for anyone to see, like many places were these days. You type in the location, and up pops a street view on your screen. Fucking amazing. Of course, the picture could be a couple of years old, so it didn't erase the need for on-site surveillance. But it sure as hell helped.

Finding the location had been a matter of putting together the puzzle pieces—the information the thug provided on the building together with what Felix had found from Quinn's phone and the results of Contrapasso's own investigating. Yeah, Contrapasso came through, turning over at least part of what they had. They still weren't entirely convinced Jack wasn't involved, but he knew that was a matter of prejudice rather than any actual cause for suspicion.

It would be Jack they blamed, not Nadia. They liked Nadia. They understood her drive for justice. They'd made it clear they'd hire Jack, too, but he knew that was mostly for Nadia's sake, knowing they were more likely to get her if they accepted him. Accepted, not embraced. No matter how good he was at his job, they saw him as Quinn did, and in their view he'd never rise far above the very guys they devoted their lives to hunting.

But they had come through. While they told Nadia that they'd lost track of Quinn in an office building—where his GPS tracker had been disabled—that wasn't entirely true. His captors had only zapped it. That was Jack's explanation. Felix had explained it in more technical terms. Point was, Quinn's captors hadn't discarded the tracker—Felix figured they wanted to study the tech. The problem was that the signal hadn't disappeared immediately. It just started to fail. That meant Contrapasso had two locations to work with: the office where Quinn's kidnappers grabbed him and the spot where the transmitter finally died twenty minutes later. Put the two points on a map, and Evelyn had been able to follow that trajectory, factor in the rest of the information and find a location.

Jack was less than ten minutes from their destination when Cillian's phone rang. He checked his watch. Shit. He'd forgotten all about the callback. Obviously they'd jumped the gun earlier, calling Cillian as soon as their goons caught up to Nadia. Now . . . Well, he wasn't really sure what the fuck they'd do now, but he was ready.

Jack answered to hear Cillian himself, breathing hard and saying, "It's me. Don't hang up, Jack. Please don't fucking hang up."

Jack said nothing.

"I'm sorry I got away," Cillian said, then gave a strained laugh. "Jesus, am I really apologizing for escaping? Fuck, this is such a mess. Such a damned mess." He took a deep breath. "Some guy found me. I made up a bullshit story, and I didn't report it or anything. I don't blame you for doing that. Don't blame you at all. I'm just lucky you gave me the antidote for that cyanide. You'd have had every right not to, after what I did."

He waited, as if expecting Jack to say it was all right. When he didn't, Cillian prodded with, "You still there, Jack?"

"Yeah."

Cillian cleared his throat. "Like I said, I understand why you did that. But as soon as I got free, I contacted a few people. Called in favors. Huge favors—the kind I've been saving all my life. Like yours."

Pause.

More throat clearing. "Anyway, I know a few things now. Things that can help. You're stateside, right?"

Jack changed lanes. Didn't answer.

"Hope so," Cillian said. "I hope you found your girl and everything's okay."

"No," Jack said. "Still looking."

"Fuck. Well, all right then. I can help. I'm going to set this right, Jack. I've called in the biggest favor I've got. A guy who can fix this for you. He knows the cartel—he's the one who put them in touch with me. If you're looking for your girl, you must be in the DC area. I asked my guy to get there right away, spare no expense, I'll cover everything."

More silence as Cillian still failed to get the enthusiastic—or even grateful—response he obviously expected.

"I'm going to give you an address," Cillian said. "I need you to get there right away. This guy won't wait forever. I can't afford that." A strained laugh. "You get to him, and he'll give you everything you need, and he'll offer to help you fix this. You can just take his information if you want, but I'm going to strongly suggest you let him help. He's as good in his field as you are in yours."

"Which is?"

"Huh?"

"His field."

"A fixer." Cillian gave a short laugh. "Which is what we need right now, huh? Someone to fix this whole fucking mess. That's what he does. Helps people connect with others and solve their problems. Which he will do for you, and I'm footing the bill. My way of saying how fucking sorry I am. And I really hope . . ." Another throat-clearing. "I'm not just trying to save my ass here, Jack. I really am sorry."

"Address?"

"I'm texting it to your phone—well, my phone. You need to get there fast. I mean that, Jack. He—"

"Got it."

Jack hung up. He glanced over his shoulder at Nadia, who'd ceded the front passenger seat to Evelyn. He'd had the phone on speaker and they'd both been silent as they listened in. Evelyn opened her mouth but stopped, seeing where Jack was looking.

"He's paddling as fast as he can," Nadia said. "Which could mean he knows exactly how much trouble he's in and he's trying to save his life. Or . . ."

"Or he wasn't rescued by a random passerby?" Evelyn said.

Jack snorted.

"Yes," Nadia said. "I'm sure you didn't leave him somewhere that would be likely to happen. Someone went looking for him and found him, and the fact that he'd lie about that says he's not—unfortunately—trying to save his life. Well, yes, maybe he is, but not from you."

Jack grunted.

Nadia smiled. "Sorry. As badass as you are, the cartels beat you, hands down."

True, and he wouldn't argue the point. What Cillian

could expect from him was two to the head. Quick. Efficient. Merciful, in its way, at least compared to what the cartels might do to him.

"We still like the cartel for this?" he asked.

He directed that one to Evelyn. Nadia didn't even try to answer—it wasn't her area of expertise.

"We do," Evelyn said. "Felix has been sending me his findings. There are a few high-level political hits on the market. He's also narrowing it down to those who employ outside contractors."

"Not many, I'm guessing," Nadia said.

"No, not many at all."

Jack made a noise in his throat. Evelyn didn't notice, but Nadia caught his eye in the rearview mirror. They exchanged a look.

"So are you ignoring the summons?" Nadia asked.

"Can't. Best way to get answers. I'll go. You two hold tight."

"And not go after Quinn? Despite being reasonably sure we know where he is, which is not likely to last much longer?"

"She has a point," Evelyn said. "Any minute now, they'll find those dead thugs, which means Dee is still in the wind. Once they realize you're in the area, they'll move Quinn."

Nadia leaned forward against the seat back. "If this meeting with Cillian is bullshit—and they even *suspect* I'm with you—they'll expect me to stick close. It's the perfect time to grab Quinn and end this."

Jack grunted.

"Yes, I know," Nadia said. "Getting Quinn doesn't end this. It ends when we figure out what was going on and put a stop to it. But with Quinn safe, they can't hold anything over our heads, right?" She paused and then added, "On the other hand, maybe we should stick close while you go to this meeting. I can provide backup—"

"No," Jack said. "It's a trap? Trap's more for you than me."

"They'll expect you to go with him, as you pointed out, Dee," Evelyn said. "Better if you're as far away as possible. Jack can handle this."

"But you'll stay in touch, right?" Nadia said.

"Course."

Chapter Thirteen

Nadia

I had all audio on my phone turned off, which included the vibration that would signal an incoming message. So I kept checking it as I headed to the building. I didn't expect to hear from Jack—he'd dropped us off barely a half hour ago—but I checked anyway.

I'd seen no signs of a trap so far. There were guards outside. Not overtly watching the building—two guys in a car near the front entrance, another two near the back, with two more inside according to an infrared device from Felix. The gadget was good; the gadget wasn't perfect. It told me how many warm bodies we had just inside the walls, as we'd circled the perimeter. To actually find Quinn, I'd need to get a lot closer to him . . . and possibly closer to more cartel goons.

I entered the building without raising a single alarm. There seem to be three basic city settings for underworld activity—offices, warehouses and industrial areas. If the buildings can be abandoned or under renovation, that's a bonus. In this case, it was neither. It seemed to be an office building, though all the blinds were drawn. A sign on the front door, as viewed through binoculars, simply and politely declared it private property.

This was no high-rise building, though. It was old, in an area where it looked as if most of the former "offices" had been repurposed. In other words, no one would bat an eye at the closed blinds and lack of business signs. Right now, as night fell, the entire block seemed deserted.

Being an old area also meant the buildings were close together. Getting in only required using the one entrance the thugs hadn't thought to cover: the roof. It wasn't exactly a cakewalk getting there. But as a sniper, I'm always looking for the highest point, which means I have a lot of experience scaling buildings and crossing from rooftop to rooftop, even if it takes a leap and a prayer to get there.

Needless to say, Evelyn didn't join me on my aerial voyage. She stayed below, covering the guards and waiting for news from Jack.

I broke open the roof door, used the infrared to scan the area and then whispered, "I'm in," through my earpiece before making that a reality.

The roof door opened, not surprisingly, to a set of stairs. I headed down them. At the bottom, I scanned again and thought I picked up a faint blip to my right . . . and then nothing. I tried repositioning a few times, but the device brought back nothing. Felix had warned me not to rely on it. Jack wouldn't even use one—and hadn't been thrilled that Evelyn brought it. To him, any reliance on gadgets meant less reliance on your senses. I knew the device's limitations, though. In an old building like this, with thick walls and rats' nests of wiring, it was even less useful than usual. But it helped.

As I moved, I kept the device in one hand and my gun in the other. At each corner, I added the infrared to the usual list of checks before I stepped around it. That blip kept appearing and disappearing, and by time I reached the stairwell, I decided the device was too distracting. I pocketed it and settled for listening and looking.

I covered the fifth floor. It wasn't a large building. Empty, too. I saw signs of renovation that reminded me of our chalet at home—the piles of wood, boxes of nails. What was missing was the smell—no hint of sawdust from cut wood or drywall from putting up new walls or even dust from cutting through old ones. And the signs of renovation were oddly random. Tools in this room, wood in that one, nails in another . . .

I couldn't tell what was going on, and there was no time to stop and ponder. I kept moving, tucking those thoughts into the back of my mind as I continued down the stairwell. At the bottom, I whispered an "all clear, still searching" to Evelyn, who told me Jack had checked in ten minutes ago saying he was at his destination, nothing to report yet.

I was about to step from the stairwell when I decided to use Felix's device for a quick scan. Sure enough, it was giving me that blip, stronger now but still not holding steady. I put the device away and searched. Empty rooms here, too. One had a sawhorse. Another had a drop-sheet and a can of paint, but again, there was no smell of actual work. The paint can had been opened and, when curiosity compelled me to check, I pried off the lid to see it was half-empty, but there was no scent of paint fumes in the air nor anything actually newly painted nearby.

On the third floor, the blip came stronger. Someone was definitely here. I found more of those signs of renovation without any actual reno. Three levels of sporadic materials and tools.

I could ask Evelyn to help me puzzle it out, but she'd just snort and tell me to stick to the job. This *was* the job, though—the circumstances were too odd to be happenstance, so they meant something.

I looked at another drop-sheet and partial can of paint.

Any ideas, Jack?

I chuckled to myself. Hey, it worked the last time. This time, he remained silent, even in my head. Silent because he would be puzzling it out. He'd take the time to consider the implications.

Okay, I'll do that, then.

Fake signs of renovation. Why?

In case someone came in and wondered why the building was empty?

Possible, but lots of buildings stood empty, either as investments or awaiting a purpose.

Because someone was visiting and they wanted it to look as if the building was being renovated?

Why? A scam? If so, they could at least slap some paint around, rip out a few floorboards. Why not bother with those basic extra steps?

I got nothing.

Untrue. I had questions, and those were almost as important as answers. Questions meant something was wrong here, and I needed to pay extra attention—

A floorboard creaked. I zipped behind the door. A moment later, a man walked by. Hispanic. Thirties. Big guy with a gun in his hand. A thug doing his rounds.

He continued past the room without slowing and went straight to the stairwell. Even after the door clicked shut, I waited for his footsteps on the stairs, to be absolutely sure it wasn't a fake out. Once his boots sounded, I slid out and silently jogged to the stairwell. It sounded as if he was heading up, but I wanted to be sure.

The door on the next level shut and his boot steps faded down the hall. I crept into the stairwell and went down to the second floor. I did a faster survey of that level. There were boxes on this one—cardboard and wood. Most were empty. A few were stuffed with random office items, like paper. And I do mean "stuffed," as if someone just dumped the supplies in, rather than actually bringing them packed for storage or use.

Nothing else on the second floor. The first level was the trickiest—I didn't need to check Felix's device to expect guards on that one. The stairs continued down another level, and I decided to just skip the first floor. At the bottom of the steps, I checked the device. Two blips together, flickering in and out, likely the guys on the first floor but I wasn't taking any chances. What interested me more was I was now picking up one steady sign of life. In the basement. Which was the best place for stashing a hostage.

The problem with the device is, of course, there's no way of seeing the actual layout of the building. So when I finally drew close to the blip, I found myself on the opposite side of a wall from it. I continued along that wall, looking for a door, but had to circle through a couple of rooms before I got reasonably close to the blip again. When I did, I found a crudely cut hole in the wall, almost like those used for passing food to prisoners in ancient dungeons. I bent to peer through it. Directly across from me, dim lighting reveals a tall guy with a light brown crew-cut sitting on the floor, his back against the wall, pretending to be asleep. I say "pretending" because short of a serious blow to the head, he wasn't going to nap while being held captive.

"Sleeping on the job?" I whispered through the opening.

Quinn's eyes snapped open.

"It's Dee," I said.

He pushed to his feet fast, something metal clattering to the floor. It looked like a spoon. Behind him, I could see signs where he'd been digging at the mortar in the brick wall.

"Nice escape plan," I said. "It'll take you a while, though."

"I'm not digging out," he said as he walked over. "Just freeing a weapon—a nice solid brick."

"Ah. Smart."

He opened his mouth to say something else. Then he stopped, his eyes widening. "Dee. Shit. No. You need to get out of here."

"Nice to see you, too. Yes, I know, this is a trap for me. Don't worry—me springing you wasn't actually their plan, and I have backup. Let's just get you out—"

"*No.*" He practically flew to that opening as I stepped away. "Don't— The door. You can't open the door. You need to get out of here. Now."

"If the door's locked from the outside, I have tools.

We can—"

"*No*. Look."

I followed his finger to see a door on the far side of the large room. And I saw why they'd cut out this opening—way over here—for communicating and passing food. Quinn hadn't just used his spoon to try prying out a brick. He'd removed the outer board from a box over the door. Inside that box? Enough explosives to bring down the whole damned building.

Chapter Fourteen
Jack

Jack was supposed to meet Cillian's "fixer" in a motel, not unlike the first place he'd rented earlier in the day. The only difference was that this place was closed—permanently, it seemed. In an apparent burst of optimism the For Sale sign had recently been replaced, but that was as far as it'd gone, the owners not even bothering to weed the parking lot.

He'd spent the last twenty minutes scoping out the situation. His options were limited. Extremely limited. The motel might be deserted, but it sat on acres of empty land, leaving no way to sneak up.

He'd spent the drive here weighing all the possibilities for what was really going on. As soon as he saw this motel setup, he knew the answer. And maybe, just maybe, he'd always known. Just hadn't wanted to believe it. He could play the hardened criminal, and ninety percent of it wasn't an act. But ten was. Maybe even closer to twenty. That's the part Nadia saw, the part that allowed him into her life, even as he told himself he had no fucking idea why she'd do that.

That part of him had not wanted this outcome. Suspected it and feared it.

But just because he hadn't wanted it to turn out this way didn't mean he hadn't considered it. Didn't mean, either, that he hadn't mentioned the possibility to Nadia while they'd been lying in bed. Now, while there was still a chance he was wrong, he prepared as if he wasn't. Then he walked to Room 7, as per instructions, and knocked.

"Come in," a voice said, deep, with an American accent.

Jack pushed open the door. The room was dark, blinds drawn.

"Keep the lights off," the voice said. "Step in, shut the door and then move away from it."

Jack did.

"Turn around. Take out your phone and weapons, and push them back behind you. Then put your hands up."

Jack set down his holstered weapon and his ankle gun, along with his knife and cell phone.

"All your weapons."

Another gun, from inside the waistband of his jeans.

"If I have to ask again—"

He took a knife from his other ankle.

"Fucking arsenal," the man said with a snort. "You

got an AK-47 somewhere, too?"

"Wouldn't fit."

Another snort. The man patted Jack down. Then he backed away and turned on a lamp. When he said, "You can turn around now," the voice and the accent had changed, and Jack had to remind himself he wasn't supposed to expect this. So he feigned shock, tensing, and then turned slowly—as if uncertainly—and when he saw Cillian standing there, he said, "Fuck," with the right degree of muted shock and consternation, and a shake of his head.

"I came to help you," Cillian said, his voice rising, eyes rounding. "Honestly. I was so upset about everything that happened that I hopped on a plane and flew here to make it right. Because I want to make it right. For you, Jack."

Cillian gave an ugly laugh and slouched into a chair. "You never did grow into that ego, did you, Jack? Or should I say your brains never quite caught up to it. Did you really think I'd fallen that far? Gotten that goddamned stupid?"

Jack wisely didn't answer that. The truth was that Cillian had never been particularly bright, having only that feral kind of criminal intelligence they called street smarts.

As for thinking Cillian had fallen so far? No, Jack hadn't realized how far Cillian *had* fallen from the man he'd been. Not until he saw the proof of it here. If there was one thing Cillian had prided himself on in the old days, it was loyalty. Playing fair. That's where Jack got it from. The one part of his career that came from Cillian. The one truly good part.

Except, when forced to face this possibility earlier, he'd dug deeper into those memories. Dug past the rose-colored tinge of nostalgia to the truth. Which was that, in Cillian, Jack had seen the veneer of honor, of loyalty. A man who'd worn those traits like platform disco shoes, to lift him above the crowd and flash at every opportunity the message, "I'm a fair man. A reasonable man. Not like those dirtbags."

Cillian had wooed Jack with those fancy shoes, the perfect enticement for a bitter young man who felt his only place in the world was at the business end of a gun, but who still held onto something that hoped he could find more in such a future. That he could be, like Cillian, fair and loyal. Then he'd caught Cillian shortchanging him on jobs and lying to him about targets. That's when Jack got out. He'd squared up, thanked Cillian and caught the next boat for America. And this was what Cillian had really taught him—if you're going to don those shoes, own them . . . and maybe tone down the glitter, just a little.

"Come on, Jack," Cillian said. "I know you don't talk much. Better to keep your mouth shut and thought a fool than open it and remove all doubt." He snickered. "But you must have something to say to me now."

"What's the game?"

Cillian blinked, clearly expecting outrage or at least a muttered curse. Then he forced another chuckle. "What? You didn't figure it out? Surprise, surprise."

Actually, Jack had. The main thrust of it, at least. But he said nothing.

Cillian reached over and opened a laptop on the nightstand. On the screen was a grainy surveillance camera video of Quinn, on his feet, clutching something silver as he looked around.

"Huh, sounds like the Boy Scout has heard something. You don't know what that could be, do you, Jack?" Cillian flipped to a still photo time-stamped twenty minutes ago. Nadia creeping down a semi-dark hallway.

"Seems she found him," Cillian said. "Excellent detective work. Excellent timing on my part, too. Having a very expensive pair of eyes in that idiot Contrapasso group helped. It still took some serious coordination, let me tell you. Of course, I had backup plans in case you hadn't found the location or decided not to head there."

"Yeah," Jack said. "You're proud of yourself. I get it. Move on."

Cillian's face mottled. "Do you know how fucking hard this was, staying one step ahead of you when you kept screwing everything up?"

Couldn't be too hard, given how *stupid* Jack was. He didn't say that. Wasn't even tempted. He might not be a genius, but he seemed like one compared to Cillian.

"Oh, look," Cillian said. "The Boy Scout is pretending to be asleep. Those footsteps must be getting closer."

Jack pushed back the panic with a reminder that Nadia would be prepared for this. When Cillian gave the signal, his thugs would swoop in to grab Nadia, but she'd be ready. Evelyn would be ready. Hell, with Nadia this close to Quinn, she could get his door open and hand him a gun, and between the three of them, they'd be fine. Not that Jack intended to let that happen. Keep Cillian talking. Get the whole plan. Then sound the alarm, warn Nadia and end this.

"You seem very calm," Cillian said. "Not so worried about your girl after all? Personally, I'd agree. She's a looker, but I'd worry she's a little *too* interested in freeing that young, burly Boy Scout."

Jack said nothing.

Cillian looked at him and shook his head. "No fool like an old fool. You didn't used to fall for the ladies, Jack."

"You want a job. A big one."

"Is that what you think this is about? A job? You already owe me one. So why the hell would I—?"

"A bigger one. Too big for your chit."

"Nothing should be too big for my chit, Jack," Cillian

said, eyes narrowing. "You cannot repay what you owe me. I *made* you. Everything you are now started with me."

"Nah. You helped. But it started with—"

"They only put your feet on the road. Made you a killer. I made you a *hitman*. A *professional*. And how did you repay me? Fucked off to America. I told myself it was temporary. You'd come crawling back. But you didn't. You stayed there and found yourself a new mentor. A woman. Do you have any idea how much shit I had to put up with for that? My prize student dumps me for a skirt?"

"Wasn't like that. Moved on. New country. New contacts."

"You owed me, Jack. Everything you are—"

"I paid you back. Before I left. Even you agreed I had. Walked away with an even score."

"I agreed that we were settled temporarily. And then I spent ten fucking years expecting you to come back. Watching your star rise and telling myself you were just busy, making a name for yourself, and you'd come back and work for me. Repay your debt. But you didn't."

Jack struggled to drum up some sympathy. Maybe even a little guilt. But for once, he couldn't find it. Cillian didn't look like a man who'd been cheated; he looked like a scorned lover. The idiot who keeps waiting, telling himself she'll come back, even after she's cleaned out her closet, settled their bills and walked away with a handshake. It had been a clean parting. Jack had no doubt of that. Even that chit was a favor; more a thank-you than an obligation.

But if this wasn't about a job . . .

Scorned lover.

Jack wheeled toward the laptop. On the screen, Quinn was rising. He said something to someone off screen, relaxed as he talked.

"Your girlfriend has arrived," Cillian said. "Maybe she'll do more than rescue him. Maybe in the heat of the moment they'll be unable to resist doing more than exchanging a hug."

Jack looked at Cillian.

Cillian laughed. "Do you really think I brought you here in hopes you'll have to watch your girl screw another guy? I owe you more than that, Jack. So much more. You're going to watch her rescue him. All she needs to do is open the door . . . rigged with C4. That, Jack, is how I'll repay you."

Cillian pulled out his gun and backed up, ready for attack.

"Okay," Jack said.

Cillian stopped moving. "If you're calling my bluff—"

"No."

"There's no negotiating here, Jack. I can't stop that explosion. The minute she opens the door—"

"Got it. You're gonna kill her. You win." Jack sat on

the edge of the bed and checked his watch. "Shouldn't be long. Then I can go, right?"

Cillian blinked.

Jack continued. "You got your revenge. I liked her. Gonna feel bad. There. You win."

Jack turned to the laptop and checked his watch again. Quinn was almost out of sight now, only his back visible as he presumably talked to Nadia through the wall. Jack resisted the urge to check his watch again—and resend the double-push that transmitted an urgent message to Evelyn, the one that said, "Stand down now!" He'd done it twice already. By now she'd have told Nadia, and that was undoubtedly what she was discussing with Quinn—Nadia saying she had to leave but she'd come back.

Unless she decided she could free him first.

Jack double-tapped the watch again, just in case. Still, he trusted Nadia. As tempting as it would be to find and open that door, if he'd sent the double-tap, she'd know it meant get out immediately.

Quinn started backing up. Nadia was leaving.

Good. Perfect. Now just—

"You want me to hurry this along, Jack?" Cillian said. "You got places to go?"

"Nah. Nothing like that." He looked over. "You said no negotiating. You sure? You could send a guy in. Stop her from opening the door."

Cillian smiled. "A little more concerned than you want

to let on?"

Jack shrugged. "I like her. A lot. Yeah. If we can figure out something—"

"You want to negotiate, Jack?"

"Yeah, I do." Jack stood. "Tell me what you want."

Cillian took a cell phone from his pocket. "I want you to suffer, you arrogant son of a bitch. No negotiations. No more waiting, either."

Cillian raised the phone and Jack knew that was the detonator. He lunged. He didn't care about the gun pointed at him. He flew at Cillian and knocked the detonator from his hand. The gun fired. The bullet went offside. Jack wrested the gun away and pointed it at Cillian's forehead. Cillian smiled. Just smiled, and as Jack saw that smile, his gut went cold. He glanced over his shoulder at the laptop and on the screen, he saw only the fuzzy gray-white blur of a lost signal.

Chapter Fifteen
Nadia

As soon as I saw the C4 rigged over the door, I took a slow step back.

"Yep," Quinn said with a wry smile. "This is not the place you want to be right now."

I didn't ask if he could defuse it. If he could, he would have. Neither of us had ever used bombs. Nor had Evelyn or Jack, so there was no use contacting them.

"I'm going to get help," I said.

"If you can, yeah. If you can't . . ." He shrugged. "I'm the idiot who stepped into a trap."

"I'm going to get help."

The smile returned, still crooked, but his eyes lighting with it as he stepped toward the hole. "Thank you. For trying. I know I've been a bit of an ass. Okay, more than a bit. I'm having a hard time with . . . If it was anyone else . . ." He straightened. "The point is that I appreciate that you haven't cut me loose. I've given you plenty of reason.

Coming after me like this? Honestly, I wouldn't have expected it."

"Then you're an idiot."

"Yeah, someone may have told me that before. But I do appreciate it. Whatever happens. And if something does happen, I just want to say—"

"Dee!" Evelyn said through the earpiece, loud enough that Quinn must have caught the buzz of it and stopped. "Out now!"

"I—"

"No. Now. Jack wants you out."

"There's C4 rigged—"

"And that'd probably be the reason."

I turned to Quinn. "You need to take cover." I looked around the room, thinking how pointless that was.

"Got it," he said. "Now go."

"You—"

"Go, Nadia."

He reached through the hole to give me a shove. I caught his hand and squeezed it.

"Dee!" Evelyn said. "Tell me you're running your ass off right now. Jack just sent a third—"

"Gone," I said, gave Quinn's hand one last squeeze and then turned and ran. I made it to the end of the hall when Quinn shouted, "Nadia! Down!" and I dove, hitting the floor as the building exploded.

Chapter Sixteen

Jack

The car didn't go fast enough. It just didn't. Jack flattened the pedal, not giving a shit if he brought a squadron of police cars in his wake. He didn't see any until he reached the scene—police, ambulances, fire trucks, all pulling up in front of the building.

When he first spotted the building, there was a moment when he thought Cillian had tricked him. That Jack had seen some prerecorded image. Because despite the emergency vehicles, the building seemed fine.

The building was not fine.

It might not be a pile of dusty rubble, but it was as if someone carved out the middle, the remaining outer walls tottering around nothing.

He'd lost contact with Evelyn after the explosion. He didn't want to think what that meant. As he roared up, though, he saw her, stepping from behind a vehicle to flag him down.

She waved him to a spot around the corner, away from the knot of first responders. As he flew out of the car, he could see she was covered in dust and hobbling. Blood dripped from a cut on her cheek.

"You okay?"

"A fucking building didn't fall on me, Jack. Right now, that means I'm fine."

He started toward the building. She caught his arm. He tried to shake her off, but she said, "No, Jack. You go that way and they'll stop you, and then you'll pull your damned gun and this will turn into an even bigger clusterfuck. Come around back. They've got the scene cordoned off, but there's more chaos there. We can get through."

As she led him, he said, "Have you heard—?"

"I would have told you if I had. But that only means the explosion knocked out the damn signal."

He'd keep telling himself that was all it meant.

"Here." Evelyn gestured to a gaping hole in the side of the building. "No one's gone in yet. Those walls aren't going to hold and they're already dealing with the two guys they found on the first floor. They'll need more equipment before they go searching for more survivors."

Jack nodded and picked his way through the rubble toward the opening.

"If they do go in, I'll tell them she's trapped," she said. "To hell with what happens after that."

Jack nodded again and looked around, trying not to assess the damage. Just find a path down to the basement.

The basement. Under a building's worth of rubble, because it had collapsed and she was down there and he'd been chatting up Cillian, so fucking confident—

"Jack," Evelyn said.

When he only nodded, she gripped his arm, tight. "Keep it together, Jack."

Another nod.

"I was just saying that if I can get them to search, I will, screw the consequences. I know that's what you want."

He started for the nearest hole. Then he stopped and said a gruff, "Thanks. I—"

"Just get down there before someone sees you."

The building hadn't entirely collapsed. That's what he kept telling himself as he pushed through the rubble. The walls still stood. Most of the building still stood. Whatever Cillian had planned, it hadn't quite worked as he'd intended.

Fucking shock of the century.

When I find her, I'll make him—

Forget that.

No, don't forget the first part. When I find her. Not if.

He would, and then he'd take care of Cillian, whom he'd left in the motel room.

Never in his life had it been more difficult not to kill someone, not to put as many bullets in him as he could. A blinding moment of rage, unlike anything since that moment he'd walked into his house thirty years ago and found his family. He'd always thought that if one of their killers had been there, he'd have emptied his gun in him. But he hadn't with Cillian. He couldn't afford the delay. And he wasn't giving that bastard such an easy way out.

Jack heard knocking. Someone hitting a pipe. He exhaled, seemingly for the first time since Cillian hit the detonator.

He made his way toward the sound. That wasn't easy. He had to crawl through impossibly small spaces. He fit, though. He made himself fit. Finally, he could see a jean-clad leg ahead. A leg pinned under a slab of concrete. He crawled through the wreckage until—

"Quinn," he said. "Fuck."

"Yeah, not who you're looking for." Quinn twisted, grimacing as he tried to lift the slab on his leg. "Go on. Find her. Just tell someone I'm here."

Jack almost did exactly that. Then he heard a creak and looked up to see a section of the wall teetering over Quinn.

"Fuck," Jack said.

Quinn looked up. "Well, that would solve one of your

problems, huh?"

Jack crawled through and grabbed the chunk pinning Quinn's leg. "On three."

Quinn helped lift, but the slab barely moved.

"Go on," Quinn said.

Jack surveyed the concrete and the surrounding debris.

"Just go, Jack. I take back the smart-ass comment about solving a problem. You tried to rescue me, I appreciate that. Now go find her."

"You're not my problem," Jack said as he moved aside rubble. "You're hers. She's trying to stay friends. You say you want to?" He shoved a steel rod under the slab. "Don't act like it. Act like a sore fucking loser."

"Thanks, Jack. That's really what I need—"

"You want to be her friend? Get your shit together. Otherwise? Get the fuck away. Only making her feel bad." He looked at Quinn. "And that's my problem."

He finished wedging in the rod and said again, "On three."

This time it worked. They got the slab shifted up enough for Quinn to wriggle his leg out. When he did, Jack said, "Broken?"

"Doesn't seem to—"

"Good. Then help me find her."

Chapter Seventeen

Nadia

I don't know how Quinn got that advance warning. Presumably something flashed on the explosive device. He'd saved my life, though, because when he shouted, I had just enough time to dive into a doorway. The hallway collapsed around me, leaving that doorframe standing.

I hadn't come away unscathed. Pieces had buffeted me, setting my injured arm ablaze and pinning down one foot and filling my lungs with dust that I suspected was very old and very toxic. But I was alive. I got my foot free, and I pulled my shirt over my mouth and nose to breathe.

And then I heard Quinn.

Well, I told myself it was Quinn. Someone was banging a pipe, and I doubted those cartel goons had rescue mission experience and knew that banging a pipe or ventilation shaft was a whole lot more effective than shouting.

The next step? Getting to Quinn. Which would be so much easier if I could get anywhere.

I was free and mobile, but when I say the hall collapsed around the doorway, I mean that literally. I was in a virtual cage, completely enclosed by broken wood and brick and concrete. I took a moment to assess. Two of the "walls" around me weren't exactly stable. Through a third I could see a faint flashing light from an approaching emergency vehicle.

I started clearing that side. It was not a speedy process. I heard sirens and shouts as the rescue crews arrived, but no one seemed in much of a rush to do any actual rescuing. Checking stability before leaping in, I assumed. Quinn kept periodically banging the pipe, but no one seemed to hear him.

I painstakingly dug my way out. With every large piece of debris I removed, I stopped and made sure the whole thing wasn't going to fall on my head.

I finally had a hole cleared that was big enough for me to wriggle through. I came out in a section of hall still mostly intact. I'd just started down it when Quinn's clanging stopped.

I went still. If he'd been seriously injured and weakening, I'd have heard that in the rhythm of his clanging. Either someone had found him or he was taking a break. Still, I picked up speed, focused on the direction I'd heard the—

Something moved off to my side. I spun and reached for . . .

Shit. My gun. It'd been in my hand when I'd been running before the blast. Long gone now.

A shape lunged at me. I twisted out of the way. Fingers grazed my arm. There was just enough light for me to see a big, burly Hispanic guy covered in dust and bloodied cuts.

I backed away, my hands raised. "Look, I'm unarmed. You're unarmed. We're in a building that just blew up and is probably going to collapse at any second. I'd suggest working together, but that may be pushing it, so let's just get our asses out of here, okay?"

He said nothing, just snorted like an enraged bull. I struggled for the few words of Spanish I knew. Before I could find any suitable ones, he said, "This is your fault, you fucking bitch."

No language barrier apparently. "I didn't blow up the damned building while I was still inside, okay? Your boss did that. Because killing me was, apparently, more important than warning his own men to get clear. If you get out of here, you can let him know what you think of that—"

He swung at me.

"Seriously?" I said as I danced out of the way. "The building is going to collapse. We survived an explosion.

Let's just get the hell—"

Another swing. This time, in ducking, I hit the wall and a chunk of the ceiling fell. As I darted aside, he caught my arm. I yanked free but stumbled, and as he swung again, I kicked him in the leg, because hey, if I was going down, so was he. Keeps the playing field fair. It also gave me easy access to my ankle holster.

I didn't pull the gun right away. He was unarmed, and he might be bigger than me, but I still hoped to reason with him. I'm an optimist. Not the best character trait in this game, but not one I'm letting go of without a fight. Speaking of fight . . .

We grappled. I managed to get hold of his chin and force his head up.

"Did you not notice the renovation stuff everywhere?" I said, grunting as he pressed down on me.

"Sure," he wheezed as I kept forcing his head up. "We brought it in."

"What's it for?"

"Renovation. You really are a stupid—"

"I'm not the stupid one. There's no renovation. It's for an insurance claim. When the place blows up, they'll find the renovation supplies, and the owner can claim it was under construction. It's a half-assed scheme by someone who's not too bright himself, but that is the plan. Blow this place up. Cash in on the insurance. And if you guys get in the way . . . Well, someone probably has insurance on you, too."

Sound reasoning, but it was like waving a red flag. He knew I was right, and it pissed him off, and since his boss wasn't here to bear the brunt of his rage . . .

Lucky me.

The guy exploded, ripped from my grip and slammed his fist into what should have been my stomach, but I'd twisted to grab my gun. I pointed it at him.

"Fine," I said. "Have it your way. If this is the only language you understand—"

He tried to take the gun. I kicked him and partially wriggled from under him.

"I really don't want to—" I began.

He pulled back his fist . . . and a two-by-four smacked into the side of his head. I looked up to see Jack standing over me.

"Thank you," I said. "I really didn't want to shoot him. He wasn't armed."

Jack shook his head. The thug started to rise. Jack whacked him again, almost off-hand. Then he reached down to help me up.

"You okay?" he said.

"Better than him," I said, nodding at the thug lying prone on the ground. "We need to get—"

At a sound, I turned to see Quinn hobbling toward us.

"I was moving too slow," he said. "Jack gave up on me."

"Rescued you, didn't I?" Jack said.

"Which you are never going to let me forget."

"You smarten up? I'll never mention it again."

Quinn rolled his eyes and gave me a one-armed hug. "Let's get out of here before the whole place comes down."

Leaving wasn't easy—back-tracking the way Jack came would have been too dangerous and we'd need to avoid any potential rescuers of the official variety. So we found a new route. At one point, we had to crawl through a narrow gap. Jack barely fit. Quinn did not.

"I'll find a way around," Quinn said. "Keep going."

Jack ducked back to the hole and said, "Go left. Saw a spot there. We'll wait."

When he straightened, I said, "Thank you," and hugged him. It was just meant to be a quick embrace, but he returned it with a fierce squeeze and then lifted my chin, saying, "Long as we're waiting . . ." and kissed me, a deep, passionate kiss that told me just how worried he'd been.

When he pulled back, he said, "Love you. You know that, right?"

I smiled. "I do." Then I whispered it back in his ear and kissed him until we heard Quinn making his way in our direction.

* * * * * *

We escaped and managed to sneak off without being seen. Then I called 911 to anonymously report the guy in the basement. He'd have killed me if he could have, but that was no reason to let him die. Jack agreed, not about the "doesn't deserve to die" part, but because the thug's survival helped us. It left someone alive who knew what Cillian had done.

Turned out the cartel angle wasn't a total fake-out. Cillian had teamed up with a small one he'd worked with before. That was how Evelyn suggested we handle this: set the cartel on him.

She was right. I didn't want Jack going after Cillian. Not because he'd have to kill an old friend. Cillian was no longer that. But Jack was more than pissed off. He was downright furious, tapping into a wellspring of rage that ran even deeper than my own. Set him on Cillian, and he wouldn't deliver a quick death, and that's what I didn't want—for Jack to vent that rage and then look back on what he'd done and suffer the guilt of acting on his anger. I knew what that was like.

Evelyn would work it so that everyone would know setting the cartel on Cillian had been Jack's revenge for coming after me. He'd sentenced Cillian to a far worse fate than a bullet to the head, and if that's what he'd do to an old friend, imagine what he'd do to a stranger who tried the same ploy.

Quinn would deal with Contrapasso. They obviously

had a leak, likely part of the issue they were still cleaning up from last fall, when we'd exposed rot in their ranks. Someone must have seen a nice opportunity for payback here.

Quinn and I talked. A long talk. I won't say he'd settled his issues with Jack. That won't ever happen. But being with Jack was my choice and Quinn agreed to finally shut up about it.

By Wednesday morning, Jack and I were heading home. Being midweek, the lodge had only a few guests, all on business and not interested in my wilderness guide services. That's normal at this time of year, and at Christmas I'd finally broken down and made it official lodge policy that in the off-season, while I do offer those services, they aren't guaranteed. That frees me for "emergencies" like this one . . . and for time to myself, or with Jack.

I still spent the first couple of hours working, making sure the guests were happy and everything was running smoothly. Then Jack and I escaped to "work on the chalet." Which meant sex in the chalet, where we kept sleeping bags and dreamed of the day when there'd be an actual bed.

It wasn't so much sex as making love. There's always been that—the more raucous fun mingled with the slower, more tender times. Normally it's the first followed—after some rest—by the second. This went straight to the slow and achingly tender, both of us expressing what came so hard in words.

Afterward, we found we had guests, the dogs having snuck in, but staying in the next room. As soon as the noise turned to quiet talk, they were there, getting pats and curling up and snuggling in around our legs.

When we heard the distant voices of wandering guests, we rose to dress.

"Know you don't want to talk about it," Jack said as he pulled on his jeans. "What happened. Mistakes I made. Danger I put you in."

I reached for my shirt. "No, let's talk. Or, rather, let me speechify. I knew exactly what I signed up for, Jack. From the start. All this tells me is that I need to be more careful. Be more suspicious. Always consider the possibility I'm being set up, especially if you aren't around. We also need alternate forms of contact. The only excuse for missing contact should be that we're physically unable, which is a big flashing red-alert. That's where we failed here. When we couldn't make contact, we presumed all was fine."

He nodded. "Yeah."

"So if you insist on apologizing again, fine. Take me to dinner tonight. Other than that . . ." I twisted to face him. "We're building something here, Jack. Literally building something." I waved at the chalet. "For us, not for me. I need to know you're going to stick around. That you won't decide you put me in too much danger and the best you can do for me is to leave, and all that complete and utter bullshit. If you aren't sure, let's stop building for a while. Take some time and work it out."

He nodded. Then he reached for a hammer and a handful of nails, walked to where we'd left off and got back to work.

Kelley Armstrong

Perfect Victim

Chapter One

Nadia

Running a wilderness lodge meant that, occasionally, there were guests I'd like to kill. The fact that I subsidized my income as a hitman made that option so much more viable. Yet in the decade since I opened the Red Oak Lodge, I had never been as tempted as I was today.

I was out at the back of my property, a gorgeous chunk of wilderness northwest of Toronto. A perfect June evening, with a fully booked lodge, and a quartet of eager New Yorkers joining me for a lesson in distance shooting on my range. Four eager New Yorkers . . . and Tyrone Cypress.

"What exactly is the point of this?" Cypress said as I instructed guests at the shooting range.

He didn't mutter the words under his breath or murmur them to himself. Cypress had only arrived this morning, but I'd already concluded that his vocal cords were permanently cranked to ten. He wasn't just loud—he boomed every word as if making a vital pronouncement. When he boomed this, my students all jumped . . . four guests who'd never handled a gun in their lives, jumping while holding loaded ones.

I quickly told them to practice unloading. As I walked to Cypress, the other guests sidled away from him. The man stood almost a foot above my five-six, with a thick, sturdy build. Grizzled brown hair hung to his shoulders, and a thick beard hid half his face.

"If you aren't interested in shooting—" I began.

"I'm just asking why you're doing this."

"I'm teaching my guests the proper use—"

"Not you," he said with a dismissive wave. "I know why *you're* here. Making a few bucks off folks who want to experience the great outdoors but don't actually know the first fucking thing about it."

"Mr—"

"It's Ty. For you, anyway. These yahoos can call me Mr. Cypress. My question was why *they're* doing this? Do any of them actually plan to hunt? If they do, are they going to eat what they kill, or just take pictures to hang in their high-rise condos?"

"We don't offer hunting at the Red Oak," I said. "But for those guests who wish to do so, we subcontract with an outfit that donates the meat to charity. What I teach *here* is marksmanship."

He snorted. "And what's the point of *that*?"

I kept my voice calm. "Sport. We also offer whitewater rafting and rock climbing. I do both of those in my free time, too, with absolutely no plans to ever be lost in the Alaskan wilderness and need to raft or climb my way to safety."

He peered at me. "You ever been to Alaska?"

"Once."

"You like it?"

I waved at the surrounding forest. "Oddly, yes, I seem to be a fan of nature."

"You're Canadian, though, right?"

"We are in Canada, and yes, I am Canadian."

"Then you should be going to the Yukon, not Alaska. Fewer people. Fewer"—he peered at the quartet—"Americans."

"I'm quite fond of people," I said. "Including Americans. But I appreciate the travel advice. Now, either you're here to shoot—"

"I don't use guns."

"All right, so you're not a hunter, either. Perhaps you'd rather—"

"I *am* a hunter. I just don't use guns. It's unsporting."

"If you like bows, we have a few of those."

"Don't mind bows. Prefer the hands-on approach, though."

"Uh-huh."

I really had to start screening guests. We'd picked up business enough in the last few years that I could afford to do that.

I continued, "Well, should you happen to encounter our local black bears, I'd strongly suggest you not try the 'hands-on' approach. Just run."

He chuckled. "If you think I can outrun any bear, you have a generous opinion of a big man's agility level. Nah, black bears aren't a problem. I've fought them off before. It's the browns that are trouble."

"We don't have any grizzlies here, so you're safe." I turned to the others. "Let's reload—"

"One more question," Cypress said.

I tensed. "Uh-huh."

"You've got a guy, right? Boyfriend?"

"Yeah," one of the Americans said. "She's definitely got a boyfriend. Sorry."

The others tittered, but Cypress wasn't hitting on me. Whatever vibes he gave off, that wasn't one of them.

Either Cypress didn't realize that the Americans were mocking him, or he just didn't care. He continued with, "You've got a boyfriend who runs this place with you, right?"

"I have a boyfriend who *works for me*, yes."

"But he's not around. That's what I heard. One of the other guests asked your housekeeper about fishing, and evidently, that's more his thing."

Well, no, Jack's "thing" was staying as far from the guests as possible. And for once, I really didn't blame him. However, he did handle the group excursions that bored me to tears, like fishing.

"Yes," I said. "John's in charge of the fishing trips, but he's not here. If you'd like, Owen can—"

"John, huh? When are you expecting 'John' back?"

"Probably not this weekend," I said. "So if you want to try fishing—"

"Oh, I know how to fish," he said as he walked off in the direction of the lodge. "I'll go when he's back. I'm booked here for the whole week."

Jack was away on a job. The same "job" that I did part-time. For him, though, it was a career, one he was easing out of. Not retiring. That implied reaching a point where he would never take another hit, and I couldn't see that happening. No more than I was ready to give up the occasional one now that I could make ends meet without the extra income.

"Making ends meet" was what got me into the business of part-time assassination. Well, no, it really started when I screwed up my career as a cop by shooting a serial killer . . . after he'd been arrested. After a very public shaming, I'd bought the lodge with my severance money and my mother's "please go away" early inheritance cash. One day, a regular discovered I was in danger of bankruptcy and offered me some side work. The regular happened to be part of a New York crime family, and his "side work" involved taking out a traitor. That became my part-time job, and I'd gained a reputation for two kinds of hits: criminal-on-criminal and what I must call vigilantism, as uncomfortable as the word made me.

I met Jack a few years later, when his mentor, Evelyn, heard of a new woman in our male-dominated field and sent Jack to investigate. He returned and suggested I wouldn't be a good student for her... and then proceeded to mentor me himself.

In the last few years, Jack had begun whittling down his clientele to those he couldn't afford to cut loose. Not "couldn't afford" financially—he was set for life there. But in a career like ours, there are clients you don't refuse, for the sake of your continued health. With the current job, a desperate former client had called him in after two hitmen failed to kill their target. Jack had done the job and was just tidying up loose ends, expected home soon... I hoped.

Chapter Two

Jack

When Jack told Nadia that he'd be late tidying up, she'd hesitated, and he knew she was thinking that his work—like hers—didn't need tidying.

"Something with the client?" she'd asked.

"Yeah," he'd said, which was true, but he wasn't going into detail until he got home. She'd be furious, and he wanted to be there for that, to watch her curse out the Sabatos in a way he could not.

The Sabatos had fucked him over. It happened. Except it never used to happen with a family like this. Which made him feel like an old man, whining about the good old days, and what was the world coming to. Nadia would roll her eyes and say that fifty-three was hardly old. Sometimes he felt like it, though, when he was out here in the world with Nadia back home at the lodge. An old man too far from the fire, chilled to the bone and world-weary.

Truth was that this job had always been full of clients like the Sabatos. Sometimes betrayal was situational; other times it was generational—the new family members disrespecting the customs of the old. And sometimes, well, fuck, sometimes you had to face the fact that being a hitman meant you worked for people who solved their problems with bullet holes and shallow graves.

If Jack was cranky about the whole thing, it wasn't even that he was genuinely upset by the betrayal so much as that he'd find it inconvenient to resolve. He should be home with Nadia by now. Instead, he had to deal with this shit.

Jack sat in Ross Sabato's night-dark living room and waited. He didn't smoke a cigarette. Didn't go into the kitchen and grab a beer. Didn't put his feet up on the furniture. Because *some* people understood the concept of respect.

At 12:30 a.m., keys sounded in the lock, and Ross Sabato walked in, talking to his nephew. A series of fast beeps as one disarmed the security system. The two men headed to the kitchen. Opened the fridge. Popped a couple of beers. And then stepped into the living room.

"Holy—" Ross began. Then he went for his gun.

"Don't," Jack said.

Ross hesitated, but his nephew continued fumbling to pull his weapon.

"Don't," Jack repeated.

Ross motioned for his nephew to stop.

"Jack. How the hell did you get past . . . ?" Ross trailed off with a strained laugh. "Stupid question, huh?"

Jack said nothing.

"The guy who sold me that security system guaranteed it," Ross said. "Guess I'll be asking for a refund."

Jack remained silent. Ross shifted from one foot to the other. Then he straightened, and the fake hearty note returned to his voice.

"David? You guys haven't met. This is Jack."

The young man started forward with his hand extended, but a headshake from Ross stopped him.

David motioned to the light switch. "Mind if I . . . ?"

Another headshake from his uncle. Then Ross cleared his throat.

"I heard you solved our problem. Not that I ever doubted it." Ross chuckled. "So I guess you're here to collect."

"No."

Three seconds of silence. Jack swore he heard Ross swallow.

"Well, uh," Ross began, "as long as you are here . . . David? Go grab two-fifty from the safe. No, make it three. A bonus for efficiency."

When David left, Jack said, "You've got a problem."

"Hmm?"

"Staffing issue. Three guys for one job?"

Ross gave a forced chuckle. "Right. Well, that's what I told the family—you get what you pay for. But with you not taking on more work, they didn't want to pay top dollar for an unknown. So they went cheap and hired internally."

"Internal's fine. Boys just need training. Let me talk to them."

Another chuckle. "I doubt we can afford your rates for that, Jack. They'll be fine."

"It's a freebie. Me and you? Worked together a long time. Built up a trust. Now I won't take your jobs? Leave you in the lurch? Bad form. Give me two days with your guys. No charge."

Sweat trickled down Sabato's cheek. Jack waited. As he did, his phone nudged his hip with the soft vibrate of an incoming call. His first instinct was to look at the clock. It'd be nearly three a.m. back home, and Nadia would only ever call at that hour for an emergency.

Time to get this over with. Fast.

Jack rose.

Ross started to back up and then stopped himself. "What's this about, Jack? I consider myself a man of some sensitivity, and I can tell something's wrong."

"Call your two guys. Now."

Ross swallowed. "All right. Let me go in the other room and—"

"Here. Now." Jack stepped forward. "Don't text. Call. Where I can hear."

"David will go get them. They'll be here in twenty minutes."

"Ghosts move fast," Jack said.

"Wh-what?"

"They're dead. The mark killed them. You told me they couldn't get a shot. Never even got past the setup. I asked if the mark saw either. You said no. Never got that close. Just, apparently, close enough to get shot by him. You set me up."

Ross's eyes rounded. "I'd never—"

"You weren't trying to kill me. You aren't that stupid. But if you'd told me two men died pulling this job? I'd have said no. Wouldn't do it."

"Sure, it was a bit more dangerous than usual, but you're careful. You weren't in any—"

"Danger? No. Because I did my homework. I always do my homework. Knew your men were dead. Still did the job 'cause I gave my word. The problem? The mark expected a hit. If I didn't do my homework? Took you at your word? Could have ended up like your boys."

David appeared in the doorway. He looked from Jack to his uncle.

"How much will it take to fix this, Jack?" Ross said. "You're right. I withheld vital information, and that was unfair. So, name your price. David can bring more."

Jack took the bag from the younger man, set it on the coffee table and counted bundles. "Two hundred grand for the job. That's what we agreed." He took that and added another two bundles. "One extra day to sort this shit. Twenty grand." He put the money into his satchel and left the rest in David's bag.

"Take that, Jack," Sabato said, waving at the extra. "Please."

"Twenty a day overtime. That's my rate. The price for your fuck-up?" He turned to Sabato. "Don't ever contact me again."

"I—"

"Not for a job. Not for anything. Don't even mention my name. I hear you did . . . ?"

Jack shrugged. That was all he did. Given his occupation, spelling it out was a waste of breath.

He hefted his satchel, walked past the two men and continued out the rear door.

Jack checked his phone as soon as he was outside. It hadn't been Nadia who called. Hadn't been an emergency of any kind, but simply a returned call from Felix, another hitman and one of the very few who had Jack's direct number. Also one of the few who Jack would consider a friend.

He waited until he was at his motel and then called

back.

"It's me," he said.

"You rang?" Felix said.

"Yeah. Ross Sabato. Blacklist him."

"Dare I ask for details?"

Jack said nothing.

Felix sighed. "Blacklisting works so much better when pros know what a client has done to deserve it."

"Just say it's from me. That's enough."

"True, but still . . . Sharing a few details helps."

"Doesn't help me. I don't give details. That's why I'm still alive."

"So am I."

"Yeah. Proof of miracles." He ignored Felix's protest and said, "Sabato misrepresented a job. The kind of misrepresentation that puts us in a grave. Or behind bars."

"Ah, got it. See? That wasn't so difficult. So, how's Dee?"

"Home."

"I asked *how* she was, not *where*." A deep sigh. "Clearly, we haven't spoken in quite some time if I actually expect you to carry on a conversation. But I must still make a token effort. Do you remember Cypher?"

Jack tensed but only gave a laconic, "Yeah."

"He was one of Evelyn's, wasn't he? Which hardly narrows it down, so I suppose you might have forgotten."

"Not him."

Felix chuckled. "Yes, it would be difficult to forget our Mr. Cypher, once met. It's been what, ten years? Fifteen? Perhaps even twenty? Last I heard, he got into some trouble on a job, pulled a kiss-and-tell."

In other words, Cypher had warned the mark . . . probably after sleeping with her. Felix was being careful with his wording. It didn't matter how secure their phones might be or that Felix himself was the tech expert who secured them. You never said more than you needed, though sometimes, Felix struggled with that concept.

"Heard that," Jack said.

"Then you also heard the rumor that he didn't survive the encounter. Our Mr. Cypher was never heard from again. Until now. He's been in contact."

Jack grunted a non-response.

"He called me asking after you."

Jack tensed again but still kept his "Yeah?" casual.

"I never got the impression you two were close," Felix said.

That was one way of putting it. Another was that Cypher had screwed Jack over on a job, and Jack had gotten him back, which should have been the end of the matter. Only Cypher seemed to think Jack's response had been disproportionate to his crime, and he'd told everyone who'd listen that he was going to kick Jack's ass "for good." There were exactly three pros in the world who could say that and make Jack start looking over his shoulder. Cypher was one of them.

"What'd he want?" Jack asked.

"Nothing. Just asked about you, how you were doing, what you'd been up to."

"And you said . . . ?"

"Nothing incriminating. You know that."

But he'd said *something*. Felix always did.

"What exactly did you tell him?" Jack said.

"Just that you were semi-retired, had left the country, that sort of thing. Do you actually remember Cypher? If you did, then you'd know I could practically hand him your address, and he still wouldn't find you. Mr. Cypher is not exactly a mental giant."

That was Felix's mistake. Cypher might not be a certifiable genius—most pros weren't. Sure, there were indeed guys who could barely write their names . . . but then there were the ones who acted that way because it was a convenient fiction. That was Cypher. And if he'd been asking after Jack, then it didn't matter how little Felix gave him—it would be enough.

Jack needed to get home. Now.

Chapter Three
Nadia

By the next morning, I'd decided that the best way—the only way, really—to deal with Tyrone Cypress was to quarantine him from other guests and bear the weight of his company alone. Given the choice between solo hikes and dealing with Cypress, they seemed quite happy to amuse themselves.

Cypress seemed equally happy to have me all to himself. I did take two others on our hike, though: our dogs, Scout and Rex.

We were heading up the ridge when Scout raced across the path in a blur of white.

"You know that's not a special breed," Cypress said.

"Hmm?"

"White German shepherds. Some fucking idiots think it's a separate breed."

"Well, fortunately—given that characterization—it's a recessive gene that people breed for, which is how new types of dogs are created. Selective breeding."

"Also leads to genetic problems. I hope you were careful picking her out."

"She was a gift, but yes, I'm sure John was careful. She's fine, as you can see."

"Seems to be. I still don't see the point in making them white. I notice you got a regular black-and-tan for the other one." He nodded at Rex.

"Yes, we like variety."

"Stupid name, though." He shook his head. "John pick it?"

"No, I did."

Which was true, but it'd been a joke. I used to tease Jack that in a world of creative noms de guerre he had to be contrary and pick the most boring one imaginable. It wasn't even really a nom de guerre—John was his real name, and his family used to call him Jack. Of course, as I'd learned later, the truth went much deeper than that. Calling himself Jack professionally was a constant reminder of what happened to his family and the role he'd unwittingly played in that. When I got him a dog, I jokingly suggested Rex, the most boring canine name imaginable. And Jack picked it.

"So I've got a question," Cypress said as we walked along the ridge top.

"Uh-huh."

"How the hell do you do this? You seem smart

enough. Someone said you used to be a cop."

I tensed. "Yes . . ."

"So why do a shitty job like this? Playing babysitter to fucking morons from the city."

"I like the wilderness . . . and I like people. Strange concept, I know. But I became a cop because I enjoyed working with people."

"Really?" He looked at me in genuine bewilderment. "I did some law enforcement shit myself, but . . ."

"You didn't do it to help others?"

His belly laugh startled Rex. "Fuck, no. I did it to help *me*."

Well, I had to give him points for honesty. As the path veered toward the forest, Rex's nose shot up, catching the wind. He gave a happy bark and tore off. In the distance, Scout crashed through the forest after him.

"Seems your pups found themselves a rabbit," Cypress said.

I nodded, but I knew it wasn't a rabbit, not with that bark, and I had to plant my feet to keep from tearing off after them, my imaginary tail wagging.

The only person they'd bark like that for was Jack.

Unfortunately, as soon as Jack spotted Cypress, he'd detour to our private chalet. Living where we also conduct business meant we had to keep a firm line between the personal and the professional, and having the guide pause a hike to hug her returning boyfriend crossed that line. Jack would back off, after making sure I knew he was home. Disappointing, but I could ask Emma to chaperone Cypress post-hike—feed him her famous cinnamon rolls—while I enjoyed my reunion.

While I didn't gape about for Jack, I'll admit I listened for him. Which was pointless. It was an old game—a training exercise for both of us, him sneaking up on me, seeing whether he could manage it. In the city, he always could, but the forest had been a new environment, one he'd been determined to master. I stood no chance of hearing him unless he wanted to be heard, and the forest remained a soft symphony of birdcalls and wind-rustled leaves.

Then something thumped to Cypress's right. He wheeled that way . . . and I looked the other, that thump very clearly being a stone thrown as a distraction. Sure enough, Jack stepped out right behind Cypress. Cypress's head jerked up as a gun pressed into his back.

"Hey, Jack," Cypress said. "Long time, no see."

I withdrew the concealed gun I carry for this exact reason: in case someone came around who *didn't* call Jack 'John.'

"You wanna lower that gun?" Cypress said when Jack didn't respond to his greeting.

"No."

"Getting jumpy in your old age?"

"No," Jack said. "Nerves are fine. Memory is, too.

You hoping I'd forgotten?"

"Forgot . . . ? Really?" Cypress shook his head. "I was playing with you."

"Playing?"

Cypress shrugged. "Job gets boring. Not nearly enough playmates on our level, you know what I mean?"

"No."

"That was always your problem. You took yourself too seriously. If I wanted to come at you, I'd have come at you. I was playing. Ask Evie. That's my idea of play." He paused. "Nah, better not ask Evie. She might give you a whole other definition, and that's more than you need to hear."

"What do you want?"

"To hire you."

"No."

Cypress tried glancing over his shoulder, but Jack pressed the gun barrel in harder.

"You sure your memory's fine?" Cypress said. "You do know I've seen what you look like. I also know what your girl here looks like. Dee, right?"

"That a threat?" Jack said.

Cypress threw up his hands. "Fuck, you are impossible to talk to. Everything's a threat. Everything's personal. I meant you might as well let me turn around since I've seen you both already. I'm here because I want to hire you, okay? That's it."

"No."

"Jack is in the process of retiring," I said, because at this rate, we'd be here all morning, Jack refusing to give an explanation that required more than three words.

I walked in front of Cypress. "That means he isn't taking on any new clients, and he's doing jobs for very few of his old ones. If you wanted to ask, though, the correct protocol would be to call."

"I don't have a phone."

I gave him a look.

"I *don't*. Been living up north for fifteen years, out where a phone is as useful as a rock. Even if I could find a pay phone around here—and these days, they're scarce as hen's teeth—any number I have for Jack wouldn't work. No one in the biz keeps a number that long."

"You mentioned Evelyn, who is *much* easier to contact and who could pass along a message."

"Yeah, no. It's harder for Jack to refuse when I'm out here, in his face. I'm good at getting in faces. Good at getting people's attention."

"By taking Jack's girlfriend hostage until he agrees to your job?"

Cypress's broad forehead screwed up. "What? Hell, no. That'd be a fucking stupid idea, considering your alternate line of employment."

"It's been tried."

He snorted. "Like I said, fucking idiots are

everywhere. Let me guess. Moron never even managed to catch you, right?"

True enough, but I only shrugged. "This might be different. I'm at home. My guard's lowered. You're a big guy. It's possible."

"If I'd planned that, I'd at least have pretended I was allergic to dogs. Get you to leave your pooches behind. You think those two would let me take you?" He shook his head. "I'm here to ask you to do a job. Both of you."

"Do it yourself," Jack said.

"I can't. It's not my kind of thing. Too much investigation. I gotta find the mark first. That isn't my talent. I'm a point-and-shoot guy. You point 'em out. I shoot 'em. Well, without actually shooting."

"Because that isn't sporting?" I said.

He only shrugged. "Either way, Jack's always done a helluva lot more research than me, and now I hear he's with a girl who's good at that stuff, too. I didn't know you'd been a cop, but now that makes sense. You've got the skills."

"You said you'd done law enforcement."

"I was the sheriff in a very, very, *very* small town. Only thing they needed was someone to kick ass and keep folks in line, which I do very well. But now a woman I care about is in trouble, and someone's gotta die to keep her safe, and finding that someone is way above my pay scale. So I'm coming to you. If you'll let me explain—"

"An hour," Jack said.

"Fine, give me an hour."

"No. Give *us* an hour. Alone. Then we'll talk."

Chapter Four
Nadia

I kicked myself for not realizing Cypress was more than a regular guest. Jack often said that the average hitman was just a thug who didn't mind killing people. Guys low on the IQ scale and high on the sociopathy one. Which seemed to fit Cypress.

Except those hitmen weren't "pros" like Jack or me or Evelyn. If guys like that knew of Jack, it was by reputation only. And those hitmen weren't still walking around at Cypress's age. That breed wasn't big on planning—they just walked up to a guy and shot him, and then repeated the process until they were caught or killed, which rarely took long. Disposable hired killers. That wasn't Cypress. Nor was I sure he fit "low on the IQ scale." He acted it, but I can, too, having learned the value of a good "dumb chick" disguise.

Cypress's cover story had made sense. "Fucking business in Toronto," he'd said. "But that doesn't mean I gotta stay in the damned city all weekend." I had regulars like him—those who didn't want to spend their off-time in hotel bars with the rest of the solo business travelers. I've even promoted to that crowd at trade shows. *Stuck in Toronto for the weekend? We're just an hour's drive away!*

And, honestly, if anyone came to the lodge for Jack, they weren't going to check in as a guest. So I understood why I hadn't suspected Cypress... but that wouldn't stop me from cursing myself now.

Lost in my thoughts, I walked to our chalet in silence, but I barely had the door closed before Jack pulled me into a kiss that made me forget Cypress. When we separated, I traced my fingers down his shirtfront.

"I hate it when you go away," I said. "But I really like it when you come back."

"Timing sucks."

"Next time you see me with someone from your past? Don't say anything. Just call me back to the chalet so I can get sex before we need to fix the problem."

He chuckled. "Good plan. Trouble is . . ." He waved, and I picked up the sound of guests laughing as they passed close to our house.

"Mmm, yes. Strike that. Only come home between midnight and six, when I can guarantee stray guests won't come knocking on our door. Well, *almost* guarantee it."

He shook his head and headed into the kitchen. "Need a fence. Electrified."

"If I thought that would stop them, I might actually agree."

Despite warning all guests that the chalet was private property—and erecting discreet signs—we found nose prints on the glass almost daily. People just can't resist the allure of a cabin in the woods. We used to keep the door unlocked until we found a couple succumbing to that allure in front of our fireplace.

Jack started the coffee machine and opened a fresh gift from the pie fairy.

"Emma's welcome home present," I said. "Though I could point out it's still morning."

"Fruit, pastry, it's breakfast food. Just gotta eat it with coffee."

"So Tyrone Cypress . . ." I said as I settled at the table.

"That what he's going by?"

"What's his work name?"

"Cypher."

I arched my brows. "Okay, I hate to give him credit, but that's kind of awesome. Much better than—"

"Yeah, yeah." He handed me a slice of pie. "Better than Jack."

"I was going to say better than Dee."

"You can change it anytime."

"Rebranding's a bitch."

He slid into the chair across from mine. "Evelyn named him."

"Ah. He's one of hers, I take it. Lover and student?"

"Mostly the former. Some training but..." He shrugged. "She never understood him."

"Hence the moniker."

"Yeah. At first? What makes him different was what got her attention. But then she wanted to fix him. He said 'fuck that.' They'd still hook up. But nothing more."

A common story in relationships, one person trying to change the other. That was one reason Jack had kept me away from Evelyn. He'd been able to accept her training while refusing her plan to turn him into a slick assassin. He'd also never ended up in her bed.

As the coffee brewed, I nibbled my pie and listened to Jack explain how Cypher found him. Through Felix, apparently, who'd been quick to buy Cypher's dumb hick routine and divulged just enough information to send Cypher in our direction.

"And there's bad blood between you two?" I said as I got up to pour the coffee.

"Screwed me over. Stole a job. So I did the same." He paused. "Well . . . not exactly the same."

"You hit back harder."

He shrugged. "Don't care for one-upmanship. But sometimes you gotta. He undercut my price. So I shot his mark."

"That's one-upmanship?"

"Shot him *while* Cypher was strangling him. Pissed him

off." Another pause. "Really pissed him off. If he claimed the hit, he had to say he used a gun. Which he wouldn't do."

"He joked about hunting with his bare hands. That wasn't actually a joke, was it?"

"Nah. Like I said, he's a little . . . different."

"Uh-huh. So you literally shot his mark out from under him in retaliation for him stealing a job. Fair enough. But he struck back, didn't he?"

"Tried to. Failed. Disappeared before he could try again."

I sipped my coffee. "Playing devil's advocate here. Is it possible he really was playing with you? I'd never disrespect the job by turning it into a game, but he seems the type."

"Maybe. Still don't trust him."

"*More* than you don't trust everyone else?"

He toyed with a piece of piecrust. "We'll hear him out."

Chapter Five
Nadia

Cypher had to wait until after lunch to talk to us. Guests paid for access to the host, which meant there was a limit to how much time I could be unavailable. Until Jack and I built the chalet, I'd lived in the lodge, partly to avoid any temptation to retreat for a little me-time. Jack had helped me see there was an unhealthy side to that, the side that felt I didn't deserve me-time. The truth was that guests didn't really expect me on call 24/7, and any debt I owed the world could not be paid off by providing an impromptu canoe trip.

We told Cypher that we'd hear him out after lunch, which kept him from breathing down our necks. He took his meal to go and said he'd be over by some ramshackle cabins on the far edge of the property.

Jack and I ate with our guests. I regaled them with life-in-the-lodge anecdotes while Jack . . . well, Jack ate. Most of what he did around the lodge was behind the scenes, slowly taking over for my aging caretaker, Owen. Jack interacted with guests for the activities I hated but otherwise kept to himself. No one bothered him. Some people just have that air about them—the one that says they won't bite your head off if you speak to them, but they don't encourage it either.

After lunch, I reminded guests about the twilight canoe excursion. Then Jack and I left to speak to Cypher.

It was a good twenty-minute hike to that part of the property. Up until a few months ago, it belonged to a neighbor. When they'd been preparing to move, Jack had approached them with an offer: he'd pay for over a hundred acres of their lot, leaving them to sell the house with five acres, which was all most people wanted—just enough to feel like they're living in the wilderness.

The ramshackle cabins had once been rental units. That was before my time, and I'd always grumbled about them being both an eyesore and a safety hazard. Guests couldn't resist wandering over to explore or photograph the cabins, which was dangerous. So Jack bought the land. We'd tear the shacks down soon and erect small cottages, expanding the business.

When we arrived, Cypher was poking around a ruined cabin.

"Careful," I called. "We've had one collapse."

"Kind of a safety hazard, don't you think?"

"We just bought the land," I said. "We haven't gotten

to the demolition part."

He grunted. "Good. I was afraid you were renting them like this."

"I should hope not."

"Never know. Where I'm from, sometimes, this is what you get."

I walked over, Jack beside me, the dogs trailing along.

"Speaking of where you're from . . ." I said. "You want us to help someone you know. But you also suggested you live someplace without easy access to the outside world. So how'd you know your friend was in trouble?"

"I have ways. It's not exactly regular contact. She's been dealing with this shit for months, and I just found out."

"And 'she' is . . . ?" I said.

Cypher settled on a log pulled over by an ancient fire pit.

"It's a woman," he said.

"I guessed that from the pronoun."

"That's really all there is to say. It's a woman. Someone from my past, from when I was young and stupid. Someone . . ." He shrugged. "Sometimes sticking around isn't an option, and as much as you might want to, you realize that the right thing to do is walk away. Doesn't mean I stopped caring. So I keep tabs on her."

"And she's in trouble."

"Yeah. You hear about that family court shit in Honolulu?"

"Hawaii?"

"Is there another one?" He planted his feet farther apart. "That's where she lives, and I'm guessing by your answer that you haven't heard of the case. Some sicko has been targeting people who work for the family courts."

"Didn't something like that happen in Australia? Years ago?"

"I don't doubt it. In our job, we get asked to do some ugly shit. To me, though, there's nothing uglier than the guys—and gals—who want us to off their exes. Not because the ex is a nasty piece of shit. Not even because they want revenge. But because of the divorce. Kill your wife so you don't have to pay alimony. Kill your husband so you don't have to sell your home. And the absolute fucking worst: kill your partner so you get the kids."

"All of which is handled by family courts," I said. "They make a ruling, and one party is bound to be unhappy with it. So that's what this is. Someone's taking it out on the court representatives."

He nodded. "Three people are dead. All had a connection to the family courts. This woman I'm worried about? She's a family court lawyer."

"You're afraid she'll be targeted?" I asked.

"No, she *is* being targeted. The damn fool—" He

shook his head. "She's put herself right in the middle of this. A lawyer's kid got killed, so he quit his cases. No one would take them except her. Then her dog..." He glanced at Scout and Rex and lowered his voice as if they could hear. "Bastard killed her dog and put a bomb in her car. Pretty soon her boyfriend—asshole coward—lit out, deciding he wasn't taking the risk. So she's lost her dog, her boyfriend, nearly lost her life, and you think she'll give up those cases? Fuck no."

"You talk to her?" Jack said, his first words since we got here.

Cypher shook his head. "It's ... complicated. Stuff like that, when you leave, you can't make contact again. It isn't safe. Or that's the excuse you give yourself, when the truth is that you know if you do call, she'll hang up. Better to say you're keeping her safe by staying away. You know how it is."

Jack grunted as if he did. When Jack and I got together, though, he'd admitted that he hadn't had a relationship since he was sixteen... right before he signed up with Irish resistance fighters, who made the IRA look like Greenpeace. After that—and the fallout from his exit a few years later—he wouldn't let anyone take the risk that came with being part of a hitman's life. Even for me, being with Jack put a target on my back, and it'd taken a long time to convince him that I was okay with that.

Right now, though, someone else wore a target, for an entirely different reason—a good and brave and righteous one.

"So this woman . . ." I said.

"Angela. Her name's Angela."

"Angela took on these cases, and now she's determined to keep them, despite the fact it endangers her life."

"Fucking stupid, huh?" Even as he shook his head, his voice swelled with pride.

"Not exactly a wise survival strategy," I said. "But she does deserve help."

"That's what I hoped you'd say. So here's the deal. I'll fly you both to Hawaii. First class, round trip, best fucking hotels they got, all expenses paid. And that's on top of the hit, which will be double your usual rate, for the inconvenience of a rush job."

Jack glanced at me. When he started to nod, I cut in with, "We'll think about it."

Jack's brows arched. He knew this was exactly the sort of job I'd want. But so did anyone who knew my professional reputation.

"One more hour," I said. "You'll have your answer in an hour."

Chapter Six
Nadia

"You want to research it first," Jack said as we headed to our chalet.

"I do."

He nodded. "Yeah, you're right. Shouldn't have jumped like that."

I looped my arm through his. "You knew I'd want it."

"You do, right?"

"All-expenses-paid first-class trip to Hawaii? Hell, yeah."

His look said I could get that anytime. I would argue that having someone else foot the bill eased the voice that fretted about how much of "his" money we spent. But I knew what he meant.

"Yes," I said. "This woman is taking personal risk to help others when no one else will. Like I said, that deserves help. And someone is killing people for doing their damned jobs? That deserves stopping—

permanently, if necessary. But I'm still worried."

"That Cypher's bullshitting. That it's a trap."

"We all have our weaknesses. We expose them with every choice we make. Anyone who's done basic research on 'Dee' knows she'd drool over this one. So there's no way I'm going to say yes until I've done some basic research myself."

Cypher hadn't been lying. There *was* a killer stalking representatives of the Honolulu family court system.

It began a year ago with the apparent suicide of a social worker. Fifty-year-old Mindy Lang had been found dead in her carbon-monoxide-filled car. The profession suffered from one of the highest incidences of burnout and depression, and Mindy had recently gone through a divorce herself, so no one questioned the initial findings.

Three months later, Albert Kim, a family court judge died in what looked like another suicide, this one death-by-gunshot. That case, though, gave the authorities pause. The deceased was a very successful judge, who'd been about to buy his dream home. Suicide didn't fit. That led to deeper investigation and the discovery that it'd been a staged murder. The police then took another look at Mindy Lang, who had often worked with the murdered judge. An exhumation and secondary examination found bruises on her neck, plus signs that she'd been unconscious when she went into the car. That meant murder.

At this point, the killer must have realized that disguising the deaths as suicides was pointless. If anyone working in family law died under suspicious circumstances, the police were going to investigate.

The next target was a lawyer, Charles Atom. The killer booby-trapped the family grill with an explosive device. Atom's teenage daughter had been the one to open it. She'd been killed instantly. Atom, who'd been standing nearby, suffered head injuries, including the loss of an eye.

Atom's injuries meant he wasn't able to handle his clients' cases. When no one at his firm would take them, Angela Kamaka stepped forward. That, as Cypher said, made her a target. Six weeks ago, she came home to find her dog dead, poisoned. A week later, someone planted a bomb in her car, but by that point, she was already checking it before she turned the ignition. She'd found the device. Then someone had fired shots into her backyard, shattering the glass tumbler her live-in boyfriend was holding. He'd packed his bags and left, while she stood her ground, living under nightly police protection.

I was surfing through articles, making notes, when Jack came in and walked up behind me.

"Pack my sunscreen?" he said.

I craned my neck to look back at him. "I think so. Is

that okay?"

"As long as you don't make me wear Hawaiian shirts."

"I won't make you wear any shirt at all." I stood and gave him a quick kiss. "Let's go talk to our new client."

Chapter Seven

Nadia

Cypher caught the next flight out. He was heading to Honolulu, which wasn't quite what I'd expected—or hoped—but that wasn't up for discussion. He would stay out of our way, but he wanted to be there. I supposed it didn't hurt to have an extra pro on hand, though I suspected I'd come to regret that.

Our guests were all weekenders, meaning they'd be checked out by noon tomorrow. They had the option of using the property until the end of the day, but with no Sunday night guests, there were no scheduled afternoon or evening events. That meant I could take off after breakfast, leaving Emma to handle checkouts.

Jack and I were on a plane Sunday afternoon. We hopped from Toronto to Vancouver and then down to Hawaii. Two long hauls, but as Cypher promised, we went first class, which helped, considering that one of us was flight-phobic. Jack could manage—flying was unavoidable for overseas jobs—but if he could drive, he did.

The time difference meant it wasn't even nine p.m. when we touched down. We'd both managed to get some shut-eye on the flight, so we were wide awake when Cypher met us at the airport.

My first impression of Honolulu was lights. Endless lights stretching up the volcanic mountain range. That wasn't quite what I expected. Every image I'd seen of the islands featured sand, surf, sun and the kind of empty paradise that I suspected was tough to find these days. The weather was gorgeous, even after dark, and I marveled at the partly open-air terminal until I realized that they didn't need to worry about winter cold, let alone snow and ice.

I put my window down as Cypher drove, and if I squinted, I could make out the ocean to my right. Soon Cypher left the highway and headed up a winding road.

"Angela lives out here?" Jack said.

"Yeah," Cypher grumbled.

I could see their concern. When I twisted to look down the mountain behind us, the view was incredible, but this wasn't some condo apartment in the city. That made it easier for a killer to get access to her. The neighborhood was residential enough, though—a proper subdivision.

"I'll drive past her house," Cypher said. "Cops are out

front in a unmarked black Jeep. Dee? Keep your window down."

I didn't ask why. The police would be on the lookout for unfamiliar vehicles. One with a woman in the passenger seat—her window down and arm out—would seem a lot more innocent than an SUV with rolled-up tinted windows.

"On your side," Cypher said. "The little gray house."

The speed limit was low enough for him to roll past slowly. I snapped shots with my camera held low. The officers in the Jeep glanced over. Cypress had his window down, too, and he lifted his fingers in casual greeting. The officers nodded, and we continued along the road.

"We *should* do it at night," Cypher said. "But those cops mean it'd be tricky. Daytime's always tricky, though."

"For what?" I said.

"Taking Angela."

"What?"

He spoke slower. "Taking Angela into protective custody while you guys find the asshole who's trying to kill her."

"I think the word you actually want there is *kidnapping*, Cypher," I said. "And the answer is: hell, no."

"Ty."

"What?"

Again, that slowed speech. "Call me Ty."

"How about I just call you crazy motherfucker? Does that work?"

Jack snorted from the back seat.

Cypher chuckled. "Sure. Wouldn't be the first time. Or the second. Or the—"

"We are not kidnapping Angela. That wasn't part of the deal."

"Because I figured it was obvious. How else are you going to keep her safe? We'll take her into protective custody for a few days. She won't be happy about it, but she'll be safe, and we'll make sure she's comfortable and—"

"And no. Hell, no." I twisted to look at Jack. "What do you say?"

"Yeah. It's problematic."

"That's one way of putting it." I glanced at Cypher. "There will be no kidnapping the woman we're here to protect. You want to know how we'll keep her safe? By watching out for her. And by catching this bastard. She's been smart enough to survive so far. She'll be fine for a few more days. I'll make sure of it."

"How the hell do you plan to do that?"

I told him.

Jack and I spent the next morning enjoying the truly spectacular lodgings Cypher had booked for us. We were outside Honolulu proper, at a five-star hotel with all the sand, surf and sun I'd imagined.

We slept soundly and woke before dawn, our internal schedules completely screwed up by the six-hour time difference. I jogged while Jack hunted down Kona coffee and macadamia nut buns, which we enjoyed on a dock, our bare feet dangling in the clear, warm water. Afterward we walked the empty beach, talking. Back to our room, with the salt-scented wind blowing in from the ocean, the sheers billowing as we took full advantage of our king-sized bed. Then, appetite renewed, it was off to breakfast, dining on a balcony as surfers headed out below.

After breakfast, we shopped. Not exactly our thing, but there was a row of high-end boutiques just outside the resort, and any good walk needs a destination. Jack insisted on buying me a pair of designer sunglasses, and I bought him a watch that I caught him admiring. Well, I *tried* to buy it. He distracted me at the till and traded credit cards, and while I'd have loved to insist on paying, the truth was that the watch would have gobbled up my entire line of credit.

They were real credit cards. "Real" in the sense that we would pay them off. They were also "not real" in the sense that they had fake names and were attached to fake addresses. It might seem tempting to just get fake cards altogether, but neither of us wanted to be the hitman brought down by defrauding the credit card company for a few grand.

A morning well spent. And, despite what it might seem, not a morning wasted in leisure. I worked my ass off. Or, more correctly, I worked my mouth off.

Being a sociable person meant that I found it easy to start conversations with strangers, and strangers found it easy to start them with me. It didn't hurt that I gave off that kind of vibe. I *looked* approachable. Thirty-five years old, dark auburn hair to my shoulders, hair with a tendency to curl, and skin with a tendency to freckle. People told me I had an open face, very genuine, very girl-next-door. Which meant that I intimidated absolutely no one. Extremely useful in my line of work. I was the person most likely to be asked for directions or just asked for the time. Also the person most likely to be asked to give up my window seat to a fellow traveler, or the person most likely to be cut off in a lineup. Those last two did not go so well. I am friendly. I am approachable. I am *not* a pushover.

So I found it extremely easy to get information from total strangers. And that was how I spent my morning, whether it was jogging on the beach or eating breakfast on the balcony or browsing in the shops. I worked through every part except, well, the sex, for obvious reasons, but I figured I'd done enough by that point to take a little time off.

Wherever we went, Jack and I talked about Angela

and the murders. Sometimes I'd use that as an opening to ask questions, like to our breakfast server. *My husband just told me about those horrible murders. Is it true?* Other times, locals would overhear us and interject a comment or an opinion. When it came to high-profile crimes, everyone had an opinion.

While Honolulu was a city of three hundred thousand, being on an island two thousand miles from the mainland made it feel as insular as a small town. It seemed as if half the people I talked to knew someone involved in the case. And they were all happy to chat. Tourism is Hawaii's number one industry, and I was right in the heart of it, which meant that the staff probably got a little tired of dispensing alohas and island charm. They seemed happy to discuss a side of their city that didn't arise in their usual tourist chatter.

Most of what I got was wild conjecture, mixed with rumor and innuendo and a liberal smattering of conspiracy theory. But there would be some truth in there, too, and I filed it all away for the next stage of my investigation, which I launched right after lunch.

Chapter Eight
Jack

"Are you fucking nuts?"

That was what Cypher had said about Jack's afternoon plans. He'd said more than that, too, ranting about how Nadia called *him* a crazy motherfucker, and if Jack screwed this up—or endangered Angela in any way—he'd nail Jack's balls to the nearest coconut tree.

Jack had let him rant. Then he'd looked at Nadia, who'd considered the suggestion. She'd opened her mouth and started, "Can you—?" and then stopped herself and said, "Sure. That's a good idea."

Can you pull it off?

That was what she'd been about to say. She hadn't finished because she knew Jack didn't take chances. He'd never been what one might call a natural risk-taker like Nadia, with her love of extreme sports. She'd taken chances on the job, too, leading to their first real fight.

He'd been furious, a shock to her, who'd never even heard him raise his voice. She'd taken an unnecessary risk, putting herself in extreme danger to catch a killer. Part of that fury—a large part—had been the mirror it reflected back on him. On his past. He saw Nadia take that risk, and he knew why she was taking it because he'd been there himself.

He had taken chances, early in his career. Huge ones that had paid off, but at the time, he hadn't really given a shit if they did or not. Hadn't given a shit if his choices landed him in a body bag. He'd gotten his family killed, and so he didn't particularly feel he deserved to keep walking around.

Nadia hadn't been suicidal—not since he'd met her, at least—but there were always threads of that in her professional risk-taking. The feeling that she owed a debt. And she could say it was because she'd shot a serial killer, but that was bullshit. Sure, there was shame and grief for the loss of a career she'd loved. But her true guilt went back to her murdered cousin, the fact that she'd failed to stop it, failed to get help in time. It didn't matter if no one else would ever hold her accountable; that kind of guilt never goes away, as Jack knew very well.

Jack's plan for today was a calculated risk that wasn't much of a risk at all. He didn't take chances these days because he wasn't just taking them for himself. He had Nadia to think about, and sure, there was the fear of her getting picked up if he was arrested, but there was also a far more selfish reason to play it safe: he was happy in his new life, and he damned well intended to keep it.

His task that day? Breaking into Angela Kamaka's house. All attacks against her—the dog, the car bomb, the shots fired—had happened at home. While he did want to get a look inside her house, he held some hope that he wouldn't be able to break in, which would mean she was safe. That was, unfortunately, not the case.

Angela lived in a neighborhood of small, older homes on large lots, and she had no neighbor to the rear. A gate at the back of her fence suggested she appreciated that openness and used the walking trails. The fence also made it easy to approach her house without being spotted.

A security camera watched the gate, but there was no reason to enter that way when the fence itself was more boundary marker than security perimeter. He hopped it easily. All right, he *climbed* it easily, being about a decade past hopping, which he'd finally admitted a few years ago when he fucked up his damn ankle on just such a jump.

Two more security cameras monitored the rear yard. They were well placed, difficult to spot, but Jack had a device that picked up their signatures. It was easy enough to slip up alongside the house and get the back door open without being spotted. Inside, he found an impressive security system, one that rivaled the Sabatos'. He disabled it and then set about tracking the camera feed to a computer in the main room. An old computer without even password protection. Jack reviewed the security video and confirmed he wasn't on it.

He took a minute to check the computer for data. That wasn't really his thing, but Nadia had been teaching him. From what he could tell, this was a basic terminal, mostly just for the security system cameras. Angela must keep her personal and professional files elsewhere, probably on a laptop.

As Jack prowled the house, he made mental notes of all the security enhancements needed to make it safer. He had to admit someone had done a decent job. If the killer was, as they expected, a disgruntled client, then he wasn't going to have Jack's skill set. Still, Jack wasn't betting a woman's life on that. The best scenario would be the one Cypher wanted—getting Angela to a safe place in the city. If she insisted on staying here, though, these security gaps had to be fixed.

As Jack walked through the house, he didn't snoop—this was already an invasion of a victim's privacy—but he couldn't help forming a fuller picture of Angela Kamaka. A visual picture, for one thing, from the photographs. Photos of a woman with her parents, with friends, with lovers. One figure featured in enough pictures to tell him this was Angela. She looked mid-thirties. Brown skin. Average height. Sturdy build. Always with a smile, one that lit up an otherwise plain face.

He focused his attention in her office, particularly on the filing cabinet. It was one you could buy at any business supply store, with a lock that only took a hairpin to open. He sprang that and looked inside.

The top drawer held personal information, and he flipped through that, skimming the carefully marked file folders to see whether there was anything that caught his eye. He checked the one for her mortgage papers and her income tax. A person's financial situation often suggested alternative answers. Like the woman who'd tried to hire him to kill her supposedly abusive husband . . . and it turned out she was neck-deep in gambling debt, and her husband wasn't eager to empty their 401(k) to pay off her bookies.

In the second drawer, he found Angela's legal files. Not the full files—those would be in her office. Here she only kept copies of the most pertinent information, presumably in case she needed it while working evenings or weekends. Past clients took up the rear three-quarters of the drawer. She kept the current ones in front. Those were the files he lifted out.

As he pulled the files, he dislodged a legal pad. On it, Angela had been making notes, doing a little detective work of her own. Jack set the files down and leafed through the notes.

Angela had made a list of all the cases she'd taken

over from Charles Atom—the injured lawyer. Then she'd cross-referenced that list with another one, presumably the names of people who also had some connection to the murdered social worker and judge. Three suspects arose. Jack pulled those files. As he took pictures of the pages, he skimmed them.

Suspect number one—Steve Forrest—was what Jack would call a classic angry white man. A middle-aged guy who ran a successful local electronics business, only to have his wife object to his sleeping around. Not only did she leave him, but she also expected half the money he'd earned while she'd stayed home to raise their kids. The social worker—Mindy Lang—had gotten involved when their seventeen-year-old didn't want to visit Forrest anymore. Then the judge—Albert Kim—had forced Forrest to divulge details of investments he'd tried to hide. Charles Atom had been the opposing lawyer in Forrest's divorce case. Last month, Forrest had shown up at his ex-wife's house and told her that if she didn't want to be responsible for more deaths, she should agree to his divorce terms. She'd captured that threat on tape, which bumped Forrest to the top of the suspect list.

Next was Louis Stanton, an engineer whose wife had left him, claiming "irreconcilable differences." Just a breakdown of the marriage. It had started amicably enough—a fair division of assets and joint custody of the kids. Then Stanton got a job offer in California, and his wife wasn't willing to leave Hawaii—she ran a business in Honolulu—so Judge Kim ordered that if Stanton wanted to retain joint custody, he had to remain here. Stanton tried taking the kids to California anyway. He lost joint custody and started having all his visits monitored by Mindy Lang. Clearly the problem was that the family courts favored women, Stanton decided, and he launched a men's rights group, dedicated to dismantling the current system—"by force if necessary."

Suspect number three was a woman who'd been denied joint custody of her children based on prescription drug dependence. Sheila Walling had a run-in with Mindy Lang over visitation: she'd been late returning her kids, and on the urging of Atom, Mindy had advised the judge to reprimand Walling, which he had. Unlike the other two, Jack saw no indication that Walling had threatened anyone involved, either directly or obliquely. While Walling was a chemist by trade—which might help with the bombs—she seemed an odd choice of suspects . . . until Jack found a note deeper in her file. Six months ago, Walling had been the prime suspect in the murder of her ex-husband's new girlfriend, who'd been killed with a gift-wrapped IED. The police hadn't found enough evidence to charge Walling, but it was obvious that they'd taken this into consideration when looking for a person committing grudge murders . . . using IEDs.

Jack flipped through the other cases that Angela had taken from Atom. Nothing else stuck out, but he knew Nadia would want to be thorough, so he snapped shots of those pages, too. Then he went back to the three prime suspects.

The cops would be investigating all of them—looking for the missing evidence that would let them lay charges. Which was a perfectly rational way to go about it, but Jack wasn't a cop, and really, he preferred a more direct approach.

Time to go and see a man about a grudge.

Chapter Nine

Nadia

Angela Kamaka was a partner at a downtown Honolulu law firm. In this case, "partner" just meant she was one of the two lawyers who worked there along with a support staff.

When I first walked in, the front desk was empty, but I'd barely crossed the floor before a young man zipped out from a side room and ducked behind the desk.

"I'd like to speak to Ms. Kamaka," I said.

"Do you have an appointment?"

"No, but I'm hoping she'll have a few moments to speak to me."

He gave me a quick once-over, and his lips tightened. "If you are a reporter—"

"I'm not here looking for a story. A mutual friend sent me. I just need a moment of her time."

He picked up the phone and turned away for a brief murmured conversation. Then, with an abrupt wave, he walked off down the hall, leaving me to follow. When we reached a closed door, he stopped and said, "I have security on speed dial."

"Under the circumstances, I'm glad to hear it."

The door opened before he could knock, and Angela stood there, one hand on her hip.

"You do know I can hear you, right, Richard?"

"As I have said before, we need to invest in better soundproofing." He walked away, raising his watch as he did, a reminder he'd be watching how much of his boss's time I consumed.

"Ignore him," Angela said as she closed the door behind me. "Everyone here is a bit overprotective these days."

"Better than the alternative." I turned to face her. "And because I know you're busy, I'm going to use that as a segue to get straight to the point. It's not just your office staff that's feeling protective. I'm a personal bodyguard, hired by a concerned third party."

She eyed me, her head tilted. I waited for her to say I didn't look much like a bodyguard, but after that assessment, she nodded, walked to her chair and waved for me to sit.

"The fact that you aren't naming my benefactor tells me it's anonymous."

"It is. I'm a former police officer, living in the Detroit area, currently working part-time as both a bodyguard and investigator." I took a sheet from my bag and set it on her desk. "My credentials and references."

They were all fake. Or fake in the sense that I'd never done bodyguard work, and my private investigations weren't something I'd put on a resume. But like the credit cards, they were real numbers. If she called them, she'd get glowing references from Quinn, Felix and Evelyn. Well, maybe not "glowing" from Evelyn, but she'd confirm I was competent enough.

Angela drummed her fingers on the paper, her lips pursed. Then she looked up at me.

"Private benefactor, huh?"

"Someone who is concerned about your situation. All my expenses have been paid. I'll be mostly acting as a bodyguard and security consultant, but I'll do some investigating as well while being careful not to interfere with the police."

She nodded. "And this benefactor . . ."

"Is paying me very well, meaning this isn't a scam where I'll later charge you for 'additional' expenses. I'll sign anything you need to that effect."

"That isn't my concern. It's . . . the benefactor. Any chance he's . . . Oh, I don't know. Male? Late fifties? Six foot five? Built like a Mack truck? Swears like a sailor? Works in the . . . extermination biz, you might say."

Oh, hell, no.

I'd run this scenario past Cypher, asking if there was

any chance she'd realize it was him.

"Fuck, no," he'd said. "Been too long."

Maybe so, but Cypher was a man who left a lasting impression.

I kept my expression under control, only my eyebrows shooting up. "That definitely doesn't sound like my client. Not unless he's had a sex change since you last saw him. And even if he had, given those stats, I think he—she—would stand out."

"Hmm."

She eyed me, her gaze boring in. Then she leaned back in her chair. "So you're here to keep me safe."

"That's what I was hired for."

"Qualifications? Besides being a former law officer?"

"I know some martial arts. No black belts, but I can hold my own. I'm an investigator and something of an expert in private security, so I can assess your current setup. I'm also a crack shot."

"Hmm."

A long stretch as she continued to study me, and I tried not to squirm under that stare.

"All right," she said. "Tell me . . ." She looked at my fake resume with my fake name. "Nancy Cooper. What is your plan here? Assess my situation."

"You face the most danger at home. That's where the perpetrator likes to strike. You've avoided attack there, though, so he—or she—may have to branch out and get more creative. Your office seems good, though I'd suggest you tell your receptionist to stay at his post—he wasn't there when I walked in. I'm sure you've instructed him not to accept parcels. I would also tell him not to let someone off the street into your office. He thought I was safe because I *don't* look like a threat. That's a problem."

"I would agree."

"With some adjustments, you'll be safe here. Same as at home. I won't hover in either place. I can stay the night if you like—"

"I'd rather you didn't. The police are outside all night. That's enough."

"Then my main job will be shadowing you when you're *not* at home or here in your office. When you're safely in one of those places, I'll be investigating. I'd like to speak to the detective in charge—Lee—so she understands that I won't interfere with her work."

"Also agreed."

"Today, when you have time, I'd like to go over your client roster, see if I can find any suspects."

"Oh, I already have a few." She reached for a drawer.

As Angela gave me the rundown on the primary suspects, I received a text from Jack, who was checking out Angela's house.

Got SF. Will get LS later.

Yes, Jack texted like he talked, which was great for privacy. Not so helpful for clarity.

SF and LS? Initials? That was the first thing that came to mind. Then my gaze flicked to the stack of files on Angela's desk . . . and my own notes.

Steve Forrest.

Louis Stanton.

So Jack was one step ahead of me.

I turned my attention back to Angela, sorting through the files and taking pages she could show me without breaching confidentiality. The suspects were all former spouses of her clients, and those clients had to be protected.

"These are the three who worked with Mindy, Judge Kim and Charles," she said.

"Did you take over all of Mr. Atom—Charles's—cases?"

"All his family court ones, but these are the three who've been questioned, so I feel comfortable giving you their information. Not the others."

"Understood."

"You'll also want to talk to Mindy's ex, Howard Lang."

"He's a suspect?"

She looked up in surprise, and it took a moment for her to answer. When she did, she gave a soft laugh. "No, not Howard. Sorry—I see how that sounded. I meant you'll want to speak to him about the case. He's a retired police officer. He took early retirement and started a security business. He's been investigating her murder."

I lifted my brows.

"Yes," she said. "The police usually frown on that, but Howard knows what he's doing, and he doesn't interfere. He still loved Mindy. It was an amicable split. No children, assets divided fifty-fifty. He was still part of her life, and her death hit him hard. So he's been investigating and sharing his information with the police. You'll want to talk to them, of course, but you should also speak to Howard."

A rap on the door. It opened, and Richard poked his head in. "Victor Walling is here for his appointment."

When he withdrew, I said, "Is that . . . ?"

She nodded. "Sheila Walling's ex-husband. It's a mediation meeting." She lifted the pages she'd taken from the files. "I'll have Richard copy these and call Detective Lee. She's lead on the case. Richard will introduce you."

As soon as we stepped into the hall, a woman barreled through the main office door. Late thirties. Well dressed. Purposeful stride. Her gaze flicked my way. Caught me. Dismissed me. Kept moving . . . and landed on the man standing beside Richard's desk. He was about her age. Thin. Balding. As soon as her gaze lit on him, he shrank back.

"Victor," she said.

"Sheila." His gaze only made it to her neck level, and he seemed to be using all his willpower not to turn and flee.

"Let's get this over with," Sheila said. "Where is—?" She turned just as another man walked through. "Good, both lawyers present and accounted for. On with the show."

She headed into a side room, leaving everyone else trailing after her. Richard rolled his eyes and mouthed something. Angela shook her head before following.

"I'll just read those pages out here if that's okay," I said to Richard once Angela was gone. I nodded to the chairs . . . right outside the meeting room door.

"Actually, I think you'll find the acoustics better in there." He pointed to an office beside the meeting room.

"Thanks," I said with a smile.

"Don't thank me. Just stop this killer before he hurts Angela."

Chapter Ten
Jack

Men never checked the back seat of their cars before getting in. Some women did. Not all, mind you, but the percentage was vastly higher than with men. Women had heard too many stories of attackers lurking in the back seat. Men heard the same tales—and figured it didn't apply to them. Which Jack had always found very convenient.

He'd been surveilling Forrest for the past hour, and when the man headed for the parking garage, there was little doubt of his destination. Jack had already located Forrest's SUV and broken in, searching for clues, so he hurried around and got in position.

He waited until Forrest backed the vehicle from its spot. Then he put a gun to his head. Forrest jumped clear off his seat. Didn't hit the horn, though. They never did, the shock of that gun barrel blasting through common sense.

"Drive," Jack said.

"T-take the truck. Just let me out—"

"Drive."

Forrest glanced in his rearview mirror. His gaze went straight to the gun, lowered but still pointed at his head.

Forrest let the vehicle roll through the dark covered parking lot. "Whatever this is about—"

"Mindy Lang. Albert Kim. Sara Atom."

"W-what? Did someone hire you—?"

"No one hires me, Mr. Forrest. Now drive."

Jack directed Forrest to a densely wooded spot. Tropical jungle, Jack guessed, and any other time, he'd have admired the beauty. Right now, though, he was kinda busy.

He ordered Forrest out of the SUV and made him walk into the dark jungle. Jack wore a disguise, but if he could add shadows, he always did. When they were far enough in, Jack walked in front of Forrest.

The man's gaze tripped over Jack and stuck on his biceps, which weren't overly intimidating, but they were a helluva lot bigger than Forrest's. Jack suspected, though, that it wasn't the muscles that gave Forrest pause. It was the scars. They were fake. Jack *had* scars, but he'd added more impressive ones to fit his look of the day. He'd blackened and gelled his hair. Bought jeans that were really too tight for comfort. The mustache might be overdoing it. The fake gold rings definitely were. It was a caricature of a middle-aged mobster. But a guy like Forrest, though—with his low-end luxury SUV and ill-fitting expensive suit—wasn't likely to have much contact with actual organized crime, and the look on his face said Jack's outfit worked just fine.

"L-look," Forrest said, his hands going up. "Whoever hired you, I can pay more."

"Hired me?" Jack let a Russian accent underscore his words. "Hired me to do what?"

"I—I don't know."

"I said, no one hires me, Mr. Forrest."

"O-okay . . ."

"Do I look like I am for sale?"

Forrest hesitated and then gave a wary, "No?"

"I am the person who hires men who are for sale. And I want to hire you."

"Wh-what?"

"I need to take care of some . . . pests. Preferably with explosives. I have heard you are the man to see."

Forrest's eyes bugged. "I don't know what you're—"

"I would prefer explosives. Yet I can be flexible, and I have heard you are a very flexible man. Cars, bullets, things that go boom . . . Such talents are valuable in my business."

"N-no. You've made a mistake."

"Do not play this game. It does not become business men like ourselves." Jack took a wad of bills from his pocket. "Haggling is a waste of my time. The rate is, I believe, fifty thousand per pest. I have one I need taken care of. I will give you five thousand now, as a measure of goodwill."

"Fifty thousand dollars? To kill—"

Jack cut him off with a frown. "Please do not use that word, Mr. Forrest. It is unseemly."

"Who the hell told you I do *that*?"

"Shall I repeat the names? Yes, I know that was not work—it was personal. But you have been very clear that it was you, and yet you have not been charged. We are impressed. We wish to hire you."

"I don't—I don't do that. At all."

Jack narrowed his eyes. "Who have you been speaking to? Is it Wilhelm? Has he snatched you from under my nose?"

"No." Forrest backed up, both hands raised. "You have the wrong guy. Totally wrong. I've never . . . gotten rid of anyone. I just said that to scare my ex."

"It was a joke?"

"Sure, yeah." A ragged laugh. "A joke."

"It is not funny." Jack looked over Forrest's shoulder. "Do you think it is funny, Bruno?"

Forrest glanced back and saw Cypher standing right there behind him. Forrest let out a yelp . . . and a wet spot spread across the front of his trousers.

Jack didn't let Forrest go quite that easily. He tried to bribe him. He tried to threaten. One way or the other, if Forrest were capable of doing what Jack asked, he would have agreed. He didn't.

On to Louis Stanton, which meant a change of both clothes and persona. Wash out the temporary black and add more gray. Hawaiian shirt. Chino shorts. Sandals... with socks, of course. Sunglasses. No scars, but a hint of a tattoo showing below his neckline. Scars and tattoos provided "distinguishing features" that people remembered for the cops. "I have no idea what the guy looked like, but he had a Mickey Mouse tattoo on his hand—that's gotta help, right?" Not if that tattoo washed off with soap and water...

Stanton was easy to get in touch with. He *wanted* to be in touch. He'd splashed his name across the Internet and invited men to join his crusade against the "tyranny" of the family law system and its "bias" toward women. Men were encouraged to contact him and share their stories. So Jack called and offered to buy him a coffee. Stanton readily accepted, which might have had something to do with Jack name-dropping a few leaders of national men's rights organizations. To be honest, Jack hadn't known there *were* men's rights organizations—and he was still a little fuzzy on the concept—but twenty minutes on the

Internet had given him what he needed to know.

He picked up Stanton in a rented Jaguar.

Stanton whistled as he climbed in. "Nice ride."

Jack shrugged. "It'll do. They didn't have much selection."

The coffee shop was within easy walking distance, but Jack hadn't suggested they do that. In his current persona, he was not the kind of man who walked.

Stanton filled the five-minute drive with meaningless chatter, growing increasingly nervous when Jack remained silent. Stanton waited until they were seated in the shop, coffees in hand, before he said, "So, tell me about your situation."

"My ex is a bitch."

Stanton laughed, relaxing into his booth seat. "Aren't they all?"

"Not until you serve the divorce papers." Jack paused. "Nah, it starts with the wedding. You get little hints of it after that, but the sweet's still mixed with the sour. That's how they keep you on your toes. One minute, it's all about how you're traveling too much, and she's tired from looking after the kids, and who's that woman calling all the time. Then the next minute, she's making your favorite meal and running out to buy you beer and showing off her new lingerie."

Stanton chuckled. "That's not just how they keep you on your toes. It's how they keep *you*. At least until they've locked you in with kids."

Jack nodded. "And then they're a lot *more* worried about that woman's number on your phone, and the next thing you know, here's a private eye's report, proving you've been screwing around, and oh, yeah, she wants a divorce and the kids and half of everything you made. Worst fucking thing? Whose money do you think *paid* for the goddamn private eye?"

"I hear ya."

Jack let this go on for a while. It was easy enough to pull it off. In the old days, he'd met plenty of guys like Stanton, guys who wanted their wives killed for no reason other than these petty outrages. Guys who mistook their marriages for ones from the nineteenth century, where they could do as they pleased, so long as they paid the bills.

Jack wished that he could say he'd never taken one of those contracts. There were *many* contracts he wished he could say that about. Sometimes, he'd only taken one, and it bothered him too much to take another like it, but even one was an indelible smudge on his conscience.

That's why he'd insisted Nadia research every job. Clients lied, and it only took one hit to lose the high ground of saying, "I've never done that." So, yeah, he'd pulled a few spousal hits back in the earliest days when he was too numb, too dead inside to give a shit. Then came the one where he'd found his mark in a playground, swinging alongside her kids, laughing and teasing, and he'd looked at her and seen his mother, and he'd thrown up in the bushes.

That marked the first time he actually stopped to think about what he was doing. Actually *allowed* himself to think about it. There'd been no spousal jobs after that, but it didn't keep him from wishing there'd never even been one.

Listening to Stanton, all he could think was "I'm glad your wife got away, asshole." That, however, was not the role he needed to inhabit today. So he played along and whined about his own imaginary ex, and then he got down to business.

"I like your platform," Jack said.

"Plat . . . ? Oh, uh, right."

"You aren't like some of those pussies, think they can change things by *talking*. Wimps who expect the system to work. It never works for guys like us. Not anymore. It's all about the women and the gays and the 'minorities.'" Jack's gaze swept over the brown faces in the coffee shop. "Well, you know what? I'm starting to feel like we *are* the minority."

"I hear ya," Stanton said, though he was careful to keep his voice lowered.

"It's time to take back what's ours. To fight for our birthright."

"It is."

"So what I'm proposing—" Jack leaned forward and lowered his own voice—"is that you help me turn your efforts here into a national campaign."

"Campaign? Oh, you mean politically."

"You could say that. The politics of force." Jack met and held his gaze. "The politics of terror."

"Terror . . . ?"

"What you're *doing* here. Fighting your own private war."

Stanton only blinked.

Jack sighed, leaning forward again. "With the court system. Blowing it to hell, if you know what I mean."

The lightbulb flicked on, and Stanton pulled back, hands wrapping around his mug.

"I can't really discuss—" he began.

"You don't need to. I'm just here to say I'm all in, and I have others who are, too. We're talking serious financial support. Whatever you need to take the next step."

"Next step?"

"Two words." Jack leaned forward and dropped his voice. "Courthouse. Bomb."

Stanton jerked back, whiplash-fast. "I don't—"

"Just tell me what you need. All eyes are on you now, Louis."

"Wh-what?"

"Big eyes. Big names. The *biggest*. They're watching, and they're waiting. You can stop worrying about how much your wife will get. You won't need that money anyway. You'll get your kids, too, and if your wife tries to interfere?" He shrugged. "Either she can be convinced or she can't. Her choice."

"No. *No.*" Stanton moved back. "You've got the wrong guy. What happened to those people? I didn't do *any* of it."

"Sure, you did. You admitted to it."

"I lied, okay?"

Jack frowned. "Is that cold feet I'm hearing? Look, you don't need to worry about being caught. You won't be. I'm taking care of all that. Just tell me what you need for the device—"

"I have no idea how to set *up* a device."

"You're an engineer."

"A mechanical engineer. I know nothing about . . . *those*. Whatever I've said, whatever I've hinted, it's bullshit. It's . . ." He waved. "Grandstanding. Promotion for the cause."

Jack leaned back. "Yeah? Well, you're not going to *have* a cause if you go to jail."

"Are you threatening me?"

"I'm just saying—"

"If I'm arrested, I have an alibi. For the night that judge died and the night someone shot at the lawyer chick. I was at a club. A private club. With lots of people who can tell you, beyond any doubt, that I was there, and

I was . . . busy. Very busy."

"Name?"

"I can't give you names of people—"

"The club."

Stanton hesitated. Then he gave it, saying, "You're not going to find it in the Yellow Pages. But if you search online, you'll see it's real. It's very, very exclusive. And that's where I was. If the police arrest me, I have an alibi."

Chapter Eleven
Nadia

Sheila Walling was abrasive, assertive, arrogant and angry. Add up those *a*'s, and people started using a word that started with the next letter of the alphabet.

Yes, as I listened to her through that wall, she sounded like a world-class bitch, but in an honest way, one that was tough and forthright, and I saw nothing wrong with that.

Sheila Walling wanted a divorce. She just wanted the damn thing done and over with. Forget alimony, forget child support, forget the fact that she'd brought their family home into the marriage. She'd happily agree to an equal division of assets. The only thing she wanted? Joint custody of their two kids.

Two doctors had confirmed she'd kicked the prescription drug habit. She'd been clean for months. So I didn't see what the issue was.

That was when they mentioned Cherise Hale.

When the Wallings left the office, I followed, as if I'd just happened to be departing at the same time. Sheila got onto the elevator. Victor and his lawyer busied themselves in conversation, as if they were too busy talking to notice that the elevator had arrived. I got on with Sheila, and the doors closed behind me.

"Bodyguard, huh?" she said as the elevator began its descent.

I looked over at her.

"I have ears," she said. "If you're here to threaten me, go ahead and get it out of your system. I need to get back to work."

"*Should* I threaten you?" I asked.

She gave a harsh laugh and then shook her head. "No, I'm not the bitch you're looking for."

The doors opened, and we stepped off. I walked alongside Sheila as she kept talking.

"I'm no threat to Angela Kamaka," she said. "I'd never poison a dog. That's just wrong."

She rounded the corner. "I probably wouldn't kill a person, either. Not unless I had to, and certainly not over a divorce. I'll get joint custody. I'm clean, and there's no other reason to deny me."

I said nothing, just kept walking alongside her heading

for the parking lot.

"I didn't kill Cherise," she said. "I know that's the real reason for the custody concern, and the only reason I'm a suspect in the rest. But I was never charged, and by point of law, they can't use 'suspicion' against me."

"True."

"Do you know why they investigated me? Because I'm a chemist, so I know how to make explosions. That's it. Oh, and because clearly if a man's young new girlfriend dies, it was the nasty old wife who did it."

She turned to face me. "Let's just get this out of the way. My husband left me because of my addiction. I suspect he'd already been seeing Cherise. Did he use the addiction as an excuse? Or was my addiction what drove him to an affair? Frankly, I don't give a damn. When Victor said he was leaving, I threw every plate in the kitchen. At the walls—not at him. Then I flushed out my pills, checked into rehab, and realized he'd done me a favor. I allowed myself to get addicted to pain meds because I was miserable. The oxy made me feel good. You know what makes me feel even better? Getting out of a shitty marriage."

She resumed walking, still talking. "I had no strong feelings about Cherise one way or the other. I thought she played the silly innocent, but there was a cunning there, too, and I had to admire that. I used my brains to get where I am. She used her pretty face. I didn't particularly want her playing Mommy to my kids, but only because she wasn't much more than a kid herself. Victor is a good dad, though, and he'd more than balance a less competent stepmom. So I didn't have any reason to kill Cherise. But no one sees that. They just see the ball-busting ex-wife and the sweet young girlfriend."

We reached a dark blue BMW. She unlocked the door. Then she turned to face me.

"Whoever sent that device to Cherise could have killed my kids. I would never have risked that. *Ever.*"

She reached into her pocket and took out a card.

"If you have questions, call me. I'm happy to answer. But I'm not your killer."

I met with Jillian Lee—the detective in charge of the case, and I got exactly the response I expected, the same one I would have given in her situation.

I explained that my primary role was as Angela's bodyguard, but that I had private investigating experience and would be delving into the case from that perspective. I would not—however—be approaching any of the suspects or witnesses. I had spoken to Sheila, but she'd been the one talking to me. In no way would I interfere with the investigation, and if Detective Lee had any concerns, she could contact me at any time, and if I had new information, I'd contact her.

Yes. That was what Detective Lee said: yes to all of that.

Yes, she was fine with Angela having a bodyguard. She wasn't thrilled that the bodyguard would also play private investigator, but she accepted it on my other conditions: that I wouldn't approach suspects or witnesses, and that any new leads would get back to her, promptly.

So we knew where we stood. She did, however, impart one last warning.

"Stay out of Howard's way."

"Howard Lang, right? Former police officer. Now private security. He's investigating, too. I'm having coffee with him in an hour."

"Good. Normally, I don't encourage private citizens to help on cases, but Howie is an exception. He's a good guy, and he's been through a lot. He loved Mindy. He's taking this hard. We all are—she was an amazing person. For Howie, dealing with her death means investigating her murder. He's turned up solid leads. I would prefer it if you two worked together. That's up to him, of course."

"If he's game, I am. He's lead investigator, though. I understand that."

"Good."

Chapter Twelve

Nadia

Coffee with Howard Lang. I suspected he'd been in touch with Detective Lee after I left her, and by the time I arrived, he was relaxed, friendly, ready to talk. Which I hoped meant I'd gotten a thumbs-up from Lee.

For me, making contact with those in charge of the case was an odd way of going about an investigation but... well, to be honest, I wasn't sure Cypher would get what he was hoping for here. He wanted the death sentence. Yet this was an active case. Usually, I was the person called in when the police gave up or when justice failed or, sometimes, when the police just weren't convinced there *was* a case.

Jack and I were still being careful here. Nothing we provided could be traced back to anyone. I wore a disguise. I used a burner phone and a fake name. All the numbers I gave as references were untraceable and would go dead after this investigation. I wasn't averse to ending the life of this multiple murderer. I just wasn't sure that was where this would lead. Where it could or *should* lead.

I was outside my comfort zone but making the best of it. This was a real case with a truly innocent person in serious jeopardy, and while I knew the police were doing all they could, they acted under restrictions that didn't apply to me.

I chatted with Howard Lang for a while. We circled each other, assessing in the most friendly way possible, which was what I preferred. Leave the stiff-legged, growling-dog approach to the guys.

Howard liked Sheila Walling for the murders, and I had to struggle not to leap to her defense. I wasn't as impartial here as I wanted to be. I saw how others reacted to Sheila, and I couldn't help feeling that her demeanor was the key strike against her. They saw a tough, blunt, assertive woman and said, "Sure, she could kill somebody." Those very people would probably never think the same about me. So I got my back up in Sheila's defense, and I had to be aware of that. My sympathy was as blinding as their prejudice.

"What was your impression of her?" Lang asked.

"Intimidating."

He laughed as he eased back in his chair. "That's a nice way of putting it. Sheila Walling scares the ever-loving shit out of me. I don't know how she ever got together with a sweet guy like Victor. Proof that opposites do attract. Thing is . . . ," he said, straightening, "I *like* Sheila. She's honest, and she's tough, and she reminds me of some of the best women I worked with on the force. Take no prisoners, and take no bullshit. I wish . . ."

He pulled at his lower lip and then shook his head. "I wish she wasn't such a damned good suspect for this."

"Is she? I got the feeling the two men were better ones."

"Between us?" He lowered his voice. "That's only because they're men. Okay, yes, it's also because they're idiotic enough to hint that they're responsible. But they're both blowhards. They don't have the brains to pull this off. Certainly not to build that device."

"Forrest runs an electronics business, doesn't he?"

"Yeah, so the theory is that he had an employee build the bomb, but then I'd expect *that* guy to blab to someone. No one has. Stanton, on the other hand, is an engineer. Sure, this isn't his exact area of interest, but I can see him making a bomb. Problem is that he's even more full of hot air than Forrest. Stanton's a loser who wants people to think he's a tough guy, and how does he prove it? By whining about his rights . . . his right to take his kids along to his new job, and to hell with his *wife's* career."

He shook his head. "Both guys are all talk, which is

what they're doing now. Talking."

"And Sheila isn't saying anything."

"Because for her, it's not about showing how tough she is. We *know* she's tough. This is about fixing problems."

"Like getting rid of Victor's new girlfriend, so he'll come back to her."

Howard laughed. "Hell, no. That was totally between Cherise and Sheila. Cherise saw an opportunity in Victor. Nice guy with some money and a wife who's not exactly a sweet-natured cover model. So Cherise swoops in. Only problem? The money isn't Victor's. Sheila is the one with the high-powered job. So Cherise hit Sheila in the only place she's vulnerable: her kids. She pushed Victor to take full custody, which would mean Sheila would pay child support. Sheila doesn't give a shit about the money, but you don't come between a mama bear and her cubs. So she took care of the problem."

"Sounds like you don't blame Sheila too much for that."

Howard made a face and sipped his coffee. "Killing Cherise was wrong. Especially . . . that way." Another face, more serious. "But I don't think Sheila meant to kill her. Did you hear how it happened?"

I did—I looked it up—but I shook my head.

"The IED was in a gift, delivered to the condo Cherise shared with Victor. An anonymous gift, complete with wrapping paper and a bow. Now, anybody in their right mind would call the bomb squad. Cherise wasn't that bright. Still, the experts said it was a miracle the IED went off. Well, I guess *miracle* is the wrong word, but you know what I mean. The device was flawed."

"You think it was a warning."

He jabbed a finger at me. "Exactly. Sheila was warning her. Instead . . ." He exhaled. "It was bad."

"And then you think Sheila did the same to Charles Atom? Sent a warning that inadvertently killed his daughter?"

"It was the same kind of device. That's the critical part. Whoever built one almost certainly built the other."

After leaving Howard, I met up with Jack and Cypher. We strolled along the marina docks, snaking past tourists waiting for boat trips.

As we walked, Cypher regaled me with the grand tale of taking Mr. Forrest into the forest.

"Jungle," Jack said.

Cypher rolled his eyes. "You have no sense of humor."

"Set that shit-show up, didn't I?"

Cypher laughed at that, a boom of a laugh that startled a nearby plover. "I'm just glad the guy didn't *really* shit. Did piss his pants, though." He shook his head. "Can't believe he bought the B-movie-mobster routine."

"Usually do," Jack said with a shrug.

I cut in. "So it seems unlikely that Forrest is our guy. Considering how much you were offering—and threatening—he would have agreed if he didn't mind committing murder. How about Stanton?"

"Jack made me skip that performance," Cypher said.

"Required a bit more acting," Jack said.

Cypher glowered. "You implying I couldn't have pulled it off?"

Jack looked at me and continued, "Same end result. Not ruling him out completely. But, yeah. Unlikely. Asshole bragging. Like Forrest. Thought it made him look tough. Call Stanton on it? Backs down fast. Says he has an alibi, too. Sex club."

"A . . ." I began.

"Sex club," Cypher said. "It's a club where people—"

"Yes, I get the idea. I was just making sure I heard right."

"You did," Jack said. "If he's arrested, he has an alibi. Now you? Walling?"

I told them about my afternoon.

Cypher nodded. "This Howard guy is on the money. Sheila Walling looks good for it. She's had enough of this Cherise girl, so she tries to spook her. Only her warning shot kills. Sheila starts thinking that wasn't so bad. She got away with it. So she goes after everyone else standing between her and her babies."

"But why? She's convinced she has a good custody case."

"That's what she *says*."

I glanced at Jack. He caught my eye and shrugged, which meant he didn't have strong feelings either way. We'd discuss it later when we were alone.

Chapter Thirteen

Nadia

I was with Angela again. It was early evening, and while I suspected her workday didn't usually end until later, she'd agreed to let me escort her home and give her house a security check. I'd assured her it'd be quick. And it would because Jack had already performed the assessment.

I had suggested Angela invite a friend to meet us there so she'd be comfortable letting a stranger into her home, but she'd brushed that off.

"I know who you're working for," she said. "And I know he hasn't hired you to kill me. No more than I'd hire another lawyer to prepare my case." She gave me a meaningful look.

I didn't respond.

"I *know* who it is," she continued. "He's an overprotective pain in the ass, but I'm not in any danger from him. He's sent you to take care of me . . . and not in the way he usually 'takes care' of people."

She pulled her car into the drive and hit the garage door opener. "Is there any chance I can see him while he's here?"

I didn't respond.

"*Is* he here?" she asked. "In Honolulu?"

"I'm glad to see you're using the garage," I said. "In your work lot, always try to park between smaller vehicles, so there's no opportunity for your attacker to slip in beside a big SUV and tamper with your car."

She sighed. "I'm not getting an answer to my question, am I?"

"If you have a message you'd like conveyed to my client, I can do that."

"Okay. For now, business. You saw the checks I performed before I got into the car. That's what Detective Lee advised. Good?"

"Yes. I'd also like you to talk to your building manager about fixing the card reader lock on the stairwell. I noticed it wasn't working."

"It hasn't been since we moved in last year, and I've been complaining since then. Even before this, though, I lock the door if I'm there at night."

"Good. Now for here, I'd like more outward security, starting with a motion sensor light at the garage door. I brought supplies."

We exited the car.

"We want to establish a standard route," I said as we walked through the garage. "You'll use one door and only one door and go the same way every time. You won't open any other doors or *any* windows while you're in the house."

"Yes, ma'am."

She locked the garage door behind us. I scoped out the area and said, "Good, you have a side door right here," as if I hadn't already known that from Jack. "This is the door you'll use. Only this one. You'll stay out of the backyard. I know that will be inconvenient."

She gave a wan smile. "I haven't used the yard since Dexter."

"Your ex. I heard someone fired a shot at him in the yard."

"Actually, Dexter was my dog. I miss *him* more." She glanced over. "Is that an awful thing to say?"

"Considering your ex's asshole move? Not at all."

"Having Cliff—*that* was the boyfriend—walk out just showed what I already suspected. That he wasn't the one."

"Does Cliff have your keys? Security codes?"

She shook her head. "I couldn't get those changed fast enough."

She pushed open the side door and led me in.

"I'm sorry about your dog," I said. "I have two."

"Better than a boyfriend?"

I chuckled. "No, I have one of those. A good guy."

"Lucky girl." She shut the door. "That will be my new dating test. If a psychotic client threatened me, would you (*a*) offer moral support or (*b*) say 'Sorry babe, I'm outta here'?"

"The correct answer is both *a* and *c*."

"*C*?"

"Offer to buy me a gun and offer to escort me to work, but don't be offended if I say no to either."

She grinned. "Exactly. I do have the gun."

"And now you have the escort."

During my fake walk-through, I made suggestions, like telling her to keep the blinds shut at all times and have multiple lights on at night so she didn't leave a trail of illumination, showing where she was in the house.

As we walked into the kitchen, I said, "The killer seems to like explosive devices, which is, unfortunately, the most frightening scenario. It could be anything you open. A door, a box . . ."

"A backyard grill . . ."

"Exactly. Plus there's the possibility of tripwires. I'm sure you've been told not to accept packages, here or at the office."

"All my mail goes through the police."

"Perfect. But while bombs seem to be the new modus operandi, we know it's not the only way this killer operates. He did fire those shots at your ex. So I have a few suggestions for home security. Yours is good—it's not foolproof."

"Just tell me what I need."

"I will. And while home security is great, the best defense against break-ins is your neighbors. I'm guessing they're on high alert? Told to report suspicious activity?"

She nodded. "They've been great."

"Good. Your backyard, though, is another matter. May I see it?"

She took me outside. I pretended to poke around while I called her attention to the issues Jack had already observed.

"Motion sensors are the big one," I said as we walked to the back fence. "There's no way to stop people from coming into your yard, no matter how high your fence, and backing onto unused property makes security tough. If you can't stop them, the next best thing is to know when someone's there. You have sensors already but . . ." I waved toward the rear deck. "Would you stand over there, please? I'm going to hop the back fence and try to get in without activating those sensors."

I climbed the fence and started experimenting. After about five minutes, she said, "Okay, I see the problem."

"Yep. If we're dealing with a total amateur, he's likely to stumble into range of your sensors. But if he can see them, like I do, and"—I started toward her—"he can get all the way to—"

Something whizzed past Angela.

"Down!" I shouted.

She didn't question. Didn't even look around. She dropped to the ground. I raced over just as another projectile flew past and hit the dirt by my feet. Then I bustled her inside.

"What was it?" she said.

I caught my breath. I knew what I'd seen—a bullet in the dirt—but I didn't tell her that. I didn't want to panic her when I had a strong suspicion panic wasn't required.

"I'm . . . not sure," I said. "I saw something fly past you. Did you see it?"

She shook her head.

"I'm going to take a look around." I squinted at the treetops. "It might have just been a squirrel dropping a nut or something silly like that."

"We don't have squirrels, but there is a mongoose."

I nodded. "That might be it. I'm going to be paranoid, though, and do a walk around. I'd like you to stay inside. Find a room without windows. Lock the door behind me. When I come back, I'll text, so you'll know it's me."

Chapter Fourteen
Nadia

From the angle of the bullet, I knew the direction of the shooter. I also knew the shot had been taken from an elevated position. Not surprisingly, that angle led me to the empty lot behind Angela's house.

I skirted her yard, coming out about a hundred meters away, in thick woods ... or jungle ... or rainforest. I hadn't exactly done my geographic research, so I could only say that the tree cover was dense, the ground choked with thick vegetation.

I was looking for a shooting perch. The trees here weren't sturdy enough for that, though, which meant that the shooter must have been on a rock along the mountainside. A rock that would provide a clear shot into Angela's backyard. After a sweep of the area, I found the one I wanted.

That's when I heard someone in the forest.

Someone *fleeing* the forest.

I ducked behind a bush. Heavy footsteps thudded off to my left. Angela's house was behind me on the right. The shooter must have waited a few moments to avoid being spotted fleeing right after the shots.

I took an educated guess about my target's flight path. Then I retreated to the street and ran along the sidewalk. I passed an elderly couple, gardening in their front yard, but they only looked over idly, as if accustomed to joggers.

When I reached the corner, I veered toward the forest. An SUV sat at the end of the road. I raced to it and hopped onto the hood.

Two minutes later, a figure emerged from the forest. He saw me sitting on the hood and stopped short.

"Nice night for a walk," I said. "You mind giving me a lift back to my hotel?"

Cypher dug keys from his pocket and resumed his approach. "I was finding a place for tonight. I've decided to stand guard."

"Uh-huh. Well, you dropped this." I held out the bullet I'd retrieved.

"Where'd that come from?"

I gave him a hard look. "You fired it into Angela's yard."

"What? Fuck no." He turned around, his hands raised. "You see a gun?"

"Where'd you stash it?"

"I don't carry a gun. And I don't lie. Ever."

"Must make things tricky, in our occupation."

He shrugged. "It adds challenge."

"You are so full of shit."

"Ask Jack. Ask Evie. I don't lie. Now, if you're asking whether I've ever *used* a gun, yes, I have. That's unavoidable. But the last time I picked one up was yesterday, when I got yours and Jack's. I haven't touched a firearm since."

"There is no *possible* way you just *happened* to be behind Angela's yard when someone fired a shot at her."

"It's not the first time that's happened, right? He's probably been out there, waiting for another chance." Cypher met my gaze. "There's a psycho who wants Angela *dead*, Dee. That's who you need to focus on. The person who just tried to kill her."

"No one tried . . ."

I trailed off. Then I looked down at the bullet in my hand. It was ice-cold. Had been since I scooped it up.

"This bullet has *never* been fired from a gun."

Cypher squinted at it. "You sure?"

"Oh for God's sake. You really *don't* know firearms, do you? What did you do? Throw it at her?"

"That'd be kinda weird."

I glowered up at him. "Did you throw this bullet at Angela, Tyrone?"

He met my gaze. "No, I did not."

Jack walked out of the forest, holding something aloft.

"Is that a . . . slingshot?" I said as I took it. I turned to Cypher. "Seriously, Tyrone? You *slingshot* bullets? Are you crazy?"

"Probably. That's the general opinion, anyhow."

I thrust the slingshot at Cypher. "Take your bullshit and go. We're done." I started walking away.

"Whoa, wait!" Cypher lumbered in front of me. A look from Jack made him lift his hands and move aside a little. "Just hold on. When you say *done* . . ."

"Job terminated," I said. "We'll repay you for expenses if you want to press the point, but I wouldn't recommend it." I advanced on him. "I came here in good faith, to protect a woman who deserves protecting, and who am I protecting her from? The asshole who hired me."

"I slingshot a bullet. At *your feet*."

"Sending us into a panic—"

"Panic? Angela never even noticed, and from the way you marched out here, you already figured it was me."

"I don't know what your game is, Tyrone, but I'm not playing it. Angela is actually in danger and—"

"And that's my point. She's in danger, and she's too damned stubborn to leave her house and go somewhere safe. You're supposed to talk her into that."

"No, I'm supposed to stop whoever is trying to kill her. That's objective number two. Number one, obviously, is keeping her alive."

"Yeah, and how about we increase those odds by getting her out of that goddamned house?"

"No point," Jack said.

Cypher glanced over, as if he'd forgotten Jack was there.

"Where you gonna put her?" Jack said. "In a cell?"

"I'd like to," Cypher muttered.

"Can't. So what's the alternative? A hotel room? An apartment? Someplace we can't control access?"

"Her house is a known quantity," I said. "We have complete control over it, and we can do anything we want to it, which we can't with a rented room. Honestly, with the police here at night, the chance of her being targeted at home again is minimal. It's much higher at work."

Cypher glowered at me. "That does *not* make me feel better."

"You know what will make you feel better? Catching this bastard. Which is what I'm trying to do . . . when I'm not dealing with idiots throwing bullets at us."

"*Slingshot*. Throwing it would be stupid. It'd just bounce off the ground."

I pitched the bullet at him and walked away.

Chapter Fifteen

Jack

They were on their second drink. Mai tais, which Jack had never had before, not being much of a drinker, and definitely not one inclined to anything that came with an umbrella. He'd been missing out. These were good. Strong, too. Which meant Nadia had relaxed and was no longer muttering about new places to shove Cypher's slingshot.

They sat on their hotel room balcony, overlooking the beach, Jack having grabbed the drinks from the poolside bar and then gone for seconds when they finished those. Nadia had hesitated—both of them knowing not to drink too much on the job. But Cypher was watching over Angela tonight as were the cops, and Nadia's only "work" involved a laptop and pages from Angela's office. So she'd accepted the second drink along with a bowl of macadamia nuts.

She'd also changed into her bikini, a new purchase

from this morning. They'd popped into a store, and he might have said, "Those are nice." She'd hesitated. Nadia really wasn't the bikini type. But then she'd said, "What the hell" and tried on a few, and while he doubted she'd wear it farther than this balcony, he was just fine with that.

Hawaii had never been on his list of post-retirement trips. Lazing around the beach wasn't his style. It wasn't Nadia's either. They liked doing things, exploring, discovering. But he had to admit, this was pretty damned close to perfect. Warm evening, a strong drink, Nadia lying beside him in a bikini while he enjoyed the scenery, his new sunglasses ensuring she didn't notice exactly where his attention lay.

When she reached over absently for more nuts, he caught her hand and squeezed it, and she smiled at him. Then he twisted the cheap gold band on her finger.

"I like this," he said.

Her smile returned. "You do, huh?"

"I do."

She opened her mouth, as if to say something, and then stopped short, and he knew she'd been on the verge of teasing him about getting a real one, and that wasn't possible. He hadn't used his real name in years, no longer had any ID under it, couldn't risk getting it. Which meant marriage wasn't an option. So she just squeezed his hand with a softer smile, before saying, "It's past dinner time.

You getting hungry?"

"Soon. Got any feelings about room service?"

"I am very fond of room service, especially if it means I don't have to dress and go out."

"Then we're eating in. Find anything there?" He pointed at the pages.

"I'm working on it. Give me another twenty minutes, and then we'll order dinner and talk."

"No rush," he said and settled into his chair, watching that gold band wink in the sunlight as she typed.

Chapter Sixteen
Nadia

I am not a detective.

I needed to write that on sticky notes and plaster them everywhere. The deeper I dug into this case, the more keenly I became aware of my overreaching. Yes, I'd solved crimes before, but only because they landed in my lap and, in every case, either no one else was investigating, or I had information the police did not. In other words, I'd had an advantage that overcame my shortcomings.

That wasn't the situation here. This was a high-profile case, being investigated by a capable metropolitan police force with the help of an equally capable private investigator. If the Honolulu Police Department and Howard Lang couldn't solve it, how the hell could I?

I'd bitten off more than I could chew, and the worst was that I'd blithely accepted Cypher's offer without even stopping to consider that.

Nadia Stafford, the professional killer who is mostly at peace with her job, but every now and then, must appease her niggling conscience with tasks that are beyond-any-doubt righteous.

Yeah . . .

I should tell Cypher that I couldn't solve this. That, instead, I would protect Angela while the police did their job.

Except the investigation had been going on for months, and I didn't have "months" to play bodyguard. I could, presumably, swap out with Jack and go back to the lodge for the weekend, but there was no way I could do that hellish commute for more than a few weeks.

As I made notes, I glanced at Jack, reclined on the patio chair, eyes closed behind his sunglasses. Relaxed, at ease and looking utterly happy. Which made me happy. It really did. There'd been a time when, if someone showed me a snapshot of him like this, I'd have said he was obviously faking it—playing tourist to throw off some unsuspecting mark. But this was real, and it looked so good on him.

And yet . . .

Oh, hell. Let's be honest. As much as I loved seeing Jack relaxed, I couldn't help but feel the dig of unspoken expectations.

"Find anything there?"

"I'm working on it. Give me another twenty minutes, and then we'll order dinner and talk."

"No rush."

If I asked for his help, he'd give it, but otherwise, in our investigations, Jack settled into the role of junior partner. I was the "proper" detective. I'd been a cop, right? He knew I'd only been a constable, but that didn't matter. To Jack, I was the one who held a legitimate claim to law enforcement. He was "just" a hitman. A guy who'd operated on the other side of the law since he was a kid. Forget the fact that he investigated each and every job to be sure his client was being straight with him. That didn't count as detective work. Not to him.

I considered admitting I was in over my head. I imagined saying the words. I imagined him lifting his sunglasses, blue eyes glancing over at me, completely unperturbed. He'd tell me I was doing fine, that I always do fine, and I'd figure it out. Which wouldn't be just a pep talk to make me feel better. He'd believe it. He had complete faith in me.

No pressure.

I sighed.

The glasses went up, just as I imagined, pushed back onto his forehead, and his blue eyes turned my way, crow's feet in the corners deepening as he squinted against the sun.

"You okay?"

"Just..."

Feeling overwhelmed. Feeling inadequate. Feeling a little bit lost.

"Just getting hungry," I said.

His eyes narrowed a fraction, studying my expression.

"You need a break," he said. "Give me what you've got, and I'll take a look while you order dinner."

"What do you want?"

A shrug. "You choose." His lips curved in a smile. "I trust you."

Yep, no pressure at all.

We were on the bed, room service trays resting precariously on bunched-up covers. I'd ordered a few dishes for us to share. Jack had put some of each on his plate, and I couldn't tell if that was because he wanted to sample them all or because he didn't want to insult my choices.

Damn, I was in a mood, wasn't I?

"You okay?" he asked after ten minutes of silence.

I shrugged.

"Something's bugging you."

I took another bite of fish.

"The case?" he said.

I managed a wan smile. "See, you should be the detective."

He snorted. "Nah. I'm just hoping it's the case. Otherwise? Well, only other thing here is me. So if it's not the case? It's me."

"It's the case."

"Talk to me."

I stretched out my bare legs, and he squeezed one before reaching for another piece of bread.

"It's just . . ."

I feel overwhelmed.

I took a deep breath. "I keep going back to Cherise Hale. Victor Walling's girlfriend."

"Okay."

I crossed my legs. "Howard Lang thinks that Cherise's death proves Sheila is a viable suspect. Cherise died when a gift blew up in her face. Charles Atom's daughter died from an IED presumably intended for her dad. Someone placed another IED in Angela's car. The devices weren't exactly the same, but there were similarities. The only connection between Cherise and the other two is Sheila."

"But you don't like her for it."

"Six months ago, she kills Cherise, accidentally, it seems, with an explosive device hidden in a gift. She's a suspect in that case, but she's never charged. Then she kills Mindy Lang, and it's ruled a suicide. Okay. Then she shoots Albert Kim and tries to set it up as another suicide, but that fails, which reopens Mindy's case, and the police realize the two killings are connected. So if you're Sheila, what do you do now? Move on to Charles Atom, using a device similar to the one that killed Cherise . . . which will then pull her death into the mix and point the finger straight at you?"

Jack grunted, his gaze going distant as he thought it through.

"Fuck, yeah," he said after a few seconds. "Makes no sense. You go after Atom? You're not gonna use an IED. It's the only thing tying Cherise to the Atom girl."

"Which then ties Sheila to the rest. Sending Cherise that 'gift' to spook her doesn't make sense. Not when her kids were there. And Sheila has never contested the divorce. She's only arguing for joint custody... Which she'd have gotten by now if she hadn't been investigated for Cherise's death."

"So what's her motive?"

"Exactly." I paused. "I want to talk to Sheila again. I worry that I'm basing conclusions on snap judgments. I spent a few minutes with her. That's not enough to judge someone's character."

"You've got good instincts."

"I've been wrong before."

He shrugged. "We all have. But yeah, talk to her tomorrow. See what you think."

Chapter Seventeen
Nadia

I escorted Angela to work. Then I met up with Sheila. I'd called earlier this morning, and she'd agreed to see me.

"I start at seven," she'd said. "I'm an early bird. That means I take my break at nine, and it's a mile to the coffee shop. You seemed to be fine with walking while talking yesterday..."

"I am. I'll meet you at nine, then."

It turned out that the *nearest* coffee shop wasn't a mile from her office. She worked downtown, at a biochemical engineering firm, surrounded by coffee shops.

"I don't like those ones," she said when I commented. "And I need the exercise. That's how I'm staying off the meds."

I nodded. "Exercise can help with pain."

"It might. But exercise works for me because I hate every goddamn minute of it, so that's thirty minutes a day

I'm bitching about something other than my shoulder."

She walked fast, long strides that had me half jogging to keep up. Those strides also kept her path clear, people making way for the grim-faced juggernaut. As we walked, we talked about Cherise. I didn't have to beat around the bush. One mention of the name, and Sheila knew what I wanted to chat about, and she was happy to do it.

She didn't defend herself again. She just answered my questions as I got a better sense of her relationship with her husband's new girlfriend.

Sheila had known Cherise before that. She'd been the children's babysitter at one time.

"World's oldest cliché, huh? But it wasn't quite like that. I don't think Victor was shtupping the eighteen-year-old sitter. She left for college, and I didn't see her for years. Next thing I knew, they were together. She was twenty-five by then. Right in that sweet spot. Young enough for a guy in a mid-life crisis, but not so young it's creepy."

She laughed, and there was no animosity in it, no bitterness.

"So he was having a mid-life crisis?" I asked. "You figured his relationship with Cherise was temporary?"

"She didn't seem like his type, long term. He seemed like *hers*, though. I have no idea how it would have worked out." She smiled. "I get the feeling Cherise might have prevailed. She had tenacity. Gumption, too, as my gran would have said."

"How did you feel about that?"

She shrugged. "Like I said, I wouldn't have been thrilled with Cherise as stepmommy, but honestly, I won't be happy to see anyone taking that role in my kids' life. Someone will, though. Victor is the marrying type."

We picked up coffees. As we started back, at the same pace, I waited a few minutes before I resumed the conversation exactly where we'd left off.

"Any chance you two will get back together?"

"Hell, no. I love Victor dearly, but I love him as a co-parent. A friend. I'm hoping we'll get back to that once they find out who killed Cherise. The sad thing, hon, is that we were exactly that—friends and co-parents—for most of our marriage. That's how I got hooked on the meds."

"You were unhappy."

"Yep. I wasn't miserable. I wasn't depressed. I was just unhappy, and so was he, and I think that bothered me more than anything. I wasn't making him happy, and I began to wonder if I ever had."

"I'm sure—"

She cut me off with a look. "I don't need a teaspoon of honey to make the medicine go down. I prefer honesty, as bitter as it might be. Victor and I met in college. Engineering. I was the only girl in the program, and I thought that would mean, for the first time in my life, the boys would notice me. They'd have to."

She laughed and shook her head. "Didn't quite work out that way. I told myself they were intimidated. I got better grades than they did. I had companies fighting for me before I even graduated. I would be more successful than any of those boys, and they knew it, so they steered clear. Truth is, I've just never been the sort of woman that men chase. Not until Victor."

"He chased?"

A smile softened her face. "He did. He wasn't intimidated—he was impressed. But he wasn't . . . Well, he wasn't my type. But I liked him as a friend, and no one else was interested so . . . Damn, that's a shitty thing to say, isn't it?"

"It happens."

Her gaze slid over me. "I'm sure you had no problem getting the boys."

"That doesn't mean I kept them. I'm a little . . . unusual."

"Aren't we all? I remember my mother telling me I just wasn't like the other girls. Now I wonder, who is? Who fits this mythical mold?"

"Guys used to say that to me. That I wasn't like other girls. I never knew what it meant—I just knew I didn't like hearing it."

"My mother meant it as a compliment—that I wasn't some insipid twit." She rolled her eyes. "I'll never say it to my daughter. She's strong, and she's unique—*just* like other girls. With Victor, I settled, and as cruel as that sounds, I think he did, too. He pursued me because I was the proverbial fish in a barrel. Easy to catch. I'd say our marriage was a mistake, but he gave me two amazing children, and he is a wonderful father."

Everything she said reinforced my first impression. Any animosity toward Cherise had been mild, and getting rid of her would only put another woman in her place—a potentially worse stepmom. Sheila didn't want Victor back. So what did she stand to gain by killing his girlfriend?

"I asked Detective Lee if I could see the remains of that device," Sheila said when I brought up the IED. "I wanted to point out all the problems with it. Then she'd see that if I'd done it, I'd damn well have done a better job."

"You'd have built it right."

"Hell, no. I'd have built it wrong *properly*. You've heard that it probably wasn't supposed to detonate, right?"

I nodded.

"If I wanted it to detonate, it would have. And if I didn't want it to . . ."

"It wouldn't have. You'd have done it wrong . . . properly."

She nodded. "I do know how to make a device like that. I won't pretend otherwise. I've worked in explosives. But I'm not going to fuck it up. I'd never send a fake bomb as a scare tactic. That's stupid. It doesn't matter if it was made to fail, it's still a criminal offense."

"What did you conclude when you saw the device?"

"Detective Lee wouldn't let me. I was a suspect. The hired expert they got"—she rolled her eyes—"was strictly amateur hour. I could have helped them figure out who might have done this. But no . . ."

"If I could get you details—"

"Sheila Walling?"

We turned to see a police cruiser stopping behind us with the window rolled down. One officer climbed out.

"Sheila Walling?" he said again. "You are under arrest for the murders . . ."

Chapter Eighteen

Nadia

Detective Lee had found the evidence she needed to charge Sheila. Not that she was telling *me* what it was—she was understandably busy interrogating her suspect. I hung out at the station, but I didn't push. I had too much respect for the police, even when I was sure they'd made a mistake.

I was still waiting at the police station when Howard Lang texted me to say they'd arrested Sheila. I got back to him and discovered he already had the details through his contacts in the department.

The police had recovered a hair from the IED left for Angela. That wasn't new—they'd had the hair from the start and been running a DNA comparison, which doesn't happen nearly as fast as Hollywood might lead us to believe. They'd compared the DNA to Sheila's, which she'd provided back when Cherise died. I was sure her lawyer had argued against volunteering that, but I could see Sheila saying, *I didn't do this, so fuck it. Take my DNA.*

That DNA matched the hair taken from the device. Lee still hadn't been quick to arrest her. She knew Sheila wasn't going to run, and she wanted more evidence. That came in today, with the results of a credit card search—the DNA match gave Lee what she needed to conduct that search. Sheila's card had been used to order bomb-making materials shortly before the IED showed up in Angela's car. It was the same material used in Angela's device . . . and also used in the previous two. That wasn't enough to charge Sheila with the murders. For now, she'd only been charged with attempting to kill Angela, but that arrest opened up Lee's search powers, and the detective was certain she'd find what she needed to connect Sheila to the murders.

I suppose it was possible that Sheila only sent the device to Angela, which explained the DNA match and purchase history. But that didn't make sense. Why would she construct a bomb to kill Angela when she was already a suspect in Cherise and Sara's bombing deaths? That was crazy. Sheila Walling was not crazy.

She was being framed.

No one as smart as Sheila was going to use her credit card to buy the materials she'd use to build an IED. She wouldn't even need to buy them—she worked in the industry, and at most, she might have to purchase a single component. As for the DNA, a hair is the easiest source to "steal." It was possible there'd been hairs left with the first two devices as well—they just wouldn't have survived the blasts.

After speaking to Howard, I called Evelyn. Normally, I'd avoid asking for her research help. Evelyn doesn't work for free. Unfortunately, she doesn't work for mere cash, either. Her system is trade. Work done for a chit owed, and Evelyn didn't cash her chits promptly. She stockpiled them as leverage.

Luckily, right now we were in a reverse-credit situation—I'd helped her more than she'd helped me. I also had leverage of my own: Jack.

If you asked Jack and Evelyn what their relationship was, Evelyn would say she was his mentor. Ask Jack, and he'd point out that she'd *been* his mentor and was now a colleague. They're also friends, but neither was the type to say that. Business was the more important relationship.

The truth, though, was that to Evelyn, Jack was the closest thing to family she'd ever have. The closest thing to a son. But he was the kind of son who didn't call home nearly as often as he should. He cared... He just got busy, and yes, sometimes he didn't have the patience for Mom's bullshit. That placed me in a position of power. I was the daughter-in-law who could encourage him to call and visit. Or discourage him. I won't say that I used my power to its full potential, but I was aware it existed, and

Evelyn was *very* aware it existed.

Today, I set her on Sheila's credit card history. I wanted that purchase order. Mostly, I wanted to know where the goods had been sent, which would take more than a phone call from a sweet old lady. That was good, because I'd seen Evelyn's sweet-old-lady impersonation, and it sucked. Her true skill required only the use of her brain and her fingers, traveling along the back channels of the wired world.

She called an hour later.

"Okay," she said. "I have . . . Damn it, Dee. Can you call me back when you have a better connection? There's static."

"That's surf."

A long pause.

"We're on the beach," I said.

"Why?"

I laughed. "It's Hawaii."

"And you dragged Jack onto the beach?"

"Uh, no. It was his idea."

A longer pause.

"We aren't surfing, Evelyn," I said. "Or sunbathing, really. Did you know people still do that? You'd think they'd never heard of skin cancer. Anyway, we're just sitting on the beach in our swimsuits, discussing the case. We might even go into the water." I paused. "Although, on second thought . . . Hey, Jack? How would you feel about surf lessons? Or snorkeling?"

"Sure," he said without looking over.

"You realize he only does these things to make you happy, Dee."

I glanced at Jack, lying on his back, face raised to the sun.

"You're right. He looks miserable. I am a bad, bad person."

Jack lifted his sunglasses and arched one brow.

"Don't worry," I said. "I won't torture him much longer. We have a case to pursue. So, on that note . . ."

"The mailing address was a house. A house that belonged to Sheila Walling's mother, who died a few years ago, and it seems Sheila is waiting out the housing market before selling. She still owns it, and it's been empty since her mother's death."

"You researched the house, too? Wow. Thank you. That is above and beyond. You're good. I don't know what I'd do without—"

"You still owe me."

"Nope, totally don't. That took you an hour. I remain in the black. I'm just heaping on the praise to make you feel good. You're old. You need a little sunshine to warm your twilight years."

"Fuck. You."

I laughed. "I do appreciate it, Evelyn. You know I do. If you can send me the address, that would be awesome.

And I think Jack wants to talk to you."

He lifted his glasses again and mouthed, "I do?"

I mouthed, "Be nice," and then passed him the phone. "Tell her how much you're secretly hating this trip."

He snorted, took the phone and said to Evelyn. "Yeah, it's awful. Good thing you're not here. Too much sand. Too much sun. Too much lazing around drinking shit with umbrellas. You'd hate it."

I motioned that I was going into the water. He mouthed that he'd join me in a minute and resumed talking to Evelyn as I scampered across the hot sand.

I confirmed that the situation was exactly as Evelyn said. Sheila's mother had passed two years ago, and she'd inherited the house. Presumably, she was waiting for a boost in the housing market. But she wasn't renting it, either. Which concerned me. One would think that if she was worried about losing money, she'd rent the place. Unless she had another purpose for it.

When I saw the house, I could tell why Sheila wasn't using it herself. I'd gone by her place earlier, and it was double the size, in a much better neighborhood. Her mother's house was tiny, barely more than a clapboard shack, and in serious need of renovation before it even saw tenants.

According to Evelyn's research, Sheila's mother hadn't

lived in it for years, instead spending her waning days in an upscale hospice. The house would need renovation to put it on the market. The neighborhood, though, was decent, the other homes in much better shape. So it might be in Sheila's best interests to leave it uninhabited and unfixed until after the divorce. Give Victor half of the current value and then renovate and sell it. It was, after all, her inheritance.

A privacy fence surrounded the small backyard, and I snuck in that way. Both a key lock and a deadbolt secured the back door. I was in before I knew it.

No alarm system inside. Or so I thought until I noticed a faint red line hovering six inches off the hall floor.

I eased back on my haunches and studied it. A laser line, like one might see in an art museum. I stepped over and traced the line along to a small box on the wall—a device that I presumed sent an alert to a remote location. I took photos and e-mailed them to Felix. Then I checked the front door and found the same laser trigger there.

Someone wanted to know whether anyone came into the house. Not a person breaking in but simply entering, even with a key. Yet it was a clumsy system. I'd spotted it during the day, and it would be unmistakable after dark.

I had an idea what that alert system meant, though. What it was being used for.

I looked for a basement first, which proved that I don't have any experience living on an island. There was only a crawlspace. I checked bedrooms next. Both were empty, like the rest of the house. Any belongings had long since been removed, leaving only dust.

So if there wasn't a basement, where could one hide . . .

I looked up.

It was a single-story house, but it had looked taller from the outside, suggesting a large attic. Sure enough, I found a ceiling hatch with a hook. I managed to snag that. Then I pulled carefully, braced to set off an alarm.

A narrow set of steps rolled down. I ascended slowly, shining my penlight up into the dark. And there it was. Right at the top. Not a laser beam but a thin thread, ready to be triggered by anyone who came up unawares.

I lifted my foot to step over the wire . . . and froze. Then I turned, following the wire. It did not connect to a tiny alert box.

I had seen very few IEDs in my life. It was a rare hitman who'd use one, both because it required specialized knowledge and because it risked collateral damage. But I knew one when I saw one. And that's what I was seeing here. It wasn't just a small bomb, either. Trip this wire, and bits of me would be scattered through the rubble of this house.

I considered withdrawing. But I had one foot over the

wire, and backing up seemed just as dangerous as going forward.

So I inched my other foot over, sweat dripping down my cheek. Once I was across, I took a closer look.

No, I wasn't exaggerating when I said tripping this device would level the house. That was the intention. If anyone tried coming up here, the whole building would come down, hiding whatever lay inside.

I stepped away from the device, shone the light around and found exactly what I expected. The laboratory where this bomb had been constructed. Where I suspected all the bombs had been constructed.

In the attic of a house owned by Sheila Walling.

Chapter Nineteen
Jack

Jack walked into Victor Walling's office dressed in a suit, newly purchased but not new. Thrift shops and consignment stores were his best source of disguise material, and yeah, partly because he hated spending a lot of money on an outfit he'd wear once, but also, second-hand clothing meant he wouldn't walk in with a stiff new suit, tag still dangling from one sleeve. For this particular disguise, slightly rumpled worked just fine.

"McCall," he said to the woman at the front desk. "I work with Detective Lee. Does Victor have a moment?"

He did not introduce himself as "Detective" McCall. His outfit and his words suggested that, though, and the young woman quickly escorted him back to Walling.

As Jack walked, he looked around, assessing. It was an insurance sales office, neither a particularly classy nor shabby one. Middle of the road, like Walling himself, seated behind his desk in a suit little better than Jack's.

When Jack walked in, he straightened, rising as he extended his hand.

"McCall," Jack said. "We haven't met. Detective Lee asked me to stop by. It's about Sheila."

Walling sighed and lowered himself back into his seat. "I heard she'd been arrested. I still can't believe it. I knew she was angry, but to kill Cherise? And Charles Atom's girl? Everyone kept telling me it was Sheila, but I thought no, they were jumping to conclusions. Not my Sheila." A slow shake of his head.

"She hasn't been charged in any deaths," Jack said. "We've only traced the device from Angela Kamaka's car back to Sheila."

"But they were all made by the same person, right?"

"We're working on that. We have a lead on a possible location for her laboratory—where she might construct the devices. That's why I'm here. Do you have access to her mother's home?"

Walling's head shot up. "Tina's house? No, that's been empty for years."

"We traced the package delivery there."

"Then that's just where Sheila picked it up. The house isn't big enough to hide a bomb lab."

"Maybe. We're working on getting a search warrant, but we've run into some complications. Detective Lee hoped you could grant access, being half owner."

Walling shook his head. "It's Sheila's. I've never had

keys. I'm sorry."

"Is there any way—?" Jack checked his phone, as if he'd just gotten a text. "Well, it seems we'll be getting that warrant in about an hour. Sorry to bother you." He nodded. "Have a good day."

Chapter Twenty
Nadia

"Don't let him see you," Howard said as I peeked over the fence.

I resisted the urge to say this wasn't my first stakeout. As far as Howard Lang knew, he was the expert here—the cop turned PI. I was just a bodyguard who fancied herself a PI and got lucky on this lead. He'd never say that—he was too nice—but that was the setup I'd given him, so I had to stick to it, and I only said, "right," when he warned me to duck.

"You should go into this full-time," he said as we waited. "You've got real talent. Two days on the case, and you solved it. We've been working it for months."

"The fact that I'm not officially a PI means I don't need to play by PI rules. *You* can't ask someone to impersonate a cop."

"But your friend never actually *said* he was a cop. That's the trick."

Maybe. It walks a thin line, though, and it could *piss off* the police and lose them as a potential source. That was a risk I'd taken, betting on a long shot. Well, maybe not such a long shot. My advantage, in this case, was that I seemed to be the only person who believed Sheila Walling was innocent. It seemed so cut and dried to others. They took Sheila at face value, stuffed her into a stereotype box and saw a cold-blooded killer.

No one had paid any attention to the *other* person connected to both Cherise and the family court victims. The person who had access to Sheila's mother's house. The person who could *get* access to both Sheila's hair and her credit card information. The person who, despite working in insurance, had gone through chemical engineering with Sheila. He just wasn't good enough to get a job in the field.

So I had Jack plant the seed. The laboratory was about to be raided . . . giving Victor just enough time to clear out anything incriminating. Victor had snatched the bait. Jack had watched him leave and called me. I'd called Howard. Now we waited as Jack periodically texted updates on Victor's location. Sure enough, he was driving straight for this house.

"Five minutes away," I said as Jack texted again.

Howard speed-dialed a call. "Hey, Jillian, it's Howard again. Yeah, we've definitely got something. Let's just say it's very suspicious. Would you happen to have a car near

Sheila's mom's house?"

A low murmur as Detective Lee answered.

"Right. Yeah. It could be completely innocent, and I don't want to go raising a ruckus, but this looks bad, and there's the possibility of an arrest. I can't tell you much more than that."

Another pause.

"Two cars would be excellent. Have them stay clear until I text you. We don't want to spook our suspect."

Pause.

"Yes, I will be careful," he said with a chuckle.

As he hung up, Jack texted me again.

"Victor's parked in a strip mall at the corner," I said. "He's walking this way."

"If he has a lick of sense, he'll come through one of these backyards. Hopefully the one on the other side, but we need to be ready to run, just in case . . ."

Footfalls thumped along the driveway.

"All right," Howard said with a sigh. "Apparently, he doesn't have a lick of sense. At least he's heading for the *back* door."

We watched Victor race into the rear yard, breathing hard.

"Yeah," Howard muttered. "Run down the street in a suit. That's not suspicious at all."

It took Victor a moment to get the door unlocked. Even from here, I could see his hands shaking. He raced through, not pausing to step over the tripwire, which I supposed made sense if he was the only person it alerted.

As Victor barreled into the house, I climbed the fence. When I perched on top, Howard looked up at me with a soft laugh.

"Ah, to be young again. I'm going to take the long way around."

He set off at a run while I jumped down. I jogged to the back door and eased the screen open. Victor had left the inside door ajar. I slipped through and stepped over the alert laser.

A rustle sounded at the front of the house, and I tiptoed that way. I peered around the hall corner, expecting to see the attic ladder lowered. It wasn't. The rustling came from an open door farther down. When Victor walked out, I backed up fast, through the living room, into the kitchen.

I was ready to keep retreating, but Victor's footsteps paused in the living room long enough for me to get out my mirror and check around the corner. He'd perched on the edge of a wooden crate as he flipped through a handful of papers.

Papers?

He'd heard the house was about to be raided and roared over to clear out the lab and then paused to retrieve . . . papers?

Shit.

I looked again. They seemed to be letters of some sort. I could see a pink envelope and a handwritten page decorated with roses.

I remembered Sheila saying she suspected Victor had hooked up with Cherise before they split. If she had proof, she could use that against Victor as proof of infidelity.

That's what he must have come back for. After Cherise died, he'd want to keep mementos of their relationship, but he wouldn't want incriminating evidence at home. He'd squirreled them away here, in a closet or under a floorboard.

Shit.

As I pulled back, a creak sounded behind me, and I turned just as Howard lifted his leg over the laser tripwire. I tiptoed to him.

"I screwed up," I whispered. "Victor isn't here for the lab."

Howard's brows lifted, and he motioned to ask where Victor was. I pointed, and he walked over and took a look. As he did, his lips formed a "Shit."

He returned to me.

I showed him a message I'd quickly typed on my phone: *I think they're love letters. From Cherise. Proof they were having an affair before he left Sheila. I'm so sorry.*

He took my phone and typed: *We knew there was a chance this wasn't the answer, which is why we don't have a team breaking down the door right now. It was a solid lead. You done good.*

He smiled at the last part and gave me a thumbs-up. A pat on the back for the newbie. Except I was less of a newbie than I'd let on, so that pat didn't make me feel better. I should have had Jack meet me here instead and just snapped photos if we did see Victor dismantling the lab. Called Howard and the police then, with the evidence.

Howard texted Detective Lee as I took another look through my mirror. Victor was on his feet now, pushing the folded pages into his pocket. Then he checked his watch . . . and headed back into the rear hall.

I took off after Victor and barely made it to the hall before I heard the creak of the attic stairs.

I turned to see Howard right behind me. He caught the same noise and his brows lifted.

"The attic," I said.

His face lit up, reminding me that he wasn't just a PI on a job. This was personal for him. Catching Mindy's killer. Now he had his answer.

So why was there a niggling voice in my head, whispering that something was still wrong here?

As Howard started to pass me, I remembered the bomb at the top of the stairs.

I grabbed Howard's arm. "Get out."

"What?"

"You need to get out. Now. Run."

His broad face screwed up.

"There's a bomb at the top of the stairs," I whispered as fast as I could get the words out. "If he's not the killer—if he's going up there for another reason—he'll trigger it, and this whole house is going to blow. I'll stay—"

"The hell you will." Howard grabbed my arm and yanked me toward the front door as Victor's footsteps continued up the ladder.

Howard reached for the front door handle . . . and Victor's footsteps continued across the attic floor.

I exhaled. "Okay, he didn't trigger it. Which either means he accidentally stepped over the tripwire or . . ."

"He knows it was there, and he's doing more than hiding old love letters."

Howard released my arm. As he texted Detective Lee, I headed for the attic ladder. I took it one rung at a time, moving slowly. When a board creaked, I froze, but Victor just kept doing whatever he was doing, the sound of rustles and clatter coming from the attic.

I crested the opening, and there he was at the workbench with his back to me. He was engrossed in his work, so I kept climbing. I moved over the tripwire as carefully as I could. As I put my foot down, though, it gave a soft thump, and that was enough for Victor to spin.

Chapter Twenty-one
Nadia

Victor saw me and went still. "Who the hell—?" He stopped as he saw my gun.

Then his gaze flew to the attic hatch as Howard Lang appeared.

"Hey, Vic," Howard said. "Gotta say, this isn't what I expected."

Victor pressed his back against the workbench. "What are you doing here?"

"Whatcha got there, Vic?" Howard said as he eased over the tripwire.

"N-nothing."

I stepped toward the bench, my gun pointed at Victor.

"Just taking precautions," Howard said as Victor stared at my gun. "You gotta admit this is a troubling situation. That"—he pointed at the tripwire bomb—"isn't exactly a welcome mat."

"Neither is that," I said as I nodded at the workbench.

On it was a device with a timer. I cursed myself for not anticipating this. Did I really think a bomber would clean up his laboratory by shoving everything into a backpack?

"Blowing up the evidence, huh?" Howard said. "You know I can't let you do that, Vic, so step away from that bench."

Victor looked at the timer, its screen black. His fingers twitched.

"Uh-uh," I said. "You make a move toward that, and I'll take you out. The police are on their way. You're about to be arrested for the murder of—"

"Me? No. I didn't kill anyone. It was Sheila. It was all Sheila."

"That story worked a lot better before we found you in the lab . . . right after you were warned it was about to be raided."

He shook his head vehemently. "I didn't build those devices. Sheila did. But when that cop mentioned the house, I knew she must have her lab here and . . ." He exhaled. "She's the mother of my children. Whatever she did, I drove her to it, and our kids shouldn't pay for our mistakes. I wanted to protect them. If that makes me an accomplice—"

"It makes you a killer," I said. "The son of a bitch who tried to frame his wife."

"No, I love Sheila. Just because we didn't work out doesn't change that." He looked at Howard. "You understand that better than anyone, Howard. Think of Mindy."

Howard's jaw clenched. "Don't bring Mindy into this, you bastard. You *murdered* her, and you're lucky I don't pull *my* gun and shoot you right now. My only consolation is knowing that when the police analyze this lab, they'll prove it was you, and you'll spend the rest of your life in a—"

Victor lunged at Howard. I held my ground. Victor wasn't armed, and I sure as hell wasn't shooting unless I had to, not when I couldn't just disappear before the police showed up.

Howard started to backpedal . . . and I saw the tripwire behind him.

"Howard!"

I didn't even get his name out before he realized what he was doing and swung to the side instead. That left the exit open with Victor heading straight for it.

"Stop!" I said, raising my gun.

Victor *did* stop, right at the trip wire. He turned to me.

"Do you know what that is?" he said, pointing at the wire.

"Yes."

"Then you know that all it takes . . ." He lifted his foot and made a motion to bring it down on the wire.

"*Stop!*"

He kept his foot poised above the wire.

"You're going to let me leave," he said. "I'm going to step over this and continue down the ladder, and you're going to let me walk away. Otherwise"—he waggled his foot—"I've got nothing to lose, do I?"

"You aren't going to do that, Victor," Howard said. "You've got two kids who deserve to know why you did this."

Victor let out a bitter laugh. "Why I did *what*? I didn't mean to kill anyone. I sent that damned package to Cherise to get her out of my life. I wasn't stupid—I knew she was just looking for a free ride. So was I. But suddenly, my ride wasn't free anymore. She wanted a ring. So I thought I'd kill two birds with one stone. Spook her and frame Sheila. Only the damned thing went off and destroyed the evidence that Sheila did it. So I tried again with that lawyer. That time, I was even more careful. I put the device in the grill, and then I was going to call in an anonymous tip, but that kid opened the grill before I could."

"That *kid* was a sixteen-year-old girl," I said. "Who you *murdered*."

"I didn't kill her. The bomb did. She opened the grill, and no one was supposed to do that. But she did, and again, boom. Sheila's hair? Gone."

"You—" I began, barely able to get the word out.

"Okay," Howard cut in. "You didn't mean to kill anyone. I get that. So, yes, I'm going to let you leave." He turned to me. "Stand down, Nancy."

I clenched my teeth. I knew Howard was right. Just lower my gun, let Victor walk away and *then* give chase. I could catch him easily enough. Still, after what he just said, it took everything in me to force my gun down, inch by inch.

"She's going to shoot me," Victor said, and he sounded so much like a petulant child that I really did want to prove him right.

I holstered my gun instead and said, "Go on."

He lowered his foot over the wire. His eyes never left mine. I stayed as calm as I could, my hand away from my gun, giving him no reason to do anything except leave. He put one foot down. Then he brought the other over and placed it on the first rung. He lowered himself down one rung . . . and stopped.

"You're going to come after me," he said, still watching me.

"Vic?" Howard said. "I've got this. You're fine."

"I want her gun." He glanced at Howard. "Yours, too. Give me the guns, and I'll leave."

"Victor . . ." Howard began.

"Sure," I said. "He can have my gun. I get the bullets. He gets the gun."

"Fine," Howard said. He took out his weapon.

I unholstered mine and started opening the chamber. And then we heard a sound. The distant wail of police sirens.

Victor looked at me. The son of a bitch looked right at me and then reached for the tripwire.

I slapped the chamber and aimed at his forehead.

"Stop," I said.

He kept reaching. Kept looking right at me and kept reaching. I heard Howard shouting, saw him start to lunge and then realize he couldn't, that the wire was between them, and he could not get to Victor without setting off the bomb.

"Stop!" Howard said. "Think of your kids. Chris and Andi. Think about them."

"Oh, but I am," Victor said. "I'm thinking of how no one will ever know exactly what happened here. No evidence. No witnesses. Just a tragic misunderstanding. An innocent man, railroaded by some bitch who roared in here, thinking she could solve a crime."

"This isn't about Nancy. I'm the one who—"

"You're the one who couldn't resist a pretty face, Howard. You never could. None of us can, really. She talked you into this, against your better judgment, and look what happened." His eyes held mine. "Boom."

"If you touch that wire—" I began.

"Oh, I'm going to do more than touch it. You think you're tough, don't you? Just like Sheila. Gotta wear the pants. Show up the men. Grind them to dust beneath your heel. Well, girlie, you know what's going to be dust here?" He smiled. "You."

He reached for the wire. His fingers started to close around it . . . and I put a bullet between his eyes.

As Victor fell, Howard hit the floor as if Victor had managed to grab that wire. But I'd been careful. I'd waited until I was completely sure he was about to do it. He never touched the wire, though, and the shot sent him toppling backward down the ladder.

The sirens screamed louder now, the police coming fast.

"Give me your gun," Howard said. "Quickly. I'll say it's mine. That I shot—"

"It's unregistered."

"Shit!"

I was about to tell him I'd handle this—I'd find some way, even if it meant just running before that cruiser arrived, but Howard jumped over the wire and tore down the ladder and put another bullet between Victor's eyes with his own gun.

"There," he said as I descended, "I did it. I shot him."

"You don't have to—"

"I had the damned gun in my hand, and I never even thought to shoot him." He turned to me. "Thank you."

"There wasn't any other way. That's what I'll tell the police when they get here. You had no choice. You saved us."

He managed a shaky smile. "I'd rather not play hero

when I didn't earn it."

"You did. You talked him down. If it wasn't for those damned sirens . . ." I turned and followed the noise. "Are those getting quieter?"

Howard strode to the front of the house. I was right. Those cars weren't coming here. Their sirens were already receding into the distance. Howard cursed under his breath. And just then, an unmarked car pulled up, and two officers got out.

"I'd better call Detective Lee," he said, "and tell her we're going to need more officers."

"If you can stall those guys while I hide my gun, I'd appreciate it."

"Sure thing."

Chapter Twenty-two
Nadia

I told the story as I'd promised. It wouldn't hold up under close scrutiny. A coroner could realize Victor had been shot twice in the same place, and that Howard's bullet was still in Victor's skull while another one made that exit wound. They might also find the hole in the wall where I'd retrieved my bullet.

But Howard was retired, meaning it wasn't a police shooting, and I suspected no one was going to go hunting for holes in our story... or holes in the wall. The bomb was there, and the position of Victor's body confirmed our version of events. Our statements matched. I only hoped it wouldn't cause any trouble for Howard when "Nancy Cooper"—the Michigan-based bodyguard who gave that statement—turned out to be a ghost.

I could have left before the police arrived. Jack certainly wished I had. But I wouldn't put Howard in that position. I'd hidden my gun, which Jack later retrieved. I hadn't touched anything in the house. I was wearing the same disguise I'd been using since I arrived, one that matched my Nancy passport. That passport and all other ID would be burned, literally, in Vancouver, and I'd fly home under a new name.

Leaving right away would look suspicious. Angela and Howard still had my number, and I wanted to wait a day or two, just to be sure all was well.

Cypher took us out to celebrate. To the beach, not surprisingly. It's Hawaii... There's a lot of beach. This time, we were on the patio of an old hotel, listening to live music, watching surfers and swimmers on Waikiki. I was having tea. A full-blown English-style afternoon tea. That was Cypher's celebration reward for me, and I didn't take umbrage at the suggestion that a female hitman needed a more "feminine" reward. It was very sweet and thoughtful, and I kinda loved putting on a sundress and a wide-brimmed hat and eating little sandwiches and sipping tea and feeling a million miles from the person who'd shot Victor Walling this afternoon.

Going into this, I didn't expect to actually pull a hit. I'd rather not have, to be honest. But under the circumstances, I was okay with it. Victor Walling had murdered his girlfriend and an innocent teenage girl, and he'd felt less guilt over their deaths than I would over his.

He tried to blow up Howard, too, a guy who'd been willing to let him walk away, a guy who'd treated him with more respect than I could ever manage.

I wouldn't have pulled the trigger if Victor hadn't reached for that wire. But I'm not sorry I did.

"How did Angela take the news?" Cypher asked when I finally heard back from her.

"She's happy," I said. "She wants to see me in person to say so. Tonight, actually."

Jack frowned and checked his watch. "Can you do it tomorrow?"

"I suggested that. She's in court all day. I know you made dinner reservations but honestly"—I waved at my three-tier tea tray—"I doubt I'll get another bite down before breakfast. I'll meet up with Angela for a drink, and if you can reschedule the reservation for tomorrow, that'd be great."

He nodded, expressionless, and I tried to catch his eye, but he was busy eating a scone, his gaze on the beach.

Jack wasn't the type to get annoyed over canceled plans. Hell, if I'd given him the option of when I met up with Angela, he'd have shrugged and said it was my choice, and I'd have driven myself crazy trying to get a preference out of him.

When I did catch his eye, he frowned, head tilting as if to ask what was wrong. His hand found my knee under the table and squeezed, and I realized that, once again, I'd been fretting over a problem that existed only in my imagination. Even after three years together, I couldn't quite accept that Jack was as happy as he seemed, and there was part of me constantly on alert for the first glimmer of trouble.

I smiled and laid my hand on his. "I can try to reschedule with Angela . . ."

"Course not. Get business done. You're right. Wouldn't eat anyway."

I tried not to exhale in relief. I wasn't unhappy with the chance to meet Angela tonight. Just like I wasn't unhappy with the chance to stay another day in Honolulu, and not just for the sun and sand.

The solution to this case bothered me. But questioning it made me uncomfortable. I felt like the new kid on the softball team, who hits a dumb-luck home run to win the game, and then thinks she has the skills to question the coach's strategy. Yes, I broke this case, but it was not through superior skills, and questioning Detective Lee and Howard Lang's theories felt like ego.

I'd talk to Angela. Settle my mind. And I'd get that over with tonight.

I sipped my tea and then looked at Cypher. "She'd like to see you. Angela, that is."

He shook his shaggy head.

"I'm not pushing you guys together," I said. "She

really did ask. Repeatedly. Including just now."

I turned my phone over and showed him her text.

Angela: *Please tell my anonymous benefactor that I'd like to thank him, too.*

Me: *I'll try. But don't hold your breath.*

Angela: *I'm not.*

Cypher rubbed his mouth. "Can you convince her it's not me?"

"I've tried. She knows."

"Try again. Tell her she's made a mistake. Tell her . . ." He threw up his hands. "Make something up. You're good at that. Make up a story for her."

"Or, maybe, you could just come with me tonight."

He shook his head again. "I can't."

"Because . . ."

"It's complicated. Now drink your damned tea."

"Yes, sir."

I was supposed to meet Angela at nine after she finished work. I'd offered to come by the office, but she'd picked a bar on the beach, one much closer to my hotel. She'd meet me there.

I went to the bar early, staked out a patio table overlooking the tiki-torch-lit beach, and I tried to enjoy a piña colada. I didn't quite succeed. I was too busy thinking.

Yes, Victor Walling murdered Cherise Hale and Sara Atom. He had confessed to those crimes. But the earlier ones—Mindy Lang and Albert Kim—didn't make sense.

With both Cherise and Sara, Victor said he was only trying to spook people, and the evidence supported that. But Mindy and Judge Kim had clearly been murdered, and Victor had no reason to kill them. While Judge Kim *had* overseen an earlier motion in the Walling custody case, he'd actually reprimanded Sheila, not Victor. And Mindy had been the cause of that reprimand . . . in Victor's favor.

The time span between "suspecting Victor" and "catching Victor" had been too short for me to pull back earlier and consider whether he worked as a suspect in all four deaths. He fit the last two, and so we'd figure out the rest later. But now no one seemed to be questioning him as the sole perpetrator. Which made me feel like that overconfident home run player questioning the pros. I didn't have the full case files. I'd barely done any investigative work. There must be aspects of the case that I just didn't know about.

Either way, did it matter, really? Victor had set the bomb for Atom. He'd planted the one in Angela's car, with Sheila's hair. Therefore Victor had been the threat to Angela, and he was gone. My job was complete.

That's what Jack would say. It's what Cypher would say. So I didn't share my doubts with them. As far as they knew, I was fine with the outcome and just meeting Angela for a celebratory drink.

Which was not why I was meeting her tonight at all. I needed information. I needed to test a theory that I liked even less than I liked questioning Detective Lee's conclusions.

I had an idea who might be responsible for the earlier murders. It was an outlandish theory with not nearly enough evidence for me to dare voice it. I felt ashamed even thinking it because the person I'd begun to suspect deserved my respect, not my suspicion. Total respect for selfless dedication to a cause. Now that I entertained this niggling doubt, I didn't feel like that overconfident softball player anymore. I felt like a two-bit thug trying to knock the pedestal from under a good person, just to bring them down to my size.

I was almost certainly wrong. But I couldn't leave until I knew that for sure.

When the server asked whether I wanted a refill, I realized I'd been sitting long enough for the ice to melt in my drink. I checked my watch. It was 9:20 p.m. I flipped through my messages. Yes, Angela said she'd meet me at nine. A glance at the bar name on the napkin. Yes, this was definitely the right place.

I sent her a text.

When five minutes passed without an answer, I called.

Her phone rang. And rang. And rang.

Voicemail picked up. I left a message. "Hey, it's Nancy. Just making sure we're still on for tonight. Give me a shout."

Another ten minutes passed. I sent another text. Made another call.

This wasn't good.

It wasn't good at all.

Time to pay my tab and get out of here.

Chapter Twenty-three
Jack

It was 9:10 p.m., and Jack had seen no sign of Angela Kamaka. He sat in a bar a few doors down from where Nadia waited, and he could see her on the patio, her back to him as she stared out at the water.

Every time Nadia shifted position, he tensed, ready to raise the drink menu and block his face. Which told him he shouldn't be here.

No, that wasn't entirely true. He *should* be here. He just should have warned her. Told her why he'd followed her. Why he was staking out her meeting with Angela. His phone weighed heavy in his pocket, needing only a single text to tell Nadia the truth. Yet it stayed in that pocket.

Victor Walling hadn't killed Mindy Lang or Albert Kim. That didn't make sense. The cops would figure it out eventually, but until then, Nadia was in danger. So he should warn her.

Yeah, it wasn't Walling. Not for all of it. Sorry. You screwed up. I know you tried, and you did great, but you're wrong. Let me take over now.

No fucking way was he saying that. Even if he worded it in the best possible language, she'd still hear: *you fucked up, and I need to fix this.*

Nadia had not "fucked up." Come tomorrow, when she relaxed and got some distance from what happened today, she'd see holes in the case. Today, she'd shot a man, and it didn't matter whether she had to do it, that still bugged her. The fact that she'd shot him before he blew her to bits, hell, she might act like that was no big deal, but Jack struggled to focus even thinking about how close she'd come to dying today.

Nadia would soon realize there was a problem with Walling as the sole perp, and Jack would have been happy to let it ride until she did. Then she set up this meeting with Angela and snared him in a dilemma. Did he warn her . . . and, in doing so, insult her? Or did he just watch over her? He knew option A was the smart choice. It was the choice she'd want him to make. Didn't mean he was making it, though. His head told him to warn her. His gut told him to shut up and watch.

One problem was that, in warning her, he'd have to admit exactly why he had a problem with this meeting. And she would not like that answer. Not one bit.

Jack didn't like Nadia meeting with Angela . . . because Angela topped his suspect list. In fact, right now, she was the only person *on* his suspect list.

Nadia liked Angela. She liked her as a person, and she liked her as a victim. Yeah, that last part sounded weird, but Jack meant that, for Nadia, Angela was the perfect victim. The exact sort of person she wanted to help. Someone who had risked her life, not for some heroic ideal, but simply because it was her damned job. Because other people needed her to do that job. A very ordinary sort of heroism, which made it all the more admirable, because there would be no medal of honor in Angela's future. The most she'd hope to gain was more clients.

For Angela, though, those clients were a godsend. From those files he'd read in her house, he knew her firm had been struggling before she took on Charles Atom's clients . . . before she gained even *more* clients from that very public act, others who heard what she'd done and wanted her as their lawyer.

Not that she had killed to get those clients. That wouldn't make sense. Walling was definitely the one who set the bomb in Atom's grill. No, if Jack was right, gaining those clients had been happenstance rather than intent.

Yesterday, after the sex-club alibi, Louis Stanton had started spouting his own theories, desperate to convince Jack that *he* wasn't responsible for the murders.

"Someone should look into that lawyer chick," Stanton had said. "The one who took on the cases."

"Angela Kamaka?"

"Everyone thinks she's a damned saint, forgetting the fact she was screwing around with the first victim's husband."

"Howard Lang?"

"Lang couldn't keep his pants zipped. That's why they split. Rumor is that Mindy put up with his shit until he banged that lawyer chick."

"Okay . . ."

"Put the pieces together." Stanton had given Jack this look, like he was an idiot for needing it spelled out. "The two women get into a catfight over the guy, and the lawyer accidentally kills the wife and then realizes how easy that was, so she goes after the judge next. He's a judge, and she's a lawyer—he must have done something to piss her off. Then she thinks, *Ah-ha, people think the deaths are connected to divorce cases, so what if I off this lawyer guy and take his cases? Then I'll make myself look like a target, so people feel sorry for me.*"

"She killed her own dog?"

Stanton had shrugged. "Maybe it barked too much."

Jack had dismissed that as a load of crap. Yeah, he knew Angela's firm was struggling, but that was to be expected for a new business. If that was part of her reason for taking on those clients, so be it. He wouldn't begrudge her the chance to make a living, especially if she was risking her life to do it. The rest was just random weird shit. Then Walling confessed to the bombs, and Jack couldn't help looking at Angela again for the other deaths.

He'd asked for Evelyn's help, and her digging confirmed the financial difficulties. She also learned that Angela had a history of problems with Albert Kim—documented animosity.

What if Angela and Mindy *did* get into a fight? Lingering resentment over Angela's affair with Howard. Angela went to confront Mindy at home, accidentally killed her and then made it look like a suicide. After that, something with Judge Kim sent her over the edge, and she killed him, staging it as another suicide. Then Walling came along, picking up on Angela's "pattern" of family court murders to frame Sheila. After Sara Atom's death, Angela knew it was safe to take Atom's cases—that there *was* no pattern of family court murders. She got extra work and looked like a hero.

It certainly wasn't a slam-dunk theory. But having Angela then want to meet Nadia at night? Alone? Yeah, that spelled trouble. Which was why Jack was staking out their meeting.

Let Angela show up. If she tried taking Nadia anyplace, he'd act. Otherwise, she might just want to talk, get a sense of whether Nadia suspected more. If so, then Nadia and Jack could talk tonight. He'd say, "Yeah, about Angela . . ." and give Nadia the evidence for them to discuss.

Only Angela wasn't showing up. It was now twenty past. He watched Nadia send a text. Answering one from Angela, he figured. Then she took a call and had a very short conversation.

Ten minutes later, another text and another call, equally brief. When she got off the phone, she flagged down a server, paid and left her table.

Angela had canceled. Jack exhaled. Okay, now he'd talk to Nadia about Angela. No more of this bullshit. Nadia wouldn't like Jack considering Angela as a suspect. It made him look like a jaded misanthrope, a guy who saw someone like Angela Kamaka and thought, *Too good to be true.* Which he hadn't, not until he had cause to dig deeper. Still, it looked shitty. It might make Nadia think poorly of him. And that was too fucking bad, wasn't it? For Nadia's safety, he had to speak up.

Jack had prepaid his tab and tip, so he hurried straight out to see Nadia flagging down a cab. He pulled back into the shadows. Yeah, she would get to the hotel ahead of him, but he could just pretend he'd gone for a walk on the beach. Then he'd sit her down and tell her what he was thinking.

A cab pulled over, Nadia got in. Jack waited as the car left the curb and ... made a U-turn. Heading *away* from their hotel.

Fuck, no.

Angela hadn't called to cancel. She'd called asking Nadia to meet her someplace else.

Fuck, no.

Jack jogged to the sidewalk and flagged down a taxi. He had the door open before it even rolled to a stop.

"Follow that car," he said, pointing to Nadia's cab.

The middle-aged driver burst out laughing.

"I'm serious," Jack said. "I need you to follow—"

"That cab I just drove past? The one that a pretty lady got in?" The driver twisted, putting his arm over the seat as he looked back at Jack. "That's not a good idea."

"I need—"

"Look, I understand. You saw her inside the bar, maybe chatted a little. But you struck out. Let it go." He nodded at the gold band on Jack's finger. "Remember your wife, okay? Don't take a vacation from your vows, too."

"That *is* my wife."

The cabbie eyed Jack and shrugged. "Maybe. But if it is? I'd suggest letting her cool down. Go buy her a lei or something. Maybe a bottle of champagne. Have it chilled for when she gets back. She'll appreciate that far more than you chasing her down after a fight."

Jack leaned forward, the gun under his jacket shifting, reminding him how easy it would be to resolve this issue. Which was the problem with guns—they made every issue far too easy to resolve. And sometimes—*most* times—that was just a fucking bad idea.

Jack hesitated only a moment. Then he swung open the door and got out of the cab.

Chapter Twenty-four
Nadia

Jack was trying to get hold of me. He'd called while I'd been in the cab, and I'd let it go to voice mail. Then he texted—he wanted to talk about the case. I replied that, yes, we should do that . . . as soon as I got back.

That's when my cab arrived at its destination, and I added a quick second text: *See you soon!* before turning off my phone.

Angela said she'd be coming directly from work to meet me. Therefore, "work" was the first place I'd look for her. I headed straight to the parking garage and found her car there, with no signs of tampering.

I sent her another text. Her phone now went directly to voice mail.

I unzipped my light jacket—easier access to my gun—and headed for the stairwell. The broken card reader meant I got in easily. I climbed to Angela's office without passing so much as a security camera.

When I reached her floor, I glanced down the hall to see her office door ajar. I took out my gun and proceeded, step by careful step, along the wall. Then I eased over and slowly pushed the door open a few inches. I listened for some response from within. The office stayed dark and silent.

Gun ready, I swung in.

The reception area was empty, lit only by the glow of the security system. The *unarmed* security system, the light solid green.

I started toward Angela's office. The door was wide open, and there seemed to be a light on inside. I rounded the reception desk and . . .

A foot protruded from behind the desk. A foot in a man's stylish leather loafer, topped by a patterned sock. I moved cautiously, gun poised. When I could see the rest of the body, I stopped. From the shoe and sock, I'd expected Angela's well-dressed receptionist, Richard. Instead, Howard Lang lay crumpled on the floor.

I hurried over. Even as I dropped beside him, I could see his chest rising and falling. He was fine.

I gripped his shoulder. "Howard?"

He groaned.

"*Howard.*"

There was no blood, no sign of injury, so I gave his shoulder a shake. He lifted his head.

"Wh—what?" he slurred as he peered around.

"Where . . . ?"

He looked over his shoulder and saw me. Three hard blinks. Then he shook his head and straightened.

"Nancy," he said. "What are you . . . ? Shit!"

He scrambled up but swayed and had to grab the desk for support.

I helped him sit and crouched beside him.

"Angela," he said. "Where's Angela?"

"I was going to ask you that. She was supposed to meet me for drinks, and she never showed. What happened?"

"She hit me over the head." He fingered the back of his skull and winced. "Damn it. I did not see that coming."

"Angela hit you?"

He nodded. "I was talking to her earlier. I had some questions."

"For Angela?"

"I . . . I hated to think it, Nancy, but I had to. There were too many loose ends. Too many holes in her story."

"You mean you *suspected* Angela?"

"I did. So I came to talk to her. And that's all we were doing. Talking. I asked about a certain case, and she came out here to check the main filing cabinet. The drawer was stuck. Or so she said. I reached to open it, and something hit the back of my head. Next thing I know, you're waking me up." He looked around. "What time is it?"

"Just after ten."

"Shit!" He wobbled to his feet. "Then she's long gone. I can't believe I fell for that. I suspected her, and still, I let her get the jump on me."

"Do you have any idea where she'd go?"

He hesitated, and I could tell it took effort to collect his thoughts. "Actually, I do. She has a place outside the city. It's kind of her secret spot, but Angela and I . . . We had a thing."

I tried to hide my surprise. "So that's why you think she killed Mindy?"

It took him at least thirty seconds to answer. "I . . . When Mindy first died, I had to consider the possibility. Angela has a temper. But I knew Angela couldn't have made a bomb, so I stopped considering her. Then we found out about Victor, and I realized there was a chance he might not have killed Mindy. So I came to talk to Angela. I never accused her of anything, but she knows me. She must have realized I was suspicious."

"Do you have a car?"

"I do."

"Then let's go."

Chapter Twenty-five
Nadia

Howard drove us outside the city. We went down back roads, parked in thick forest and then crept through it to find a place that was little more than a shack.

"Angela bought the property cheap years ago," Howard said. "Her dream was to tear this down and rebuild. For now, it's not much. But hardly anyone knows about it. She'd feel safe here. And, yep, there's a light on."

A dim one, barely more than a glow.

"We should split up," I said. "I'll take the back."

"I'd . . . I'd rather not. You already saw how I respond under pressure. I freeze up. You should take the lead."

I nodded and started forward. He fell in behind me. I'd gone five steps when I felt cold metal against the base of my skull.

I swore under my breath.

Howard chuckled. "You don't sound surprised."

"I'm never surprised."

"I bet you aren't. You're not just some chick who decided to play bodyguard, are you? I saw the way you handled Victor. I hesitated. You didn't. A perfect, cold-blooded shot."

"Just take me to Angela."

"Oh, believe me, I'm about to."

I started walking. I probably should have *tried* to seem more surprised, but really, I didn't see the point in faking it. I'd started suspecting Howard the moment I realized Victor wasn't the sole killer.

I remembered Angela's reaction when she first mentioned Howard, and I thought she meant he was a suspect. She'd hesitated before laughing it off and correcting me. And I thought she'd just been surprised, but then I began to wonder. Which is why I'd wanted to talk to her tonight. I'd hoped I was wrong. I liked Howard. Maybe I'm a romantic at heart, but I also liked the idea that he'd still cared enough about his ex to single-mindedly hunt down her killer. And then doubt had set in as I'd twisted the situation around. What if *Howard* killed Mindy? What better way to ensure he wasn't caught than to investigate her murder as the grieving ex?

I'd known exactly why he brought me to this shack, and I'd been relatively certain this place never belonged to Angela. It was just a convenient place to stash her . . . and now me.

I continued on to the house. Then I turned around, faced him and reached for my gun.

"Are you crazy?" he said, pointing his weapon at my forehead. "Or do you really think I didn't realize you'd taken the bullets out of my gun?"

He turned the barrel aside and fired.

Oh, shit . . .

When I'd seen him on the floor of Angela's office, I'd emptied his gun before I roused him. That's why I hadn't been too worried about him holding me at gunpoint . . . until now.

Howard prodded me to the shack, opened the door and shoved me into a dimly lit room. It took a moment for my eyes to adjust. Then I saw Angela. Bound, gagged and furious, her eyes blazing.

I started toward her.

Howard shook his head and waved the gun. "A little more distance between the ladies, please."

I glanced around. It was a one-room shack with a single door and windows. Not even an indoor bathroom. The only furnishings were a couple of lawn chairs, one broken, the other rotted.

"Put your hands out," Howard said.

I did. He stuffed the gun into his holster, eyeing me the whole time, waiting for any sign of attack. I stood patiently, hands extended as he wrapped thin nylon rope around my wrists. Only when he had my hands secured did he relax. And I kicked him in the kneecap as hard as I could.

He flailed, hands windmilling to find his balance. I managed to snag the grip of his gun with my bound hands, but I didn't get a good enough hold to pull it out before he recovered. His first reaction was to grab his gun, which I was still holding, albeit awkwardly. That meant that we pulled it out together. Then I let go and slammed my bound hands up into his.

He fumbled the gun. As it fell, he went for it, but Angela was right there, and maybe she couldn't do a whole lot, being bound and gagged, but she was on the floor, which meant when she slammed into his legs, he tumbled overtop her.

Angela kicked the gun aside. Howard scrabbled up and went for it again, but now I rammed into him with my shoulder, hard enough that pain ripped through it. I hit him again, this time a head butt that sent him staggering back. I was about to strike again when the door flew open and Jack swung in, gun raised.

"Stop," Jack said.

Howard twisted to look over at him. He eyed the gun. Eyed Jack . . . and then lifted his hands over his head.

Chapter Twenty-six
Jack

Jack followed Nadia out of the cabin. Inside, Howard had taken Angela's place, bound and gagged on the floor. Angela wanted to speak to Howard alone, in hopes of negotiating a way to turn him into the police without involving Jack. So after they made sure Howard was secure, Jack and Nadia went outside.

"Well," Nadia said once they were away from the cabin. "At least I had the *foresight* to empty his gun."

"You didn't think he'd notice?"

"Hey, the guy was nearly blown to smithereens and never even raised his weapon. I hoped that meant he'd fail to notice his weapon seemed a whole lot lighter. It was worth a shot. I still sent you that text as a backup plan, though. I guess Felix's GPS app in my phone worked, huh?"

Jack hesitated. Shit. Right. Felix had installed an app in each of their work phones, which was supposed to let them track each other in an emergency. Felix had warned it might not work well, so Jack had forgotten all about it.

The truth was that he'd played a hunch that Nadia might go to Angela's office—which was in the direction the taxi had been heading—so he'd hot-wired a car and arrived just in time to see Nadia leaving with Howard. He'd relaxed . . . until he'd gotten her text. He'd followed Howard's car and then . . . Well, the problem with jacking a nice ride is that it might have an ignition kill. The owner had realized that his—or her—car was gone and shut it down. Jack had set off running, and fortunately, within a mile, he'd spotted Howard's car.

He nodded. "Yeah, GPS worked fine. Didn't matter. You had it under control."

"I appreciated the save, though. Nice work."

Jack was about to answer when Angela came out of the cabin.

"Okay, negotiations complete," she said. "I'll tell the police that I came along willingly, which saves Howard from the kidnapping charge. In return, he won't mention either of you. I followed him here, hoping to get him to confess to the murders. We fought. I won."

"You don't have to do that," Nadia said. "He *did* kidnap you."

"The murder charges are more important. Of course, he's convinced he can duck those, which is why he's agreeing. He won't get out of this. I'll make sure of it."

She glanced back at the cabin. "I'll admit, I was almost glad when he brought you through that door, Nancy. At least then I knew it was a straight-up kidnapping and not anything... else. He came by my office when I was getting ready to meet you. I really didn't want to be alone with him, so I said you were expecting me. That's when he knocked me out."

"He must have thought you knew something and were about to tell me. Then he pretended *he'd* been knocked out—by you—to get me here."

"I didn't know a damned thing, except that Victor didn't kill Mindy and Albert. That's what I wanted to talk to you about. Just discuss my doubts. When I woke up in that cabin, I was worried it wasn't about the case at all."

"You never had an affair with Howard, did you?"

She sighed. "Did you hear that old rumor? I thought—hoped—it died long ago. There was no affair, but not for lack of trying on his part. Howard fooled around, and Mindy ignored it... until she realized it wasn't the women doing the pursuing. *Hard* pursuing. In my case, I was about to file a stalking complaint when Mindy found out. We talked. That's why she left him. Because when a woman said *no*, Howard heard *maybe*."

Nadia made a face. "Ugh."

"That was Mindy's breaking point, but they stayed friends. I think she hoped their divorce would teach him the error of his ways. I thought it had. He certainly backed off me after that. I'll admit that after we found out Mindy had been murdered, I immediately thought of Howard. I couldn't see any reason why he'd kill Albert, though, so I told myself I was being silly. Obviously, I should have trusted my instincts."

Jack waited in the woods with Nadia until the police arrived. Then they slipped off and began the long walk back to the city.

"You didn't track me on GPS, did you?" she said when they were far enough away to talk. "I noticed that flash of confusion when I mentioned it. I just wasn't going to call you on it back there."

He told her everything, starting with watching her at the bar and ending with following her to the cabin.

"You thought Angela was the killer?" she said when he finished.

"I know you like her."

"Sure, but I liked Howard, too, and I still suspected him. But you thought Angela killed her own dog?" Nadia shook her head. "I can't imagine anyone doing *that*."

To which Jack, who had seen people do much worse, wisely decided not to respond.

"The upshot, though," she continued, "is that we both knew Victor didn't fit for all the murders, and we both had other suspects in mind. It would have been a hell of a lot easier if we'd just, you know, talked." She looked at him. "We need to work on that."

"Yeah, we do."

She slipped her hand into his, squeezed it, and they continued walking.

Chapter Twenty-seven
Nadia

I met with Angela for an update the next day.

The police already had a theory connecting Howard to Albert Kim's death. It seemed that e-mail correspondence between Kim and Howard suggested the judge had reason to believe Mindy Lang didn't kill herself.

"So first Howard killed Mindy," Angela said as we had our belated drink on the beachfront. "I'm going to guess that he borrowed the truth for his accusation against me. He got into a fight with Mindy, accidentally killed her, and staged it as suicide. Then something led Albert to think it was murder. He contacted Howard to raise the possibility. To say, 'Hey, I think someone killed your wife.' Howard shoots him to shut him up and stages it as a suicide because that worked the first time. Only this time, it doesn't, which leads to reopening Mindy's case."

"He would have been better to just talk Albert Kim

out of it," I said. "Convince him he was mistaken."

"Which would have worked, I bet. I'm sorry Albert died, but he was a corrupt bastard. I wouldn't be surprised if Albert *did* suspect Howard and was just hoping for a cash payment to make it all go away. Instead, Howard shoots him. And then Victor, who has accidentally killed Cherise, sees an opportunity to frame Sheila for the deaths and ends up killing poor Sara Atom."

"In the lamest frame-up job ever. Which wouldn't have gone anywhere, except, by that point, Howard was on the case, working hard to solidify the link between all the murders, because that was in his best interests. Prove Sheila killed Sara Atom and Cherise Hale, and pin the others on her, too."

"Men," she said. "They can be such bastards."

I laughed. "Which is not really the moral of this story, but in this case, yes, the boys were to blame."

"Speaking of men . . ." She twirled her umbrella. "He's not going to come, is he? My anonymous benefactor."

"I . . . I've passed on the message."

Angela sighed. "Okay, well, can you pass along another?" She looked me in the eye. "Tell my father I would really like to see him."

"Father?" Jack said as we walked along the beach, one

last time before our red-eye flight home.

"That makes more sense than former lover if you think about it."

"Guess so. Just . . . father." He shook his head. "Think he'll go see her?"

"I hope so. But, like he said, it's complicated."

"Yeah." Jack watched kids run across the sand. "When you take this job, you can't get out of it. Not really. Ty quit the life years ago. Doesn't matter. You can't go back. Can't erase the jobs. Or pretend they never happened. Not if it affects someone you care about. It's fucking complicated." He lifted our hands and touched my fake wedding band. "Can't do this."

"I know."

"Part of me says screw it. Chances anyone will find me? Near zero. But not zero. Never zero."

I squeezed his hand. "I know that. Marriage means using your real name. You burned that long ago, and you can't risk claiming it again."

"Wouldn't put you through that."

"The issue for me isn't what you'd 'put me through.' It's that I'd lose you, and there is no way in hell marriage is worth that. We're a committed couple. That's enough."

He glanced at the matching band on his finger. "Yeah, I know. I just . . ."

"You like that."

"Yeah, I really do." He took a deep breath. "Which is

why I'm going to ask. Not for a wedding. Not for a legal marriage. Just . . ." He took a box from his pocket.

I stopped walking.

"Yeah," he said. "Even *that'd* be complicated. I shouldn't ask."

He started shoving the box back into his pocket. I caught his wrist and pulled it out.

"That wasn't a no, Jack."

I took the box and opened it. Inside were three rings. Two gold bands and a diamond solitaire.

I looked up at him. "Are you asking me to fake-marry you?"

He sputtered a laugh. Then he went serious and took the diamond ring. "No, I'm asking you to be my wife, Nadia. In every way that counts."

I held out my hand.

He tilted his head, blue eyes meeting mine uncertainly.

"That's a yes, Jack," I said. "God, you can be—"

He cut me off with a kiss. A long, sweet kiss, and when I finished, I had a diamond ring on my finger. I took the larger band from the box and picked up his hand.

"Will you marry—" I began.

"Fuck, yeah."

I laughed and threw my arms around his neck and kissed him. Then I pulled back, took out my phone and placed a call.

"Hey, Emma?" I said when she answered. "It's Nadia. We'll be home tomorrow, but something happened, and I wanted to tell you in advance."

I winked at Jack as Emma's voice rose with concern.

"No, no, it's fine. We're fine. It's just . . . Well, it turns out John had an ulterior motive for this trip. He asked me to marry him."

I held out the phone so he could hear her screech.

"I said yes, obviously, and then we were walking past this adorable chapel, right on the beach, and I know, we should have waited, but we couldn't. So we're married."

I held out the phone again for her response, and Jack shook his head, chuckling.

"No, we don't want a party," I said. "Fine, okay, a small party. Very, very small."

I resumed walking along the beach, my hand in Jack's, as Emma chattered her plans, and I smiled. I just smiled.

ABOUT THE AUTHOR

Kelley Armstrong is the author of the Cainsville modern gothic series and the Rockton crime thrillers. Past works include the Otherworld urban fantasy series, the Darkest Powers & Darkness Rising teen paranormal trilogies, the Age of Legends fantasy YA series and the Nadia Stafford crime trilogy. Armstrong lives in Ontario, Canada with her family.

Visit her website at www.KelleyArmstrong.com

City of the Lost (excerpt)

Enjoyed the Nadia Stafford stories?

Try Kelley Armstrong's new mystery series.

To read the first three chapters of

City of the Lost,

just turn the page!

Kelley Armstrong

CITY OF THE LOST
CHAPTER ONE

"I killed a man," I say to my new therapist.

I've barely settled onto the couch . . . which isn't a couch at all, but a chaise lounge that looked inviting and proved horribly uncomfortable. Like therapy itself.

I've caught her off guard with that opening line, but I've been through this before with other therapists. Five, to be exact. Each time, the gap between "hello" and "I'm a murderer" decreases. By this point, she should be glad I'm still bothering with a greeting. Therapists do charge by the hour.

"You . . . ," she says, "killed a man?"

The apprehensive look. I know it well—that moment when they're certain they've misheard. Or that I mean it in a metaphorical way. I broke a man's heart. Which is technically true. A bullet does break a heart. Irrevocably, it seems.

When I only nod, she asks, "When did this happen?"

"Twelve years ago."

Expression number two. Relief. At least I haven't just killed a man. That would be so much more troublesome.

Then comes the third look, as she searches my face with dawning realization.

"You must have been young," she says. "A teenager?"

"Eighteen."

"Ah." She settles back in her chair, the relief stronger now, mingling with satisfaction that she's solved the puzzle. "An accident of some kind?"

She's blunt. Others have led me in circles around the conclusion they've drawn. You didn't really murder a man. It was a car accident or other youthful mishap, and now you torture yourself with guilt.

"No, I did it on purpose. That is, pulling the trigger was

intentional. I didn't go there planning to kill him. Manslaughter, not homicide. A good lawyer could argue for imperfect self-defense and get the sentence down to about twelve years."

She pulls back. "You've researched this. The crime. The sentence."

"It's my job."

"Because you feel guilty."

"No, it's my job. I'm a cop."

Her mouth forms an O of surprise, and her fingernails tap my file folder as she makes mental excuses for not reading it more thoroughly. Then her mouth opens again. The barest flicker of a smile follows.

"You're a police officer," she says. "You shot someone in the line— No, you were too young. A cadet?"

"Yes, but it wasn't a training accident." I settle on the chaise. "How about I just tell you the story?"

An obvious solution, but therapists never suggest it. Some, like this one, actually hesitate when I offer. She fears I'm guilty and doesn't want me to be. Give her a few more clues, and she'll find a way to absolve me.

Except I don't want absolution. I just want to tell my story. Because this is what I do. I play Russian roulette with Fate, knowing someday a therapist will break confidentiality and turn me in. It's like when I was a child, weighed down by guilt over some wrongdoing but fearing the punishment too much to confess outright. I'd drop clues, reasoning that if I was meant to be caught, those hints would chamber the round. Magical, childish thinking, but it's what I do.

"Can I begin?" I ask.

She nods with some reluctance and settles in.

"I'd gone to a bar that night with my boyfriend," I say. "It was supposed to be a date, but he spent the evening doing business in the back corner. That's what he called it. Doing business. Which sounds like he was dealing coke in some dive bar. We were actually in the university pub, him selling vitamin R and bennies to kids who wanted to make it through exam week...."

CHAPTER TWO

Blaine and I sat at a back table, side by side, waiting for customers. His fingers stroked the inside of my thigh. "Almost done. And then . . ." He grinned over at me. "Pizza? Your place?"

"Only if we get enough for Diana."

He made a face. "It's Friday night, Casey. Shouldn't your roommate have a date or something?"

"Mmm, no. Sorry."

Actually, she was out with college friends. I just wasn't telling Blaine that. We hadn't had sex yet. I'd held him off by saying I was a virgin. That was a lie. I was just picky.

Blaine was my walk on the wild side. I was a police recruit playing bad girl. Which was as lame as his attempt to play drug lord. On a scale of bad boys, Blaine ranked about a two. Oh, sure, he claimed he was connected—his grandfather being some Montreal mobster whose name I couldn't even find with an Internet search. More likely the old guy played bookie at his seniors' home. Blaine's father certainly wasn't mobbed up—he was a pharmacist, which was how Blaine stole his stuff. Blaine himself was pre-med. He didn't even sample his merchandise. That night, he nursed one beer for two hours. Me? I drank Coke. Diet Coke. Yep, we were hard-core.

A last customer sidled over, a kid barely old enough to be in university. Blaine sold him the last of his stash. Then he gulped his beer, put his arm around my shoulders, and led me from the pub. I could roll my eyes at his swagger, but I found it oddly charming. While I might not have been ready to jump into bed with Blaine, I did like him. He was a messed-up rich kid; I could relate to that.

"Any chance of getting Diana out of your apartment?" he asked.

"Even if there is, the answer is no."

He only shrugged, with a smile that was half "I'll change your mind soon" and half genuine acceptance. Another reason why I wasn't ready to write him off as a failed dating experiment—he never pushed too hard, accepted my refusals with good-natured equanimity.

We started walking. I wasn't familiar with the campus area. I was attending the provincial police college outside the city and spending weekends with Diana, a high school friend who went to the local community college. Neither of us was from here. So when Blaine insisted that a dark alley was a shortcut to the pizza place, I didn't question it . . . mostly because I was fine with what he had planned—a make-out pit stop designed to change my mind about getting Diana out of our apartment.

We were going at it hard and heavy when I heard the click of a gun. I gasped and pushed Blaine back. He looked up and jumped away, leaving me with a 9 mm pointed at my cheek.

"I only have fifty bucks," Blaine lied—the rest was stuffed in his sock. "She has some jewelry. Take that and the fifty—"

"Do we look like muggers, Saratori?"

As the gun lowered, I saw the guy holding it. Early twenties. Dark blond hair. Leather jacket. No obvious gang markings, but that's what this looked like: four young guys, one with a gun, three with knives.

I couldn't fight them—I didn't have a weapon, and martial arts doesn't work well against four armed attackers. Instead, I committed their faces to memory and noted distinguishing features for the police report.

"Does the old man know you're dealing?" the lead guy asked.

"I don't know what—" Blaine began.

"What I'm talking about? That you're Leo Saratori's

City of the Lost (excerpt)

grandkid? Or that you were dealing on our turf?"

Blaine bleated denials. One of the guys pinned him against the wall, while another patted him down. They took a small plastic bag with a few leftover pills from one sock and a wad of cash from the other.

"Okay," Blaine said. "So we're done now?"

"You think we want your money?" The leader bore down on him. "You're dealing on our turf, college boy. Considering who you are, I'm going to take this as a declaration of war."

"N-No. My grandfather doesn't—"

A clatter from the far end of the alley. Just a cat, leaping from a garbage bin, but it was enough to startle the guy with the gun. I lunged, caught him by the wrist and twisted, hearing the gun thump to the ground as I said, "Grab it!" and—

Blaine wasn't there to grab it. He was tearing down the alley. One of the other thugs was already scooping up the gun, and I was wrenching their leader's arm into a hold, but I knew it wouldn't do any good. The guy with the gun jabbed the barrel against my forehead and roared, "Stop!"

I didn't even have time to do that before the other two slammed me into the wall. The leader took back his gun and advanced on me.

"Seems we know who's got the balls in your relationship," he said. "The pretty little China doll. Your boyfriend's gone, sweetie. Left you to take his punishment." He looked me up and down. "A little too college-girl for my tastes, but I'm flexible."

I thought he was joking. Or bluffing. I knew my statistics. I faced more danger of sexual assault from an acquaintance or a boyfriend.

"Look," I said. "Whatever beef you have with Blaine, it has nothing to do with me. I've got twenty dollars in my wallet, and my necklace is gold. You can take—"

"We'll take whatever we want, sweetie."

I tugged my bag off my shoulder. "Okay, here's my purse.

There's a cell phone—"

He stepped closer. "We'll take whatever we want."

His voice had hardened, but I still didn't think, I'm in danger. I knew how muggings worked. Just stay calm and hand over my belongings.

I held out my purse. He grabbed it by the strap and tossed it aside. Then he grabbed me, one hand going to my throat, the other to my breast, shoving me against the wall. There was a split second of shock as I hit the bricks hard. Then . . .

I don't know what happened then. To this day, I cannot remember the thoughts that went through my brain. I don't think there were any. I felt his hands on my throat and on my breast, and I reacted.

My knee connected with his groin. I twisted toward the guy standing beside us. My fingers wrapped around his wrist. I grabbed his switchblade as it fell. I twisted again, my arm swinging down, and I stabbed the leader in the upper thigh as he was still falling back, moaning from the knee to his groin.

Afterward, I would piece it together and understand how it happened. How a response that seemed almost surreal was, in fact, very predictable. When the leader grabbed me with both hands, I knew he was no longer armed. So I reacted, if not with forethought, at least with foreknowledge.

Yet it was the lack of forethought that was my undoing. I had stabbed the leader . . . and there were three other guys right there. One hit me in the gut. Another plowed his fist into my jaw. A third wrenched my arm so hard I screamed as my shoulder dislocated. He got the knife away from me easily after that. Someone kicked me in the back of the knees, and I went down. As soon as I did, boots slammed me from all sides, punctuated by grunts and curses of rage. I heard the leader say, "You think you're a tough little bitch? I'll show you tough." And then the beating began in earnest.

*   *   *   *   *

City of the Lost (excerpt)

I awoke in a hospital four days later as my mother and the doctor discussed the possibility of pulling the plug. I'd like to believe that somewhere in that dark world of my battered brain, I heard them and came back, like a prizefighter rising as the ref counts down. But it was probably just coincidence.

I'd been found in that alley, left for dead, and rushed to the hospital, where I underwent emergency surgery to stop the internal bleeding. I had a dislocated shoulder. Five fractured ribs. Over a hundred stitches for various lacerations. A severe concussion and an intracranial hematoma. Compound fracture of the left radius. Severe fracture of the right tibia and fibula with permanent nerve damage. Also, possible rape.

I have recited that list to enough therapists that it has lost all emotional impact. Even the last part.

Possible rape. It sounds ludicrous. Either I was or I wasn't, right? Yet if it happened, I was unconscious. When I was found, my jeans were still on—or had been put back on. They did a rape kit, but it vanished before it could be processed.

Today, having spent two years as a detective in a big-city Special Victims Unit, I know you can make an educated guess without the kit. But I think when it disappeared, someone decided an answer wasn't necessary. If my attackers were found, they'd be charged with aggravated assault and attempted murder. Good enough. For them, at least.

As for my injuries, physically, I made a full recovery. It took eighteen months. I had to drop out of police college and give up the job waiting for me. As the victim of a serious crime, I was deemed no longer fit to serve and protect. I didn't accept that. I got a bachelor's degree in criminology, a black belt in aikido, and a flyweight championship in boxing. I aced the psych tests and, five years after the attack, I was hired and on the fast track to detective.

My parents had not been pleased. That was nothing new. When I'd first declared I wanted to be a police detective, their reaction had been pure horror. "You're better than that," they said. Smarter, they meant. Not geniuses, like them. While they considered my IQ of 135 perfectly adequate, it might require extra effort to become a cardiologist like my dad or chief of pediatric surgery like my mom or a neuroscientist like my sister. Still, they expected that I'd try. I wanted none of it. Never had.

After I had to leave police college, they'd been certain I'd give up this nonsense and devote myself to a meaningful career, preferably with a string of letters after my name. We argued. A lot. They died in a small plane crash four years ago, and we'd never truly mended that fence.

But back to the hospital. I spent six weeks there, learning to walk again, talk again, be Casey Duncan again. Except I never really was. Not the Casey Duncan I'd been. There are two halves of my life: before and after.

Four days in a coma. Six weeks in the hospital. Blaine never came to see me. Never even sent a card. I'd have ripped it to shreds, but at least it would have acknowledged what happened. He knew, of course. Diana had made sure of that, contacting him while I was in emergency. He hadn't asked how bad I was. Just mumbled something and hung up.

When I'd seen him run away in the alley, my outrage had been tempered by the certainty that he would get help. Even as the blows had started to fall, I'd clung to that. He must have called the police. He must have.

The last thing that passed through my mind before I lost consciousness was that I just had to hold on a little longer. Help was on the way. Only it wasn't. A homeless guy cutting through the alley stumbled across me, hours later. A stranger—a drunk stranger—had run to get help for me. My boyfriend had just run.

Blaine did need to speak to the police after I woke up and had told them what happened. But in Blaine's version, he'd created the distraction. I'd been escaping with him, and we'd parted at the street. The muggers must have caught up and

City of the Lost (excerpt)

dragged me back into that alley. If Blaine had known, he'd have done something. To suggest otherwise, well . . . I'd suffered head trauma, hadn't I? Temporary brain damage? Loss of memory? Clearly, I'd misremembered.

I didn't call him when I got out of the hospital. That conversation had to happen in person. It took a week for me to get around to it, because there was something I needed to do first. Buy a gun.

Blaine's routine hadn't changed. He still went jogging before dawn. Or that was what he'd say if he was trying to impress a girl: I run in the park every morning at five. It wasn't completely untrue. He did go out before dawn. He did run in the park. Except he only did it on Fridays, and just to the place where he stashed his drugs. Then he'd run back to campus, where he could usually find a few buyers—kids who'd been out too late partying, heading back to the dorms before dawn, in need of a little something to get them through Friday classes.

I knew the perfect place for a confrontation. By the bridge along the riverbank, where he'd pass on his way home. The spot was always empty at that time of day, and the noise of rushing water would cover our discussion.

Cover a gunshot, too?

No, the gun was only a prop. To let him know this was going to be a serious conversation.

I stood by the foot of the bridge. He came by right on schedule. Walking. He only jogged where people could see him.

I waited until I could hear the buzz and crash from his music. Then I stepped out into his path.

"Casey?" He blinked and tugged at the earbuds, letting them fall, dangling, as he stared at me. "You look . . ."

"Like I got the shit beat out of me?"

"It's not that bad."

"True. The bruises have healed. There are only ten stitches on my face. Oh, and this spot, where they had to shave my head to cut into my skull and relieve the bleeding." I turned to show him. "Plus a few teeth that will need to be replaced after my jaw's fully healed. My nose isn't straight, but they tell me plastic surgery will fix that. They also say I might walk without the limp if I work really, really hard at it."

He listened, nodding, an overly concerned expression on his face, as if I were an elderly aunt detailing my medical woes.

When I finished, he said, "You'll heal, then. That's good."

"Good?" I stepped toward him. "I almost died, Blaine. I had to drop out of police college. I'm told I'll never be a cop. That I'll never move fast enough. I might never think fast enough."

Another long pause. Then, "I'm sorry this happened to you, Casey. I gave you a chance to run."

"No, I let you run. You did, and you never even called for help."

"That's not how I remember it." He pulled himself up straight, ducking my gaze.

"No?" I said. "Does this refresh your memory?"

I took the gun from my pocket.

I'd envisioned this encounter so many ways. All those nights, lying in a hospital bed, fantasizing about it, I'd realized I didn't want him to break down and beg forgiveness too quickly. I wanted to have to pull the gun. I wanted to see his expression. I wanted him to feel what I'd felt in that alley.

Now I pointed the gun at him, and he blinked. That was it. A blink. Then his lips twitched, as if he was going to laugh. I think if he had, I'd have pulled that trigger. But he rubbed his mouth instead and said, "You're not going to shoot me with your training weapon, Casey. You're smarter than that."

"Did I mention I had to drop out? This isn't my training weapon. Now, I want you to think hard, Blaine. Think back to that night, and tell me again that you let me run."

"Oh, I get it." He eased back. "You want me to confess on some hidden tape so you can—"

I yanked off my jacket. It wasn't easy. My left arm was still in a cast, and my shoulder blazed with the simple act of tugging off clothing. But I got it off, and I threw it at him.

"Check for a recorder. Pat me down if you want. I'm not taping this. It's for me. I want to hear you tell the truth, and I want to hear you apologize."

"Well, then you're going to have to pull that trigger, because I don't have anything to apologize for. We ran, and you must have doubled back."

"For what?" I roared. "What in fuck would I double back for?"

"Then they must have caught you. You were too slow—"

"I did not run! You know I didn't. I grabbed him, and you were supposed to pick up the gun he dropped, but you ran. Like a fucking coward, you ran, and you didn't look back, and I nearly died, and you never even called the goddamned hospital to see if I was okay."

"You are okay. Look at you. Up and about, waving a gun in my face. Well, actually, I'm not sure I'd call that okay. I think you need help. I always did. You're messed up, Casey. I bet a shrink would say you have a death wish."

I went still. "What?"

He shifted forward, as if he'd just remembered the missing answer in a final exam. "You have a death wish, Casey. What normal girl wants to be a cop? Does that martial arts shit? We get mugged in an alley, and I'm trying to play it cool, and what do you do? Grab the guy. Hell, thank God I did run, or I'd have had the shit beat out of me, too."

I hit him. Hauled off and whaled the gun at the side of his head. He staggered back. I hit him again. Blood gushed. His hands went to the spot, eyes widening.

"Fuck! You fucking crazy bitch!"

"We were not mugged," I said, advancing on him as he backed up, still holding his head. "You were selling dope on some other guy's turf. Apparently, you knew that. You just didn't give a shit. I grabbed that guy to save your ass, and you ran. You left me there to die!"

"I didn't think they'd—"

"You left me there."

"I just thought—"

"Thought what? They'd only rape me? A distraction while you escaped?"

He didn't answer, but I saw it in his face, that sudden flush right before his eyes went hard.

"It was your own fault if they did rape you," Blaine said. "You couldn't leave well enough alone. Now give me that—"

He lunged for the gun. I shot him. No thought entered my head as I pulled the trigger. It was like being back in that alley.

I saw Blaine coming at me. I was already pointing the gun at his chest. So I pulled the trigger.

The end.

CHAPTER THREE

"And he died?" the therapist says.

I swing my legs over the side of the couch and sit up. Her expression is rapt, as if she's overhearing a drunken confession in a bar.

"And he died?" she prompts again.

"I called 911 on his burner phone. By the time I got through, he was gone." No, not gone. Dead. Use the proper terminology, Casey. Don't sugarcoat it.

"What did you tell the operator?"

"Dispatcher," I say, correcting her automatically. "I said I heard a shot, and I raced over to see two men fleeing the scene. One had a gun. I gave descriptions roughly matching

City of the Lost (excerpt)

two of the guys who beat me. I said I was going to follow them to get a closer look. She told me not to, of course, but I was already hanging up."

"You'd thought it through."

Her tone should be at least vaguely accusatory. Instead, it's almost admiring. She's been abused in some way. Bullied. Harassed. Maybe even assaulted. She's fantasized about doing exactly what I did to whoever hurt her.

I can't even take credit for "thinking it through." A situation presented itself, and I reacted. One therapist explained it as an extreme response to the primal fight-or-flight instinct. Mine apparently lacks the flight portion.

"What did you do with the gun?" she asks.

"I wiped it down and threw it in the river. It was never found."

"Have you ever pulled the file? As a cop?"

She doesn't even bother to say "police officer" now. All formality gone.

"No, that could flag an alert," I say. "It didn't happen here anyway."

"Was his family really connected? Like capital F family?"

She says it as if this is an episode of The Sopranos.

"I guess so," I say, which is a lie. I know so. The Saratoris aren't major players, but Blaine's grandfather Leo is definitely part of the Montreal organized crime scene.

"Don't you worry they'll find out and come for revenge?"

Every day of my life, I think, but all I grant her is a shrug.

"Biggest therapist fail ever." I down a shot of tequila two days later, my first chance to have a drink after work with Diana. "I might as well have confided in that chick over there." I point at a vacant-eyed girl in the corner. Hooker. Crack addict. If she's old enough to be in a bar, I'll turn in my badge.

"Remind me again why you put yourself through that,"

Diana says. "Oh, right. You're a sadist."

"Masochist," I say. "Also, possibly, a sadist, but in this situation, it's masochism."

She rolls her eyes and shifts on her stool. She's already sitting on the edge, as if placing her ass—even fully clothed—on the surface might result in lethal contamination. At least she's stopped cleaning her glass with an antiseptic wipe before drinking from it.

Another shift has her sliding off the stool, and she does a little stutter-jump to get back on, tugging down her miniskirt as she does. One of the guys across the bar is checking her out. Or he's checking out her hair, blond with bright pink tips. He squints, as if suspecting he's had too much to drink. They don't see a lot of pink hair in here.

"So how was work?" I ask. Diana is in accounting. Her exact title seems to change by the month, as she flits about, not climbing the corporate ladder, but jumping from rung to rung, testing them all for size.

"We're not going to talk about your therapy session?"

"We just did."

I down my second shot of tequila. The bartender glances over and jerks his thumb at the soda fountain. It's not a hint. Kurt knows I have a two-shot limit. I nod, and he starts filling a glass.

"So work . . . ?" I prod Diana.

Her lips purse, and that tells me that's not a good question. Not today. I just hope it doesn't mean she's been demoted again. Lately, Diana's career hopes seem to all be downward . . . and not by choice.

"Is work . . . okay?" I venture.

"Work is work." She gulps her drink, and there's an uncharacteristic note of bitterness in her voice.

I try to assess her mood. We haven't always been best friends. In high school, it'd been on and off, the ebb and flow that marked many teen friendships. It was the attack that

City of the Lost (excerpt)

brought us closer. She'd stood by me when all my old friends shied away, no one knowing what to say. After I shot Blaine, she'd found me frantically changing out of my blood-splattered clothing, and I'd told her everything, and that cemented our friendship. Forged in fire, as they save. Fire and secrets.

"Let's talk about something else," I say. "Did you bump into that guy at the coffee shop? The musician, right?"

She shrugs and runs a hot-pink fingernail around the rim of her martini glass . . . which is actually a regular whiskey glass, but it's currently holding a lemon-drop martini. I know she has something to say. Something about therapy, I presume, but I pretend not to notice, as Kurt brings my Diet Coke.

"You staying till closing?" he asks me.

"Maybe."

A smile lights his eyes. When I stay until closing, I usually end up in the apartment over the bar. His apartment.

"You should," he says. "Looks like you could use a break."

I'm sure he's about to make some smutty suggestion about ways to relieve my stress. Then his gaze slides to Diana, and instead he heads off to wait on another customer. He thinks he's being discreet, but Diana knows about us, and she's just as horrified as he suspects she'd be. Diana does not approve of casual sex, especially not with an ex-con bartender who works at the docks by day. She has no idea what she's missing.

Normally, she'd make a smart comment as Kurt walked away. But tonight she's lost in the mysteries of her lemon drop.

"You okay?" I ask.

"It's . . . Graham."

"Fuck," I mutter, and sit back on my stool.

Graham Berry is Diana's ex-husband. Respected lawyer. Community pillar. Also one of the most goddamn brilliant psychos I've ever met. He knows exactly how to stalk and torment her while keeping his ass out of prison. Restraining orders? Sure, we can get them. But any cop who's spent time in SVU knows they're as useful as cardboard armor in a gunfight.

She downs her martini and signals Kurt for a refill. Diana rarely has more than one, and when he comes over to deliver it, he gives me an Is everything okay? look.

"Rough day," I say.

When he says, "Maybe tomorrow will be better," I know he isn't talking about Diana.

"It will be," I say.

"Graham's in town," she blurts out when Kurt leaves. "He claims he's here on business."

"And he wants to see you, because he loves you and he's changed."

I look her in the eyes as I say this, steeling myself for the guilty flash that says she's considering meeting with him. Like many abusive relationships, theirs is a complicated one. He'd beat the shit out of her, and then he'd be so very sorry, and she'd go back to him, and the cycle would start again.

It's been two years since she left him and convinced me to move to a new city with her. I'd resisted, not because I was reluctant to help but, honestly, because I expected I'd relocate my life for Diana and then find myself alone in that new city when she went back to Graham. But I'd decided to give her one last chance . . . and she'd finally decided he'd had enough chances. She's been free and clear of him ever since, and now I don't detect any guilt in her eyes, any sign that she wants to see him.

"Okay, step one," I say. "You'll stay at my place tonight and work from there tomorrow. Call in sick."

I brace for her to suggest she stay longer. When her lease came due, she hinted—strongly—about moving into my place instead. She'd gotten very little in the divorce, having signed a prenup, and had long since run through it. The demotions haven't helped her ever-worsening financial situation. I'd pointed out that my single-bedroom place wasn't big enough,

City of the Lost (excerpt)

but still I feel like a selfish bitch. I help by footing the bills when we go out and "loaning" her bill money that I never expect to see again.

She doesn't suggest a longer-term stay, though, and I feel like a bitch for that, for even thinking it at a time like this, as if she'd manufacture a story about Graham to move in with me.

"With any luck," I continue, "it'll take him a while to track your home or work address, and if he really is on business, he won't be here long . . ." I catch her expression. "He's already found you."

"He—he stopped by the office. The usual crap. He just wants to have coffee, talk, work things out."

"And then?" I say, because I know there is an and then. In public, Graham plays the besotted ex-husband. But as soon as no one is around . . .

"He waylaid me in the parking garage."

I reach for her wrist, and she flinches. I push up the sleeve to see a bracelet of bruises.

"Goddamn it, Di!"

She gives me a whipped-puppy look.

"Graham showed up at your office, and you didn't call me? You walked into the goddamn parking garage—"

"Don't, Casey. I feel stupid enough."

Her eyes fill with tears, and that's when I really feel like a bitch. Blame the victim. I hate it so much. But Diana never seems to learn, and I'm terrified that one day I'll get a call that she's in the morgue because she gave Graham another chance and I wasn't there to stop her.

"He's going to do it one of these days," she says, wrapping her hands around her glass. "You know he is."

I don't want to follow this line of thought, because when I do, I think of Blaine and how easy it was to kill him. I fear that one day I'll decide there's only one way to protect Diana. No, really I'm afraid she'll ask me to do it. I don't know what I'd say if she did. I owe her for keeping my secret about Blaine.

But I don't owe her enough to repeat the mistake with someone else. Not even Graham.

"I've been researching how to disappear," she says.

"What?" I look up sharply.

"We could disappear. You and me."

I don't ask why she includes me. When she'd asked me to relocate and I'd resisted, she'd pointed out the ugly truth—that I'd had no reason to stay. That hasn't changed. I have a furnished apartment I've never added a picture to. I have a lover whose last name I've never asked. I have a sister I speak to three times a year. I have one friend, who is sitting in front of me. I do have a job I love. But that's all I care about. My job and Diana. The job is replaceable. Diana is not.

"Let's just focus on keeping you safe for now," I say. "Graham will give up and go home, and then we can discuss how to handle this long-term."

I put money on the table and catch Kurt's eye as he deals with a drunk. He mouths, "This weekend?" meaning he can see something's up and tomorrow probably isn't going to be better. I nod, try for a smile, and then turn to Diana and say, "Drink up, and let's go."

Printed in Great Britain
by Amazon